Stem Cell Symphony
A Novel

By Ricki Lewis, PhD

Order this book online at www.trafford.com/07-2401
or email orders@trafford.com

Most Trafford titles are also available at major online book retailers.

© Copyright 2007 Ricki Lewis.
All rights reserved. No part of this publication may be reproduced, stored in a retrieval system, or transmitted, in any form or by any means, electronic, mechanical, photocopying, recording, or otherwise, without the written prior permission of the author.

Note for Librarians: A cataloguing record for this book is available from Library and Archives Canada at www.collectionscanada.ca/amicus/index-e.html

ISBN: 978-1-4251-5402-8

Photography by Drs. Dennis Steindler and Eric Laywell of the McKnight Brain Institute

(cover: astrocyte precursors [green] and young neurons [red] in the brain) and Dr. James Comly (back cover).

We at Trafford believe that it is the responsibility of us all, as both individuals and corporations, to make choices that are environmentally and socially sound. You, in turn, are supporting this responsible conduct each time you purchase a Trafford book, or make use of our publishing services. To find out how you are helping, please visit www.trafford.com/responsiblepublishing.html

Our mission is to efficiently provide the world's finest, most comprehensive book publishing service, enabling every author to experience success. To find out how to publish your book, your way, and have it available worldwide, visit us online at www.trafford.com/10510

Trafford PUBLISHING   www.trafford.com

North America & international
toll-free: 1 888 232 4444 (USA & Canada)
phone: 250 383 6864 ♦ fax: 250 383 6804 ♦ email: info@trafford.com

The United Kingdom & Europe
phone: +44 (0)1865 722 113 ♦ local rate: 0845 230 9601
facsimile: +44 (0)1865 722 868 ♦ email: info.uk@trafford.com

10 9 8 7 6 5 4 3 2

ALSO BY RICKI LEWIS

Human Genetics: Concepts and Applications
(McGraw-Hill Higher Education)

Life (McGraw-Hill Higher Education)

Discovery: Windows on the Life Sciences
(Blackwell Scientific)

Dedicated to hospice volunteers and their patients.

ACKNOWLEDGEMENTS

I'd like to thank the many people who helped tell this story. Stem cell researchers Dennis Steindler, Bryon Petersen, John Gearhart, and Sally Temple provided ideas and encouragement. Larry Lewis, Wendy Josephs, and Edith Swetsky offered valuable advice on early drafts. Many thanks to Barbara Ardinger for her expert editing. Many, many thanks to my wonderful friends at hospice and to my patients.

This book is a work of fiction. Names, characters, places and incidents are products of the author's imagination or are used fictitiously. Any resemblance to actual events or locales or persons, living or dead, is entirely coincidental.

1

AMES NURSING HOME, PHILADELPHIA, ROOM D317

Stuart had been watching the tattered Polaroid peel away from the corner of the mirror for four days, six hours, and seventeen minutes. The photo had been in the room as long as he had, about seven years.

The peeling had begun on Tuesday. First, Elvin the janitor had whacked his dreadlocks against the mirror as he turned to chat with Reginald, although the shriveled old soul who shared Stuart's room hadn't shown much sign of life in months, even during the dutiful visits by his equally shriveled wife. The swinging dreads had jostled the photo just enough to dislodge it from the corner of the glass. Then a three-hour lapse in the air-conditioning following a late afternoon storm had let in enough humidity to unglue the tape that had held the yellowed photo in place. Stuart had been monitoring the slow-motion unfurling ever since.

Except for the occasional flash of cleavage when an aide bent to wipe away his drool, the photo was one of the few things of interest in Stuart's limited visual field. He could no longer turn his head to look toward the window where Reginald lay, nor the other way toward the door. But he could hear the swish of gliding wheelchairs and clanking walkers as the more mobile residents made their thrice-daily migration to the dayroom for meals. About a year ago, Stuart's head had begun to stiffen, gradually locking itself into place so that now he could only move it slightly up and down or side to side. That gave him a vocabulary of "yes" and "no."

Though the photo's ungluing was distressing, Stuart dared not indicate his anxiety, especially on the weekend. He'd learned that the hard way. Grunting and grimacing—about the only means of communication left to him except blinking and nods—spelled agitation to the nurses' aides who were more or less in charge from the Friday night shift until 7 A.M. on Monday. The newer ones didn't even realize that the grimaces were out of his control, part of his disease. Agitation thus meant Ativan, and oblivion. He didn't want that. And Samantha, the only nurse who seemed to understand what he could and couldn't do, wouldn't be back from vacation until Monday.

Eight months ago, when Stuart could still speak, he'd asked Samantha to mark off the days on the calendar that hung on the wall to the left of the mirror. He could also (but just barely) see the clock, which was off to the right, and he could hear it ticking. Knowing the day and time gave a context to the relentless monotony. Stuart had gotten the idea from the movie "Cast Away", in which Tom Hanks' character, a harried FedEx employee stranded on a tropical island after a plane crash, had made a ritual of scratching a hatch mark for each passing month into the wall of the cave that he had made his home. Like the modern-day Robinson Crusoe in the film, Stuart also tracked time to stay sane. That was how he knew that the photo was into its fifth day of peeling.

But how could he save it?

"Hey, Reggie, hey, Stuart. I'm back!" A tall, olive-skinned nurse who always wore her hair in a long, swinging, brown braid wheeled in two breakfast trays on a small cart.

Samantha! Stuart's eyebrows shot up. He'd missed her.

"Now don't all speak at once," she said. "I got called in last minute to help with an admission, and figured I'd stick around for an extra shift. How're you boys doin' since I've been away?"

As Samantha went about checking Reginald's vitals, adjusting his oxygen leads, and propping him up, Stuart's mind raced, trying to think of what he could do to indicate the peeling photo which, he'd calculated, had less than a day left. Samantha would crank him up further, shovel in his eggs and pureed sausage, and hope he wouldn't choke to death, then pack him in so he would be sitting straight up for an hour. Stuart waited patiently for his chance.

Good. She was through with Reginald and was pushing the tray toward him. Samantha bent forward and gently removed Stuart's hands from beneath the covers, where they'd been tucked in, to check that his nails were short, and then examined the healing scratches on his face. Although the disease was so advanced that it stilled him most of the time, he'd jerk unpredictably now and then, injuring himself or whoever happened to be near. But comparative immobility was better than when he moved all the time.

As Samantha leaned over to brush a strand of hair from his eyes, he saw his chance.

Stuart began to blink furiously. *Three blinks, pause, one blink. Repeat.* Samantha got the message and took his hands.

"Come on, Stuart. What is it? Focus. Show me with your eyes. You can do it!"

Stuart's tongue darted in and out as he shut his eyes in deep concentration. Reginald farted loudly, as he often did, but Samantha and Stuart didn't even notice the rippling sound. And then, suddenly, Stuart's head bucked forward several times in the direction of the mirror. Samantha turned.

"Oh! Of course. Your family! I'll be right back."

As Samantha went in search of tape, Stuart collapsed back against the pillow, the faintest hint of a smile on his face.

It wasn't really a very good photo. It was, in fact, out of focus, as if the photographer had been shaking. Children were playing among the wood and metal swings, slides, seesaws, and monkey bars of a playground built long before the elaborate canvas castles of today. A little girl in the foreground was pushing a small, dark-haired boy on a swing. Stuart didn't know if being on that swing was actually his earliest memory, or if he just thought it was because Jim, Sheila, Will, and Livvie had talked about it so many times. Or simply because he saw the photo every day.

They'd been at a picnic that day, with aunts and uncles and cousins on their father's side of the family. Jim was the only one old enough to remember his grandparents, who had died in a car crash in their forties. The Mathesons were a boisterous bunch, always attracting attention, several of the great aunts in perpetual, seemingly purposeless motion, some of their gyrations smooth and almost dance-like, some jerky. A few younger relatives moved, too, but more subtly. One aunt waved her hands about in graceful, repetitive, endless patterns, while her brother repeatedly flexed his fingers and one leg. Yet some of the relatives were perfectly fine. They didn't yet realize that the family members with the odd, constant movements had inherited a disease that struck anyone with one affected parent with 50:50 odds.

The frenetic, staggering elders didn't upset the kids too much, for they'd grown up with it. Stuart and his brothers and sisters were actually a lot less troubled by their father's constant moving than they were by the reactions of people seeing it.

On that glorious, late summer day, the Matheson kids had been playing when their father burst out of the wooded picnic area. He lurched towards the playground, arms waving wildly, face contorting, staggering and yelling their names in garbled speech. All the children on the playground turned to stare.

"Hey, kids. Time t'eat. C'mon."

"It's Dad!" said Jim. He jumped down from the monkey bars and ran to round up his siblings.

"Oh, no." Sheila tried to move back. "Is he coming?"

"Is he?" echoed Will.

"Looks like it." Jim waved frantically. "Hurry up!"

"C'mon, Livvie," Sheila yelled. "Hurry up, get Stuart out of there!"

The Matheson kids approached their father, who lifted the Polaroid camera that had miraculously escaped being bashed to the ground or hurled heavenward as he gyrated.

"Hold still. Lemme getta picture."

They stopped and posed, knowing that the sooner they did so, the quicker they could get out of there. But it was too late.

Just as their father stopped wobbling long enough to get off the shot, two women came running over and dragged their offspring away, stage-whispering to them about public drunkenness. Ignoring them, Jim, Sheila, Will, and Livvie gathered around the camera as the photograph came sliding out, Stuart hanging back to watch the other kids leave. Then they took their father's hands and walked back toward the picnic area.

Stuart knew the memory was real. He remembered something the others didn't. When his brothers and sisters took his father's hands, he'd fallen behind, and by the time he'd caught up, everyone was busy getting food. He'd looked up and seen Uncle Todd, leaning against a tree and rhythmically extending and contracting his fingers, over and over again in the precise same pattern. And as Uncle Todd glanced from the spasming elders to the youngsters, tears slid slowly down his cheeks. Stuart wondered why.

2

ALTOONA, PA.

Kelsey Raye had been dreading the funeral, feeling more guilt than sadness. She stood next to her sister, Jennifer, awaiting the guests. Only a year apart, they looked like twins, although Kelsey refused to tame the wild red curls that Jennifer had gotten under control. Perhaps it was because Jennifer was a nurse that she had single-handedly cared for both their parents as they had unsuccessfully battled cancer, or perhaps it was also that she'd never felt a need to bolt from small town life the way that Kelsey had.

Snowflake-brushed mourners began to arrive. Looking about, they recognized and approached Jennifer, hugging her, murmuring a few comforting words, then walking slowly down the church aisle as Jennifer turned to the next person. Kelsey, smiled at politely or generically greeted, wanted to disappear behind a mound of snow. Finally, a young woman with sleek black hair pulled back in a severe bun, but with a face so pretty that she could pull the look off, approached. She hugged Jen, then turned to Kelsey, her face lighting up.

"Hi! You must be the other sister. Kelly?"

"Close. Kelsey."

"Oops. Right, of course. With all I've heard about you from Jen, I should have gotten that right. I'm Teri, your dad's hospice volunteer." She offered her hand and then grabbed Kelsey for a quick hug. "I'm so sorry about your father. I'm glad you could make it today."

"Thanks. Maybe we can talk after the service? I'd like to learn more about what you did. With Dad, I mean."

"Sure. I'll find you later." Teri patted Kelsey's arm.

The organ music began. Kelsey looked around uneasily, then grabbed Jen's arm. "It feels weird to be in a church," she whispered. "We never went as kids."

"No, not much."

"All I remember is Dad making fun of people who went to church every Sunday."

Jennifer was silent a moment. "He'd changed, you know, since Mom died."

"Oh." What else could she say to that? "Well, we'd better go sit down."

✲

After the service, at which Jennifer delivered a moving, memory-drenched eulogy, the hugging and comforting continued at her nearby home. Family and friends, mostly local, gathered for the post-funeral feast. Kelsey was standing off to the side when Teri approached.

"C'mon," she said, "let's go sit on the stairs."

Relieved to have someone to talk to, Kelsey allowed herself to be guided. "So, Teri. Tell me what you did for Dad. Is hospice your job?"

"Oh, no. I'm a fourth grade teacher. I volunteer for hospice."

"I don't get it. You just sort of show up at the bedside of a sick stranger?"

"Not quite. We're trained. Psychology. Spirituality. Medical stuff. Then we visit patients in nursing homes or hospice facilities, but mostly in their own homes, like your dad."

"But isn't hospice just giving up? It sounds so morbid. Why do patients do it? Why do you do it?"

Teri laughed. "We get asked that all the time. Actually, our motives are rather selfish."

"Huh?"

"Most of us do it initially because hospice helped us with a loved one. Then, when we start visiting people, we notice how good we feel afterward, knowing we are helping. At first we think it's weird to feel good, you know, talking to a dying person, but when we talk to each other about it, and to other volunteers, we realize that we crave the appreciation." She laughed again. "It's hard to explain. But we get more out of it than we give. They told us that at training, and none of us really believed it then, but it's so true."

Kelsey moved aside to let a barrage of little kids run up the stairs. "Oh. I guess I misunderstood. When Jen mentioned volunteers coming to visit Dad, I imagined Girl Scouts. I don't quite get it, but thank you." She took Teri's hands in her own. "What did Dad talk about, you know, these past few months? I didn't get to visit much."

"Your father was wonderful. Calm, not afraid, always concerned that others would worry too much about him. And he was so proud of you, of your writing. He talked about your trips. Where were you this time?"

"Hawaii. For a stem cell conference. That's why I was delayed." Kelsey paused a moment. "Can I ask you something?"

Teri nodded. "Sure."

"Did he resent my work? After all, it kept me from being with him. Jen was always there for him."

"I don't think he saw it that way, Kelsey. Did he compare you two when you were growing up?"

"No." Without warning, she found herself sniffling. She suddenly hugged Teri. "Thank you."

3

MARKET STREET, PHILADELPHIA

Checking her watch, Kelsey zigzagged through the rush hour crowd. With the first autumn chill she'd finally abandoned her summery skirts for khaki pants. She took her earbuds out and stashed her iPod in her purse as she dashed up the six steps at the corner of Market Street and 38th. She slipped through the revolving doors and waved at Ralph, who spent his days signing people in and out, part of the post-9/11 protocol. She squeezed into a packed elevator and stared at the shiny specimen of male pattern baldness a few inches in front of her for the thirty seconds it took to reach the second floor and the offices of BioTech USA.

Once through the glass doorway, she passed the framed magazine covers that lined the walls and turned into her cluttered cubicle. Shoving her bag under the desk, she punched a computer key and then hit speed dial.

"Yes, this is Kelsey Raye from BioTech USA. Dr. Holloway, please." She glanced at a few e-mails and deleted a penis enlargement ad while she waited.

"Hi, Dr. H. Are we on for coffee later? Okay. And thanks for the neurosphere slide. It makes a great screensaver." She looked over at the bluish-green rotating cellular globes displayed on the screen. "Great. See you soon."

She swiveled toward the screen, hit a key to banish the neurospheres, and began typing. Tony Moretti's head popped up over the divider. It was quite a handsome head, and Kelsey had had the beginnings of a thing for him back when she first came to the magazine, but only for a day or two. She'd realized they wouldn't be able to work together well if they'd gotten involved.

"Another stem cell article, Kel?" he asked.

Kelsey nodded, eyes still glued to the screen as she typed away and grunted something that sounded like a yes.

"What's your angle this time? Aren't you getting sick of those little suckers?"

"Cancer," she said. "From Dr. Holloway's lab at Franklin. I met him in Hawaii last winter, right before the funeral. He e-mails me when something's up."

Grinning, Tony pointed to an article with a photo attached and tacked onto Kelsey's corkboard. "That him?"

"Who?" said Kelsey, busy scanning her screen.

"Dr. Gorgeous. Quite the hunk, especially for a nerd. Nice toupee."

"The ponytail's real, Tony. And so's my deadline."

"Chill, Kel. I have to bang out another microarray article. But it's only Monday, so what's the rush?"

"I've got an appointment."

"Aren't we being mysterious!" Tony smirked as he slowly sank back down to his desk.

※

Downing an iced venti no-fat sugar-free vanilla latte as lunch, Kelsey looked about the tidy, bright office as she waited for the volunteer coordinator, Emily Josephs, to finish her phone call. Framed awards and notes from grateful families decorated the walls. She picked up a tattered copy of *World Medical Mysteries* from the small table next to her chair, and was soon immersed in a gory story on teratomas, the tooth-and-hair-sprouting tumors that sometimes grew in place of an embryo. Realizing within two paragraphs that the tabloid was just recycling and hyping a well-known medical oddity, she put the magazine down and admired Emily's outfit. The tailored shirt and jacket were of colors that Kelsey would never have put together – aqua and purple -- but somehow they looked fabulous on the fortyish woman with the chiseled, almost handsome, features and shock of short red hair.

"Yes," she was saying into the phone. "Tonight. Can you do 6 to 9? Great. Yes, it went to her brain. Liver too." Emily scanned a list of names as she listened. "No, she didn't tell her family, and didn't have any treatment. But she couldn't hide it anymore. She's been on hospice only a week, and she's scared. Thank you so much." Emily gently put down the phone and looked across her desk at a suddenly teary Kelsey.

"Are you okay? Hit too close to home?"

Kelsey nodded.

"That's why we require that new volunteers wait a few months after a personal loss. And maybe you shouldn't see cancer patients right away."

Kelsey looked puzzled.

"Your application. You wrote that your parents had cancer, right?"

Kelsey nodded.

"Well, it might be better if we matched you with patients who have nervous conditions. Dementia? Parkinson's? We have plenty of those."

"Yes, that would be okay."

Emily chuckled and got up, holding out her hand. "Oh, forgive me for not introducing myself. Kelsey, I'm Emily Josephs, volunteer coordinator."

Kelsey leaned forward and took her hand. "I figured. Nice to meet you."

"You look so familiar. Not just your face, but your name. I just can't place you …" Emily said as she sat back down.

"Oh, it must be the newspaper. I write a column. They run a photo, although not a particularly good one."

"Of course! The essays on science behind the headlines."

"Right. That's me. But my day job is at a biotech magazine for scientists and venture capitalists."

"Yes. I saw that on your application, too. You have quite an impressive academic background. But if you have a doctorate in genetics, why aren't you in a lab curing diseases or inventing glow-in-the-dark cats?"

Kelsey laughed. "You probably won't believe this, but for that oh-so-impressive Ph.D., I worked with flies that had legs growing out of their heads. Not much of a demand for that, I'm afraid." She gave a wan smile. "More seriously, I've been writing all my life. I finally decided I prefer the constant changing of topics in journalism to the intense focus on one problem in science—such as the organization of parts in a fly embryo."

"That's very interesting," Emily replied. "And unusual. It'll be great to have a volunteer with your background. Was it your parents' final illnesses that brings you to us?"

Kelsey nodded and was silent a moment. "Yes. I really didn't do enough to help when they got sick. My sister did it all. She was happy to stay in Altoona, where we grew up, while I couldn't wait to get out."

"Did hospice help you and your sister? And of course your parents?"

"Yes and no. Or rather no and yes. My mom got sick first, and her oncologist thought she'd freak out if he even mentioned the "h" word. So she never had hospice. Nor did Jenny or I have any idea how close she was to the end. Jenny's nursing experiences hadn't taken her beyond snotty-nosed grade schoolers."

"So how did things go with your mom, in the end?"

"I wasn't there much. But I remember Jen saying that time got weird. Like it was too fast and too slow, all at the same time. I guess Mom just got weaker and weaker, until she was sleeping all the time. She died in the hospital with liver failure. I got there the day before," Kelsey said quietly, "but I don't think she even heard me say goodbye."

"Oh, I'll bet she did. Hearing is the last sense to go. What about your dad?"

"That was different. When his cancer came back, he was too weak for more chemo. The doctor told him, and Jen, about hospice. A team would come in and keep dad comfortable at home. And they did. A nurse, a social worker, even a doctor who was on call. Dad sent the religion guy away, but he really liked the volunteer, Teri. I met her at the funeral. She's the one who told me about hospice. And volunteering."

"We hear some variation of that story often." Emily turned the page on Kelsey's application and frowned slightly.

"You're an atheist?" she asked.

"Yes. Is that a problem?" Kelsey straightened.

"It's unusual for a hospice volunteer. Were you raised without religion? Or is it because you're a scientist?"

"I was raised Methodist. And giving up God isn't a prerequisite for becoming a scientist. Forgive me if I sound rude, but why is this important?"

"I'm wondering if you would be able to comfort a religious person."

"I suppose that depends on what exactly you mean by comfort. Pray?"

"Maybe."

"Wouldn't my praying be dishonest?"

"I don't think so, if you did it for the patient. Didn't your parents' deaths chip away at your atheism just a little?"

"Oh, no." Kelsey bristled, nervously twisting at her curls. "If anything, their deaths reaffirmed it."

Emily raised her eyebrows but stayed silent.

"I remember watching Mom in the hospital. I thought if there really was a God, that would be a good time for Her to appear. Was that praying? Because if it was, it sure didn't work. I'm afraid that when it comes to life and death, we're no more important than the tiniest bacterium."

"Kelsey, that's the biologist talking. There's more to life, and death, and humanity, than biology."

"With all due respect, I just don't think you understand."

"Maybe not." Emily set the application down. "But you need to resolve your lingering anger, or be able to put it aside, to comfort a patient."

Kelsey sat quietly for a few minutes, absently looking sideways at the cover of *World Medical Mysteries*. "I can do that," she finally said. "But I don't know about the prayer and scripture part. Me reading the bible? I can't see it. But I'd do the best I can. It would be a little like acting."

"It sounds like in your case it might be a lot like acting." Emily laughed, breaking the tension. "But it might come more easily than you think. Spirituality isn't really about prayer and scripture. It's about who you are."

"What do you mean?"

"You'll see."

"So I'm in?"

"Training starts next week." Emily shuffled a stack of papers together, glanced at her watch, and rose. "Not everyone makes it all the way through, but I have a good feeling about you." She gave Kelsey a quick hug. "Sorry, but I have to run. We have a meeting with a new family. Huntington's disease. We don't see that very often."

"Huntington's disease? I actually know—"

"Sorry to cut you off like this, Kelsey, but I'm already late. You'll have to fill me in next time. See you next week!"

Kelsey looked perplexed as Emily rushed out. She stopped a moment to look in the mirror hanging on the office wall and pat her frizz. As she walked out the door, she bumped into a man and woman entering the hallway. With curly dark blond hair and light brown eyes, they looked remarkably like each other.

4

HOSPICE OFFICE

Jim and Sheila Matheson looked nervously at each other as they glimpsed the number of people gathering in the atrium. When they'd spoken with Emily, the friendly volunteer coordinator, they hadn't imagined that so many people would be present when they discussed their brother Stuart.

Dr. Pram, the family's neurologist, had noticed changes in Stuart's symptoms and had recently suggested hospice care. Although Stuart would still live at the nursing home, being on hospice would mean that he'd get more visitors, something Jim and Sheila wanted. Even though they tried to visit often, they knew it wasn't enough, and that Stuart was lonely. But it was hard. They both worked long hours, but even more than that, their memories of visiting Will and Livvie in the same place for so many years were still too fresh. At least Stuart didn't thrash about the way Will and Livvie had, at least not anymore. Sheila and Jim had once thought "rubber room" was just an expression. But then, since restraints were considered inhumane, poor Livvie had been put in one to keep from hurting herself. Stuart's stillness was equally disturbing, like he was already half gone.

With its bay windows, potted ficus trees, miniature topiaries, and baskets of blooms, the atrium had the feel of the outdoors. As Jim and Sheila were admiring the plants, Stuart's hospice team came forward to introduce themselves. A pretty, willowy blonde named (appropriately) Lori Reed was the R.N. case manager. Dr. Pram was there, as well as Kate Sorenson, a social worker they'd met at Ames. They'd thought she was a student because she was very young and petite. In contrast, a tall, sinewy man with longish hair in the back but impending baldness beneath the carefully combed strands at the front held Sheila's hand and gave her a warm smile. He introduced himself as Timothy Green, the hospice chaplain.

A woman who looked like a younger, redheaded version of Martha Stewart approached and gave them each a hug. "Hi!" she said. "I'm Emily Josephs, volunteer coordinator. We spoke on the phone. I'm glad you could make it so soon."

"We were a little alarmed when Dr. Pram mentioned hospice," Sheila replied. "But before we panicked, we wanted to get some more information."

"Yeah," her brother added. "We didn't have hospice with Will or Livvie."

Emily gently touched Sheila's arm and motioned for her and Jim to sit on the couch that faced another couch and several overstuffed armchairs. "From what Dr. Pram has told us," she began, "their cases were difficult to predict. Your brother and sister had been in the same condition for so many years, it was hard to tell how long it could go on."

Sheila took Jim's hand. "But Stuart's different?"

"He seems to be changing now, yes," Lori the nurse answered as she also touched Sheila's arm. "Why don't we start by gathering information about the family?" she added as Emily put some bottles of water and a tissue box on the coffee table. "Would either of you like to tell us about Stuart? About your family?"

"Well," said Sheila, "our family has HD. Huntington's. And Stuart's the baby." She had that bleak look on her face that always appeared when she spoke about her family. "Jim and I are the only ones to escape it. Lucky, I guess."

"But we sure don't like feelin' lucky when we have to watch our brothers and sisters die," Jim added.

"Which of your parents had HD?" asked Kate, as she filled in the circles and squares in the social work genogram on her clipboard.

"Dad," Jim and Sheila said in unison.

Dr. Pram looked through a thick chart. "I see he died quite young. How did that happen?"

"He was run over," said Jim. "Little wonder, with his moving all over the place like he did. He just careened in front of a car one day. Poor lady. Scared the crap out of her. He came reelin' out of nowhere."

"When did his symptoms begin?" the physician asked. "I mean, about what age was he when the movements started?"

"Hard to tell. We were little. At first, we thought he was just drunk a lot. And the moving really didn't seem strange, 'cause our aunts did it too." Jim imitated the fidgeting and flailing.

"We only really started to think he was sick when other people tried to get away from him," Sheila added. "Like on the playground. And at school."

"Yeah," Jim echoed.

"So you must not have known it was HD for awhile, is that right?" Dr. Pram gently asked. "What about your grandparents? Your father's parents. Did they have it?"

"We don't know," Sheila replied. "They died in car accidents, too. We don't remember if they moved funny, but we probably wouldn't have noticed much." She gave a little shrug. "Kids don't."

"How did you find out about Huntington's?"

"Cousin Ginnie. She went to Berkeley. A bio major. She read a book about Woody Guthrie, the folksinger. You know, Arlo's dad. She thought that their family sounded a whole lot like ours, only they had fires instead of car wrecks. Most of us read it, right, Jim?"

"Yeah. So us cousins started to think it might be this Huntington's. And we all knew our thrashing parents didn't much like going to doctors. So maybe they didn't even know."

"What would've been the point?" Sheila's voice was gruff. "You can't do anything. And they'd already passed the bad genes on to us. Some of us, that is."

They were quiet for a moment. Sheila reached for a tissue and dabbed her eyes. "But then Livvie started to fidget. She couldn't help it. Oh, she tried hard not to. She'd sit on her hands to keep them still. But soon enough, we could tell she was beginning to get *the sickness*, which is what we called it. And cousin Barry, too."

Dr. Pram looked up from the file. "But you eventually found out who had the mutation and who didn't. How did you learn about the test, if your family didn't see doctors often? After all, it's a pretty rare disease and a rather odd sort of genetic test."

"Ginnie again," said Jim. "She read about a government study—it was 1994, I think—where we could all get tested for free. Even if we didn't have the sickness yet."

"Yeah. The government researchers especially wanted to test Jim, Stuart, and me," Sheila explained, "because we weren't sick yet, and they wanted to see if the test they'd invented could predict if any of us would be. But I don't think we quite understood that at the time, certainly not how upsetting it would be, to get results either way. Anyway, that's how we found out Stuart was gonna get it. And that we wouldn't. And by then we didn't need a fancy gene test to tell us about Livvie and Will."

"And Stuart started showing symptoms—when? In 1998?" Dr. Pram asked.

Stuart's brother and sister nodded.

"He was very young when it started," Sheila said in a low voice. "Never finished college, because things got too embarrassing. He couldn't hold jobs. He lost the one at MacDonald's when he threw a drink at a customer. He didn't really throw it, of course. He said he knew his arm was flinging the soda, but he just couldn't make it stop. The boss didn't believe him."

"Who took care of him?" asked Kate.

"He split his time between Jim and me," Sheila said. "We each had a room for him, and we sorta knew what to expect. Until now."

"He's been at Ames for seven years?" asked Dr. Pram.

"Right." Jim and Sheila looked at each other. "But, doctor, we don't really understand why hospice is coming in if he's stopped moving. Couldn't that mean he's getting better?"

"Sheila," the doctor replied in a quiet voice, "people don't get better from Huntington's."

"I know, but—"

"The stillness means his body is exhausted. *It* wants to move, but *he's* just too tired. His muscles are simply running out of energy. But every once in awhile, he will jerk about. That's why he sometimes injures himself, unless he's restrained with blankets and sheets and his nails are kept short."

Jim shook his head. "But isn't it better than when he was crashing into the walls and hurling himself to the floor?"

"It's probably safer," said Lori, the nurse. "And we can help make him more comfortable. Take care of the anxiety." She smiled. "And he'll be less lonely."

Jim and Sheila looked at each other again and nodded. "How could hospice help?" Sheila asked.

"Well," Lori replied, "we will be Stuart's team. And Emily will assign a volunteer to visit him, too."

"Can you send a lady?" Sheila asked. "A pretty one?"

Emily smiled and leaned forward. "We usually send a same-sex volunteer, but I think we can make an exception. I have someone special in mind."

"Would Stuart like me to visit, too?" the chaplain asked.

"No, sir," Jim said. "No offense, but he isn't really into church."

Sheila turned to Emily, who was smiling at Jim's honesty and writing on her clipboard. "When can the volunteer start?" Jim asked.

"I'll call her right away. She's taking our training class next week, so hopefully right after that. I think she's perfect for Stuart."

5

AMES NURSING HOME

The nurses and aides had gotten Stuart out of bed early. After the new aide, the Britney Spears look-alike, had cleaned him up from breakfast, and that badass Nurse Smithies had changed his Depends and gotten his meds into him, Samantha and her swinging braid had come in with the Hoyer lift and they'd begun the daily ritual of hoisting him up and depositing him in his chair. It wasn't a wheelchair, more a recliner-on-wheels. But it was better than being stuck in bed, where, if someone forgot to put him upright, he'd go nuts staring at the ceiling. And the Hoyer gave him an opportunity for cleavage gazing at Brit, given that his head was momentarily and conveniently right at nipple level.

The ride down the hallway took only seconds, and then he was parked in the dayroom, where a curious assortment of humanity assembled each day. They were more his family than his actual family, whom he saw only once a week, if that. Jim and Sheila were pretty much the only ones left. Oh, yes, and cousin Ginnie.

Samantha always took great care to dress Stuart, selecting from his collection of concert T-shirts to match what the radio was playing in the hallway. Today he wore sweatpants and a Pink Floyd tee, one of his favorites. It made him think of the song *Comfortably Numb*, which more or less described his current state.

He settled in to await lunch. Time in a nursing home is strictly measured by the meals: before, during, and after, times three. Stuart watched, as best he could, trapped in his limited visual field, as the nurses and aides came and went, wheeling in more residents. A group of old ladies sat in their wheelchairs huddled around a TV in one corner, enraptured with Jerry Springer and the two whores wrestling over some obscenely ugly dude. A man with an oxygen tank also sat within Stuart's sight; he was meticulously aligning paper clips on the armrest of his chair. Stuart couldn't see most of his hallmates, who simply stared into space, their morning meds having made the nurses' jobs easier. He was growing bored with the scene when Elvin the janitor, finished for the moment with wiping up fresh barf, came over. Stuart hoped he'd tell him a few dirty jokes.

"Hey, Stuart," the janitor muttered, "looks like the show's about to start. Here, lemme turn you so's you don't miss nothin'."

Gradually, the song playing on the radio faded as a low, ominous rumbling rose. Stuart and several of the others smiled in anticipation. And then it began.

"Ahhh, ahhh, ahhh."

The foghorn-like sound was coming from a surprisingly small woman, sitting in a wheelchair, surrounded by two others.

"Shuddup! Shuddup! Shuddup!" yelled the lady to her left.

The residents started to clap.

"YOU shuddup, you moron! She can't help it!" yowled the third woman.

And so the mantra repeated: *ahhh ahhh ahhh, shuddup, shuddup, shuddup, you-shuddup-you-moron-she-can't-help-it*, the residents now stamping with glee. Stuart's eyebrows shot up and down.

After a few minutes, Nurse Smithies came charging in, and broke up the trio. Stuart was certain that the old farts were always parked together intentionally because the staff recognized their entertainment value. But the show wasn't over.

"Lemme turn you some more," said Elvin. "Wanna watch Cornelius?" He turned Stuart's chair to face an elderly man, brow furrowed in concentration as he tore pages from the *Philadelphia Reporter* and folded the pieces into tiny boats. Then one boat fell.

"Man overboard! Man overboard! Women and children first!" the man howled until an aide retrieved the paper boat. Then he calmed down. Stuart suspected Cornelius came from some sort of nautical background. Or maybe he was just nuts, like most everyone else.

Lunch would be coming soon. Stuart could tell, even though he couldn't see the clock, because *The Price Is Right* had just ended, and the commercial that ran just before noon every day blared yet again:

"Got an idea? Share it and earn $10,000! Call 1-800-555-TELL. World Medical Mysteries."

"Lunch!" bellowed Nurse Smithies, right on cue, as if they were in summer camp and everyone could just run on over to the mess tent. The scowling Smithies pulled a tray carrier into the dayroom, barking orders to the kitchen crew, who couldn't give a rat's ass what she wanted. The aides started handing out the trays. Stuart couldn't figure out why nobody ever called Smithies by her first name, like the other nurses. He hated the old bitch.

6

HOSPICE OFFICE

The thirty-five-ish, elegantly beautiful woman with flawless ebony skin, almond-shaped eyes, and dozens of long, sleek black braids sat on the dried grass in the center of a circle of a dozen people, sheltered by the leafy canopy of vibrant elms and oaks. The weather was so spectacular that they'd set up chairs right outside the atrium. The eclectic group—a pair of soccer moms, a hippie type with long Cher-like hair, and a few very sad-looking people—had come to learn if they had what it takes to comfort the dying. Also present (for a refresher course) were a few nurses, a minister, and a nun who was wearing normal clothing. And Kelsey Raye. The woman in the center cleared her throat and the chattering stopped.

"Welcome! I'm Lydia Johnson, hospice director. Thank you for signing up to be volunteers. The training is all week, and will get a little more intense each day, culminating with an unforgettable personal exercise on Friday. If you make it through the week, you'll do fine as a volunteer. We'll meet in the atrium when the weather isn't this glorious. I thought I'd talk a little about hospice first, and then we'll introduce ourselves, okay?"

The volunteers all nodded, their attention riveted on Lydia.

Hospice began in the Middle Ages, she told them, when religious pilgrims who were ill would gather at rest stops until they felt well enough to continue their journeys. Soon it occurred to people to actually care for them at the rest stops.

"Fast forward," Lydia said, "to England in the 1960s." Over the years and with the advent of antibiotics, transplants, and chemotherapy, the medical profession had become obsessed with treating and curing. Anything less was regarded as failure. But with all the medical progress, nobody was paying attention to the chronically ill or the dying. Dame Cicely Saunders, an English doctor, did pay attention. She saw dying patients stuck at the ends of hallways and ignored.

"And she wouldn't stand for it," Lydia continued. "So she championed the special needs that people face at the end of life. Medical. Psychological. Emotional. Spiritual."

"The first modern hospice facility, St. Christopher's, opened in London in 1967. In 1974, the first hospice in the U.S. opened in New Haven, Connecticut. The project was spearheaded by Elisabeth Kubler-Ross."

"The psychiatrist who published *On Death and Dying*, with the five stages of dying?" one of the soccer moms asked.

Lydia nodded. "Yes, right. Since then, thousands of volunteers, everyday people like yourselves, have helped families navigate this most difficult journey. Which brings me to *you*." She looked around the circle. "Does anyone want to talk about why they're here? And please introduce yourself first." She pointed to the soccer mom who'd just spoken. "Why don't you start?"

"Sure. I'm Janet Moore. I'm a substitute English teacher, and my boys are seven and nine. My mother died of ovarian cancer last year, and that's why I'm here. To help someone else."

"Me, too!" a few voices echoed.

"OK," said Emily Josephs, the volunteer coordinator, who was team-teaching the class with Lydia, "hands up for those sharing Janet's experience of recent loss." She counted hands, then pointed to Kelsey.

"Me? I'm Kelsey Raye. I'm a science writer. My parents died of cancer, my dad about a year ago, my mom two years before that."

"I lost a child. Leukemia," said a woman who looked little more than a child herself. "Oh. I'm Lisa."

"I'm sorry," several voices murmured.

One of the men looked around the circle. "I'm Stan," he said. "Retired chemist. And my wife died eighteen months ago. Of Alzheimer's. She also had Parkinson's."

"Many of our patients have those disorders," said Lydia.

The woman with the Cher hair looked up, wearing dramatic eye make-up that also suggested the exotic singer. "I took care of my father. He had Parkinson's but died of a stroke. About a year ago. I'm Marsha Berne. I'm a buyer for Urban Outfitters and Anthropologie."

Several pairs of female eyes widened.

"That's my favorite store," Janet said. "The Anthropologie in Rittenhouse Square."

"Mine too," said Lisa.

"Well, me too," said Lydia, laughing. "But can we move on? Anybody else?"

A younger man spoke up. "My name is Eric. My partner died fifteen months ago. Of AIDS. I'm a student at Temple."

Lydia looked around at the group. "Thank you. The rest of you are here for continuing education, right?" The others nodded.

"I can introduce you. Simon is a minister at Faith Baptist in South Philly. Sister Camelia lives at St. Anne's. And Sue, Connie, and Pat are fabulous hospice RNs. Sue will teach us about therapeutic touch, and Connie's a recent nursing school graduate," Lydia continued as she walked around the circle, handing out paper and pens.

"Now we can start. Hospice training is practical. You'll learn how to turn an oxygen tank on and off. How to manipulate a hospital bed. Do mouth care. You'll learn how to tell when death is weeks away, days away, even hours away. But it's much more than that. The process begins with knowing yourself. We'll start by answering a few questions. Please take your time."

Kelsey glanced down at the questions, and grew uneasy.

- *What role has faith played in your life?*
- *When do you read the Bible?*
- *Who has meant the most to you?*

- *How do you cope with personal loss?*
- *Do you believe in an afterlife?*
- *How often do you think of loved ones who have died?*
- *How often do you attend church?*
- *What is your favorite place to pray?*

Kelsey looked at the others, who were all writing feverishly. Except Marsha, the store buyer. Unexpectedly, they looked up at the same instant. From underneath her fringe of bangs, Marsha rolled her eyes. Kelsey suppressed a giggle.

Lydia gave them both dirty looks. "Is there a problem?" she asked in a stage whisper.

"No, sorry," Marsha muttered.

Lydia nodded. "OK," she said a minute later. "Please hand in your papers, and we'll take a ten-minute break."

The group splintered and wandered off, some to admire the waning vegetable garden out back, others heading for the front of the building. The three nurses huddled together on the sidewalk, furtively lighting cigarettes. Stan and Eric seemed to be having an intense conversation. Marsha and Kelsey walked over to a bench near a weeping willow and sat down together.

"I'm getting a bad feeling about this," Marsha said. "You, too?"

"Yeah," said Kelsey. "I don't like the religious stuff. It makes me feel strange. All the assumptions. I take it you aren't religious, either?"

"Nope. Raised Jewish, but I lost interest way back in Sunday school."

"Why? Anything in particular?"

Marsha laughed. "It seems funny, now. I asked the rabbi where Cain and Abel's wives came from. Were they people? Apes? Neanderthals? It seemed a logical question then. And it still does."

"What was the answer?"

"I was told to be quiet. And when I persisted, I was shushed again, and a note was sent home. I know that's hardly typical of the Jewish way of thinking, but it happened, and was enough to turn me off. What about you?"

"My folks were marginally Methodist."

"I know what you mean. We have a version of that, the revolving-door Jew."

"What's that?" Kelsey asked.

"In with Rosh Hashanah, out with Yom Kippur. The equivalent of the Christian who only shows up at church for weddings, funerals, and Christmas is the Jew who ventures to synagogue only during the high holy days. Thank God—well, whoever—my parents didn't force me to have a bat mitzvah." She shuddered.

"I've heard about those," Kelsey said. "Wasn't there a movie about how ridiculously lavish they can be? What exactly is a bat mitzvah?"

"A bar or bat mitzvah celebrates officially entering the faith, but it is usually a keep-up-with-the-Finkelstein's event." Marsha didn't even bother to keep the scornful tone out of her reply. "Sometimes at nauseating cost."

"Well, I guess the part-time religious folk are better than the ones who try to convert you."

"That's what I don't understand. Jews don't do that. We don't try to 'save' people who don't think like we do. It's so arrogant." Marsha looked up. "Oops. Looks like the boss lady's calling us. C'mon. Time to go over our answers and have them pass judgment on us. Can't wait."

※

"Thank you for sharing your loss timelines, and especially for including your pets," said Emily as a group activity ended on the fourth day. The past sessions had been filled with the minutiae of symptoms of the top ten causes of death in the U.S., talks by all the types of professionals associated with hospice, several films chronicling specific cases, and a travelogue of sorts about the option to go to South Africa to work with AIDS orphans. That was certainly different than the cancer, heart disease, dementia, and COPD they'd most often encounter in Philadelphia. After all the discussions and exercises, the group had become pretty tight.

Kelsey's mind wandered, her 3 PM caffeine low making her drowsy. The day had become so overcast that they'd moved indoors. She noted that the volunteer coordinator was again wearing a combination of colors and textures that no fashion savvy woman would dream of mixing—a skirt with a large floral print paired with a blouse with small flowers—but on Emily, as always, it worked. Must be her exquisite facial bone structure, Kelsey thought absently.

"Now I'll turn the discussion over to Lydia and Chaplain Timothy. Our final topic for today is spirituality and faith," Lydia continued.

Marsha rolled her huge, brown eyes and Kelsey examined her shoelaces.

Lydia looked around the group. "How many of you attended church regularly as children?"

Many hands went up.

"Does synagogue count?" Marsha whispered.

Lydia, sitting to her left, heard. "Yes, of course," she said. "That's what I meant. How about, how many of you attended religious services regularly?"

The same hands went up again.

"OK. What did you like about going to church? And synagogue?"

A long discussion ensued of church memories. Marsha's otherwise striking eyes glazed over and Kelsey continued her intense scrutiny of the color pattern of her running shoes. Ten interminable minutes passed, apparently nobody noticing that the two women were the only ones not participating.

"Thank you all," Lydia said, looking pointedly at Marsha, "for sharing. Chaplain Timothy? What have you to add?"

The very tall man who seemed to be having trouble folding his frame into the chair straightened and checked instinctively to feel for the hair on the top of his head. He cleared his throat. "As hospice chaplain," he began, "I often observe the relationship between people and their God. As we've heard here, people perceive God in different ways. And your patients will, too. Some will feel abandoned, others at peace, even joyful."

Pat the nurse raised her hand. "I've seen people very angry at God. Is that normal?"

"There's not really any *normal*," the chaplain replied. "Feelings vary. Yes, for some people anger and despair become rage, perhaps as a response to their suffering. But some people feel oppositely. That is, they've left God, for whatever reason, and when the end is near, they wish to reestablish the relationship. And that's where you, the volunteers, can come in."

At this, Kelsey and Marsha began to fidget in earnest. Their eyes met, and they seemed to be deciding which of them would dare speak out first. Kelsey couldn't control herself an instant longer.

"Um, I'd like to bring up the, um, "A" word. Actually, two "A" words."

Everyone turned to her. What was she talking about?

"*Atheist*," she said in a voice slightly louder than necessary. "And *agnostic*."

"That's three "A" words," Marsha stage-whispered to Kelsey as Connie, Pat, and Simon gasped. Sister Camelia squirmed and crossed herself. Lydia and Emily exchanged concerned glances. Chaplain Timothy met Kelsey's gaze head on and opened his mouth, but Connie, the recent nursing grad, beat him to it.

"What did you say?"

"Atheists. Agnostics. We exist, too."

"What?"

"You've been assuming everyone is religious," Kelsey explained. "*Christian*, actually. Well, that's not true. And that assumption is responsible for a lot of the problems in the world today, don't you think?"

"Huh? I know there's Jews," said Connie, defiantly twisting a curl that had escaped her frizzy brown ponytail. "And Muslims. And others. I guess."

"No," said Kelsey, and Marsha nodded. "That's not what I mean. Not everyone believes in God."

"Well," Connie blurted out, "they don't count. Volunteering for hospice requires having ethics, and people without God can't have ethics. Those atheist types just aren't appropriate for this organization."

Trying not to explode, Kelsey silently counted to 10. She did her yoga breathing. Then she decided to try reasoning with the self-righteous nurse. "I'm confused," she said softly. "Aren't we supposed to accept our patients' differing viewpoints? Doesn't that extend to us, too?"

With great drama, Connie stood up, walked over to Kelsey, shoved her way onto the couch next to her, and put her arm around her. "Do you mean to tell me that you haven't accepted Jesus Christ as your Savior?" she asked.

"Who are you? Mel Gibson?" Marsha snorted.

"No, Connie, I haven't."

"Well, then, how can you expect to help a patient if you deny God? I don't understand."

Transfixed by this unanticipated confrontation, everyone in the room leaned forward.

"No, Connie," Marsha finally said. "You sure don't understand."

Kelsey, now beet red and sweating, turned helplessly to Emily and then to Lydia. "Please. You two are in charge. This is ridiculous. Why does Connie think I need to be saved—whatever that means—because I don't think, pardon me, *believe*, as she does?"

Emily stood up and crossed the circle to take Kelsey's hand. "I think we're getting off the topic. Kelsey, just by being here, you are demonstrating ethics as well as spirituality." She gave everyone in the circle an even look, then turned back to Kelsey. "You have a right to your opinion and your own beliefs."

"Thank you. I think."

Emily turned to the others again. "That's enough for today. Tomorrow is our last session. It won't be easy. We will imagine our own deaths."

Everyone got up to help put the chairs away, then Marsha put one arm around Kelsey's waist and they walked out together, clearly apart from the others.

"Sounds like a barrel of laughs tomorrow. Can't wait. Wanna go get a drink?"

"Sure. I need one."

7

"Hey, who goes there?" asked the disembodied voice from somewhere within the yellow rain slicker. Despite the attire, Kelsey could easily see Marsha's remarkable eyes peering out from the shiny vinyl raincoat.

"It's me. Kelsey. Marsha, is that you in there?"

"Yup. Great weather, perfect for death class. How do you like my gear?"

"Very fourth-grade." Kelsey smiled at her new friend. "I'm glad it's you!"

"Thanks." Marsha pulled her hood back enough to show her face. "You may have noticed I'm into high couture. Why're you glad it's me?"

"Well, I'm not exactly winning any popularity contests after our last session. Official class godless heathen."

"I wouldn't worry about it." Marsha took Kelsey's arm as they both looked up at the multihued leaves swirling down with the high wind and filling the air with an earthy aroma. They headed towards the door. Inside, everyone was chatting as they hung dripping jackets and raincoats on hooks on the wall and stowed their umbrellas. The group then settled in facing Lydia and Emily, who sat on one of the couches on either side of a short, balding man with thick black glasses and a nervous facial tic.

Lydia wore her mini-braids like Princess Leia, coiled into bagel-like growths on either side of her head. Kelsey admired her sense of style.

"You've almost made it!" Lydia began. "Today is our last, most intense session. Before we examine our personal feelings about death, Dr. Zimmerman here will review the signs of active dying. He has privileges at several area hospitals and is a professor of geriatric medicine at Franklin Medical College. Welcome, Dr. Z!"

The doctor nodded and cleared his throat. "Thank you for inviting me. Lydia's told me that you've learned about major causes of death and recognizing and treating end-of-life pain. Whatever the cause, the last two weeks tend to be similar as the organ systems shut down."

Dr. Zimmerman stood up and walked among the volunteers, looking each in the eyes and handing a sheet of paper to each of them.

"This is a list of the signs of active dying. They often occur in this order, though this is not an exact science. With different individuals, things might be different. Or only some of the signs may appear. And of course if the heart stops or any other catastrophic event occurs, due to generalized weakness, the person may not have a chance to develop these signs at all."

As the doctor spoke, Kelsey studied the list, wondering how with all her training in biology, no professor had ever discussed what happens when life ends. The list spelled it out:

- *Social withdrawal*
- *Loss of appetite*
- *Irritability*
- *Pulling at linens*
- *Irregular breathing*
- *Cool to touch*
- *Sleeping most of time*
- *Altered mental status*
- *Skin mottling*
- *"Death rattle"*

"So these are the basic steps," Dr. Zimmerman said, taking his place in front of the group of volunteers. "You may witness what we call *nearing death awareness*. This is when the person has a foot in two worlds. He or she may speak to a deceased loved one, or even think you are that person."

Janet raised her hand. "Is that the same as seeing the white light on the other side?"

"No," said Lydia, "that's a near-death experience, which is more likely to happen with a violent hospital death."

The doctor nodded. "Good question, though. Any others?"

"What should we do if a person thinks we're someone else?" Marsha asked. "My luck, the patient'll think I'm Elvis."

Even the doctor smiled at this. "It's okay to just go along with it," he said. "There's even a name for it: *therapeutic fibbing*. Don't feel dishonest about role-playing. Also don't try reasoning. It's comforting for them to think you are the long-lost loved one."

Lydia stood up to shake the doctor's hand. "If there aren't any other questions, and I don't see any, then let's move on to the final exercise. Dr. Z, thank you so much."

The doctor gave a little stage bow, smiled again, and left the room, softly closing the door behind him.

Lydia turned to the class. "OK. Let's move the chairs out of the way. Everybody grab a box of tissues, a pen, and a mat, and spread out on the floor along the walls."

As the volunteers took their places, Emily and Lydia handed fifteen squares of construction paper to each person, five red, five green, and five yellow.

"Now," said Emily, "take a deep, cleansing breath. On each of the red squares, write the name of a loved one."

Everyone thought for a moment, wrote names, then looked up.

"Great. On the green squares, write your five most important possessions."

More writing.

"I think you get the idea. Now on the yellow squares, put down your five most meaningful activities."

Emily sat down again. "Now Lydia is going to read you a story. Listen. It is, for now, *your story*."

All eyes focused on Lydia, who opened a well-worn book.

> *"It's morning," she began, "and you are getting ready for work. You have an important meeting, so you take extra time with your hair. Looking in the mirror, something catches your attention, a dark mark, just at the edge of your scalp. You never noticed it before. It's multicolored, with irregular borders."*

One by one, the listeners put down their pens.

> *"A few days later, you again notice the mark at your hairline. You phone your doctor. You go for a visit, and she probes your scalp. Then she refers you to a dermatologist. 'I wouldn't wait,' she tells you. 'It could be a melanoma.'"*

Most of the volunteers were now looking down. They seemed to be curling into themselves as Lydia continued.

> *"The minute you get home, you look up melanoma on the Internet. And you panic."*

Lydia looked up. "Now, please take one of your yellow activities squares, turn it face down, and lay it aside. You are taking this activity out of your life."

Pretty quickly, they all selected the yellow squares to be placed aside.

> *"The dermatologist finds two other spots on your head and biopsies them along with the first one."*

"Take away a green square, a possession," Lydia said.

The volunteers set aside green squares. They were still looking at the floor, obviously uncomfortable.

> *"An anxious week passes. The dermatologist calls. He has bad news. The spots are indeed melanoma."*

Lydia's voice did not change. "Take away a red square. A loved one."

Most of the listeners studied their red squares and then, looking distressed, slowly removed one. A few people, unable to choose, pulled a piece of paper at random. Marsha gave Kelsey a skeptical look. Kelsey met her gaze but she seemed upset.

A half hour passed, and the scenario grew grimmer. Kelsey sat in a corner with all but one of her squares overturned, as Lydia continued.

> *"You can no longer tell day from night. You're long past wanting to eat. You're hot, then cold. You think people are with you, but you aren't sure. You do know that you are at home, in your own bed. You whisper goodbye to your loved ones. You are at peace. You drift off to sleep."*

Lydia paused, listening to the sniffling of her volunteers.

"Now take away your last loved one."

Some of the volunteers were crying; nearly all looked shaken. After several long moments, Lydia spoke again.

"Take your time to collect your thoughts. Once you submit your health forms, we'll be calling you as soon as you're needed. If you feel ready, of course. You may need to wait a few weeks, or even months. Sometimes it's just too soon after a personal loss to volunteer. But I'm sure you will all be great." She gave them her brightest smile. "And we need you! Thank you."

Slowly a few of the volunteers pushed themselves to their feet. They blew their noses, wiped their eyes, collected themselves. No one spoke. After a minute or two of indecision, they got their rain gear on. Marsha grabbed Kelsey's arm and led her quickly outside.

"What a crock of shit!"

Kelsey wiped her eyes. "I don't know, Marsha."

"Huh?"

8

Kelsey sat on the couch, feet up on the coffee table, one cat on each side. Next to Chester was a pile of *Nature* magazines, and next to Foghat, a pile of *Sciences*. On the coffee table sat a third feline, Nirvana, and a pumpkin carved into a scary face, about all Kelsey's lack of artistic abilities would permit. She was typing away at her laptop, writing her bimonthly column for the *Philadelphia Reporter*. This one was about a group called Citizens Against Stem Cell Research which was threatening to sabotage various labs without apparently having the faintest idea of what the research was about, or even what an early human embryo actually looks like—a microscopic ball of cells.

When Kelsey's interview with a researcher on the use of discarded human foreskin as a tissue culture aid had taken less time than expected, she'd left the office early and was now finishing the column at home. But she'd forgotten that it was Halloween. As if to remind her, the doorbell rang. She got up, put her plastic pumpkin full of candy outside the front door, came back in, plugged in her iPod and sat back down.

Usually, Kelsey worked more efficiently at home, surrounded by felines but no chattering humans to break her concentration. She also preferred the rock concert posters on her walls of the apartment to the magazine covers and article reprints festooning the walls at the office. She'd made an exception on her walls at home for framed tearsheets of her series on Huntington's disease. They were the first *real* newspaper articles she'd written, not for the student paper, but published in an actual newspaper just before she'd gotten her Ph.D. A few weeks after the articles had appeared in the small Indiana newspaper, she'd received a letter of thanks from a nice lady in New York City. She'd stuffed the letter in the back pocket of her jeans, then washed them, only to find the letter, the print barely visible, weeks later.

This time, she had paid attention to the signature. Marjorie Guthrie. Realizing the connection instantly—Marjorie was Woody Guthrie's second wife—Kelsey had written back, which led to meeting Marjorie, as well as her son, Arlo, in the offices of the Committee to Combat Huntington's Disease. Her first articles remained her favorites.

Just as Kelsey finished the column, her cell phone, buried under journals on the coffee table, made a meowing sound, thoroughly confusing the cats. Kelsey dug out the phone and flipped it open while calming the frazzled felines.

"Hello? Hi, Emily! No, I just finished writing. Perfect timing."

Kelsey scratched Nirvana behind the ear while she straightened up the journals and listened to Emily.

"A patient?" Kelsey replied. "How old is she? Is she demented? Oh, a man? Only thirty-two? In a nursing home?" Kelsey frowned. "What's wrong? What's he got?" As she listened, her frown deepened. "Huntington's? Was that the family coming in the other day?"

Purring, Nirvana slunk back onto the coffee table and wound himself around the pumpkin.

Kelsey was no longer paying any attention to the cat. "Isn't that kind of young?" she asked Emily. "How awful. Okay, I'll go see him soon. I was starting to tell you the day we first met—I know about that disease. I've written about it. And I helped out with a family support group. What's the patient's name? How violent are his movements?" She listened intently.

"I see." She sighed. "Or maybe I don't, that *is* unusual. Can I stop by the office tomorrow at lunchtime to read his chart? I remember you said you can't mail that info out because of the HIPPA regulations." Kelsey listened a few moments, stroking Nirvana again.

"Oh, Emily, can I tell Marsha about the patient? I won't use his last name. Okay, I'll see you then!"

⊙

Kelsey sat in Emily's office looking through a sheaf of papers and jotting notes on a legal pad. She quickly sketched the Matheson family pedigree, filling in the symbols for Stuart's father, but writing question marks over the symbols for his parents, Stuart's paternal grandparents, killed in a car crash. They'd died too young to have shown symptoms of Huntington's. She filled in the shapes representing Livvie and Will and Stuart, indicating their losing hand in the inheritance game. That done, Kelsey flipped through several pages of medical information, then settled on a page that actually told her something about Stuart as a person:

Religion:	Raised Protestant, atheist
Occupation:	Cabdriver, bartender, construction
Interests:	Sports (Eagles), rock music
Education:	High school, some college

Kelsey looked up, thinking, then looked back down. Then she opened her purse, took out her iPod, and stared at it.

⊙

AMES NURSING HOME, DAYROOM
It had been a relatively calm lunch. Stuart was glad he still had some control over his mouth. That made him able to refuse the meatloaf sandwich that had been passed through a blender before emerging as something resembling diarrhea. Yet he'd happily kept his mouth open for the ice cream and pureed fruit. Since it wasn't a choking day, he also drank the Ensure. He actually felt full for once.

The aides were busy shoving the trays back in their metal carriers and wiping off the tabletops and residents. Poor, demented Mrs. Foofnagel had nodded off into her applesauce again, possible only due to her deafness because Mrs. Rinehart, next to her, was breaking the sound barrier with her belches. An impossibly tiny woman who was younger than the others sat in front of the fish tank, mesmerized by a bright yellow tang that swam in circles around a plaster figurine of Ariel, the Little Mermaid.

Doc, who had Tourette's syndrome, was nodding, barking, and repeating the steps of the Krebs cycle over and over. *Citrate-isocitrate-alpha ketoglutaric acid-succinyl-succinyl CoA-fumarate-malate-oxaloacetic acid. Repeat.* Yesterday it had been Moh's scale of hardness for minerals. Stuart suspected that Doc had not been a medical doctor, but a scientist of some sort whose mind had melted, except for the brain circuits devoted to lists he'd once committed to memory.

A TV soap opera droned in the background, momentarily distracting all the bickering old biddies with the drama of siblings Nick and Victoria discovering that their spouses were having an affair. Again. Stuart glanced past the TV to the clear partition separating the dayroom from the nurses' station. Someone new was getting off the elevator, which was barely in his field of vision. She walked right into Elvin, whose dreads merged with the mop he was carrying out of the janitor's closet to clean up the regurgitated remnants of lunch.

※

"Ooh! I'm so sorry!"

"No problem." Elvin, peeking out from the mop and extending his hand, grinned at the woman who had bumped into him. "Hi. I'm Elvin," he said, quickly retracting his hand. "No, better not touch my hand. You don't wanna know where it's been lately. Can I help you? Visiting someone?"

"I'm looking for Stuart Matheson. Am I on the right floor?" Kelsey glanced into the dayroom. "Everyone here looks positively ancient."

"Mostly everyone is," Elvin replied. "'Cept poor Mimi, the fish lady, and Stuart. Over there." Elvin pointed to what was apparently the only male resident under the age of eighty. "That's him. He had a nice lunch today. Didn't even barf once. I'll take you on over."

"OK, thanks. I think." Kelsey sniffed. "Does it always smell like this?"

"Like what?"

"Uh, it's hard to describe. Like the air isn't moving. And dirty laundry. And a sweetness."

"Part of it could be lunch. But you get used to it. I don't even notice the smell no more, 'cept of course when someone heaves or craps themselves. Let me bring you's over to the boss lady. Hope she ain't too crabby today."

Kelsey followed Elvin a few steps to the nurses' station. "She's here to see Stuart," Elvin said, then stepped back.

Nurse Smithies took a few moments to finish counting pills, then looked up at Kelsey. She frowned slightly, then pointed in Stuart's direction. "He's all yours, honey. He don't get too many visitors, but I'd cover up a bit more if I was you." Elvin slapped a hand over his mouth, but the laughter shone in his eyes.

Kelsey fidgeted with her shirt, but the nurse kept staring at her.

"You look familiar," she said. "Been here before?"

"No," Kelsey answered, hesitantly.

"You're sure? I could swear…"

"Oh, you might've seen my photo in the paper. I write a column. On science."

"Then you should visit with our resident geek, Dr. Fleming, or Doc, as we call him," said the nurse, warming a little.

"Was he a doctor? Or a scientist?"

"Same thing, ain't they? Doc sputters long names, mostly chemicals. Shouts out lists that might make some sense to some other nerd. You might wanna give it a listen, seein' how you write science."

"OK." Kelsey said. "I'll keep an ear open for someone reciting a biochemical pathway."

Nurse Smithies came around the counter and glared briefly at the janitor. "Elvin, you can get back to work. I'll bring her over." The nurse took Kelsey's arm and led her into the dayroom. "Like I said, Stuart has a real thing for the ladies, especially young and skinny ones like you," said the slightly rotund nurse.

Kelsey greeted each resident she passed with a friendly nod until they were standing right in front of Stuart. He stared at her without raising his head, his eyes widening, mouth twitching, and eyebrows raised.

"Told ya," whispered the nurse. "He could look up at your face if he really wanted to."

But Kelsey didn't hear her. The patient's eyes did just that, they turned up to meet hers. His mouth opened and closed, in what she sensed was deep frustration. He couldn't speak because of his disease; she couldn't either, but she didn't know exactly why. Some sort of instantaneous and overwhelming force seemed to be drawing them together. The overbearing nurse, the friendly janitor, the pervasive stench, the blaring TV, the distant moaning—all faded as her mind seemed to hurtle her back in time. Her imagination filled in the gaunt planes of his face, fleshed out the sticks of his legs, revealed where his thin sweat pants rippled, added muscle to the skeletal arms that poked out from his loose Phish T-shirt. She could sense that he still saw himself as he once was, which was *hot*.

After what seemed an eternity she found her voice, although it was scratchy. "Hi Stuart. I'm Kelsey. Is it okay if I come by sometimes to visit you? Dr. Pram thought it would be nice. It looks like you don't get to be around many people your, I mean, *our*, age. Would that be okay?"

Stuart grimaced with the effort of trying to move forward toward her. She took his gnarled hands, the fingers clawlike from the years of uncontrollable clenching, drew them together, and covered them with her own. Then she began to gently move her thumb back and forth on his hands as she leaned in closer. She thought she could feel his fingers slightly relax and warm to her touch.

"Would you like to hear some music?"

Stuart moved his eyebrows up and down.

"OK." Kelsey released his hands and pulled a chair closer, and sat down. She pulled her iPod from her purse, unwound the earbuds, and scrolled through the settings. "Don't worry," she told him. "This is just an iPod. It won't take your blood pressure or give you a shot or anything. And we can share it."

Kelsey placed one earbud in her ear and reached over to place the other in Stuart's. "The doctor told me you like rock music. Me, too. So I tried to think back to what you'd know from high school. Remember this?" She clicked the iPod, sat back, and smiled.

Stuart's face registered shock, then suddenly transformed as "Smells Like Teen Spirit" resounded through the tiny earpieces. A huge grin fleetingly though definitely broke out, and Kelsey thought she could see his turned-in, deformed feet move just a little. She didn't doubt her eyes, though, when he lifted his arms up, his meaning unmistakable. Kelsey didn't hesitate to hug her new friend.

"You remember Nirvana! I knew you would! How about Pearl Jam next?"

※

AMES NURSING HOME, NOVEMBER 2

Kelsey exited the elevator on D3, this time looking both ways. She'd stopped in on her way to work. It was between breakfast and lunch in nursing home time.

A few of the healthier residents ambled back and forth using their walkers, the contraptions personalized with ribbons and nametags. Many of the others were parked in their wheelchairs along the hallways. A very old man was folding papers into boats and hurling them onto the floor, looking distressed, then folding more boats. Another man aligned paper clips along the arm of his chair. In a corner, a black woman cradled a black doll, and next to her a blond woman combed the hair of a blond doll. The room doors were all partially open, and Kelsey glimpsed residents waiting their turns to be sprung, if only to the hallway or dayroom. Most were staring into space, the morning drugs having kicked in. Halloween decorations were still up, soon to be replaced with cardboard turkeys and cornucopias. Kelsey wondered how many of the residents resented being treated like children.

She looked around the hallway for Stuart, but didn't see him. It was probably harder to get him into his chair than it was to guide a pleasantly demented resident, who still had control over his muscles, into a conventional wheelchair. She finally found Stuart's room. His nameplate had a little heart sticker on it, alerting the staff that he was now on hospice care, and therefore would have more traffic going in and out. The heart symbol was used to maintain his privacy because the other residents wouldn't know that the symbol meant anything. Sometimes even the person on hospice didn't know it, if the family agreed it would be better not to tell him.

Kelsey wondered if Stuart knew or not, although the "H" word was printed on her id badge. Still, in case he didn't, she hadn't volunteered the information. She slowly pushed his door open and peeked in. Reginald lay deathly asleep, drool shining on his face. Stuart was awake, staring straight ahead, his eyes focused on an old photograph taped to the corner of the mirror.

Today he was wearing a Philadelphia Eagle's cap and a Grateful Dead T-shirt. Faded and tattered, it was the real deal, not some knock-off. The bedsheet covered his legs, but she could tell they were bent and skeletal because his Nikes stuck out at odd angles. That nice nurse with the swinging braid, Sam, had told her that Stuart grew distressed if he didn't wear running shoes. A tattoo of a snake on his neck looked alive as it pulsed along with the movements of his carotid artery. On the wall behind Stuart's head hung a Woodstock poster, placed there so he could see it reflected in the mirror. A few small Beanie Babies sat on the dresser, in front of several framed photos of Stuart (in healthier times) with various women. *Star Trek* blared on the TV, the original. Mr. Spock was raising his ears. And eyebrows. Periodic buzzes, beeps, and yells up and down the hall maintained the cacophony of nursing home normalcy.

Kelsey walked to the foot of the bed and stopped in Stuart's narrow line of sight.

"Hi! Remember me?"

As a grin flitted across Stuart's face, Kelsey thought she could hear a slight noise in response. He lifted his arms for another hug.

"Wanna hear music?" she asked. "Last time I chose the songs, but I can put it on shuffle and see what comes up." Kelsey fiddled with the controls, then placed the earbuds in Stuart's ears. He was still looking at the TV screen.

"That's U2. 'I Will Follow'. Like it?"

Stuart smiled again, this time with half his mouth.

"Shuffle's supposed to be random," she told him, "but it really isn't. This iPod came pre-loaded with U2, but even so, there are some songs that I know are on here that've never come up, yet others pop up often. I don't get it. Maybe there's some sort of algorithm built in based on song popularity." She knew she was babbling. Stuart was absorbed in the music and not listening to her.

She caught herself. "Sorry. Sometimes I just keep on talking. It's like I'm trying to fill in for you, but I guess I don't really need to do that, right?" She paused as if he were answering. "Right. Okay, let me hear too." She bent over and took out one earbud. Stuart's eyes moved down toward the open top of her shirt.

"You can tell U2 right away," she said, standing up straighter. "Can you hear how the guitar starts going back and forth so fast? There's a word for that, *archipelago* or *alopecia* or something like that. Anyway, that's U2's signature. A lot of bands copy that. You probably remember 'Pride: In the Name of Love'? I'll find that."

As Kelsey clicked on the song, Stuart's eyebrows arched as he shut his eyes. Smiling as she twiddled her braid, Samantha watched from the doorway.

9

Kelsey's Diary, November 2

Emily suggested we keep a hospice diary, so this is my first entry. Stuart Matheson is only 32 and has HD, but he's had it so long that he's stopped moving, or so they say. If you watch him closely, it's clear that he uses whatever movements he has left to communicate. He has his own language of raised brows, blinks, partial hugs, and I think I even have heard him say "uh" for "yes." He loves the iPod. We listened to Nirvana the first day, U2 today. It must be better than that background radio or the droning TV.

Maybe I can make playlists that tell a story or have a theme. Musicians-who-died-at-26 day. Kurt Cobain, Jim Morrison, Janis Joplin, Cass Eliot, that guy from Blind Melon. Musicians-who-died-in-plane-crashes. Buddy Holly, Jim Croce, Lynyrd Skynyrd. This could be fun! Fun? In a nursing home?

Nurses' Notes, November 3. Stuart had a peaceful night without usual agitation. No meds needed.

Kelsey's Diary, November 4

The nursing home has its own economy based on stuffed animals, with Beanie Babies the preferred currency because fewer arguments over size are likely to erupt. That explains old Tom, who hoards his winnings and won't let anyone near them, and Evelyn, who arranges them in accurate phylogenetic order on her bedspread, the bugs and crabs before the starfish, which comes before the reptiles and amphibians, birds and mammals, with primates, of course, last. She must have been a biologist. Bunnies and bears predominate. Currency is earned or lost at the Tuesday bingo game, held in the second floor cafeteria. That's where I found Stuart today.

At first I was alarmed that he wasn't in the dayroom or his room, but Elvin pointed me in the right direction to the game. Stuart was immobile, of course, with three bingo cards on his scrawny lap, and a bevy of nurses' aides, probably thrilled to be caring for someone not only under the age of 80 but significantly so, listening and placing the markers whenever and wherever he got a hit. He'd apparently won a few times, because he had a purple hippo on his chest and an ostrich straddling his knee. I got rid of the aides. Stuart smiled. For me?

Nurses' Notes, November 4. Ate more than usual for dinner, shortly after hospice volunteer left. No choking. Seemed more animated.

Nurses' Notes, November 5. Stuart slept most of today. When he awoke, he had a small dinner. Was agitated after. Gave Ativan.

Kelsey's Diary, November 5

I didn't get over to see Stuart today, but I got a chance to stop in at Urban Outfitter's and talk to Marsha. So far she hasn't had such great experiences with hospice. She's had 3 patients. One in home care, 2 at the nursing home, and each died in just a few days. Cancer. She never connected with them. She got really upset after the first one, because no one had let her know that the lady had died. So Marsha had shown up on a Sunday afternoon, when things at the nursing home are usually, excuse the expression, *dead*. When she got to her patient's room, the bed was stripped, the photos, stuffed bears, some clothing, and the birthday card from the local congressman packaged neatly into a small box left in the center of the bed. It freaked her out. She said it reminded her of the old *Star Trek* episode where crew members were arbitrarily killed and their biochemicals reduced to a small white box. Her patient had become a box of possessions.

I guess I'm very lucky to have gotten assigned to Stuart.

Nurses' Notes, November 6. Stuart spent most of the day in the dayroom staring at the elevator. Awaiting volunteer? She arrived late afternoon.

Kelsey's Diary, November 6

I think Stuart noticed that I missed a day! I won't let a deadline get in the way again. Got a nice welcome. Smile and grunts. Today's playlist was on the roots of Crosby, Stills, Nash and Young, although Stuart had on an Allman Brothers tee. I played Buffalo Springfield, the Hollies, and the Byrds, and pointed out the individual voices. I think he liked it.

I try to imagine what his days are like. Could I stand it? Every day the same, except the weekends, when it's even more boring. What is it like when suddenly a neighbor is gone? Or someone cries out in pain? Or when people get no visitors, and have to watch everybody else with their families? Maybe it is better to be one of the patients who live mentally in the past. Most of the dementia patients seem at peace, but a few will scream suddenly, as if reliving an old terror. The nurses and aides seem mostly kind and dedicated, providing good care. And it's true that the residents couldn't really survive at home without round-the-clock help, which nobody can afford. But I don't think I could stand being warehoused away like they all are.

As I was leaving, I saw a rare sight—an actual M.D.! And this wasn't just any M.D., but one with an entourage of students. I politely sidestepped the group and then stood out in the hallway and listened. The doctor was a neurologist, the nursing home's counterpart to Dr. Pram, Stuart's family's physician. He was explaining to the students how Stuart's symptoms differ from those of his siblings because he had survived with the disease longer than they had.

On impulse, I introduced myself to the doctor on his way out. I told him I was a geneticist and Stuart's hospice volunteer, then asked if I could see the family's medical records. He wasn't very impressed with my Ph.D., as MDeities generally aren't, but I did get the go-ahead to look through the chart, which I hope has the extended family history. Maybe that will give me something else to talk to Stuart about. Indirectly, of course. I can ask him yes/no questions.

At first I thought I'd have trouble carrying on one-way conversations. Sometimes I can't seem to shut up, but that happens to me even when people *can* answer. I wonder if I'm actually annoying him?

No.

We connect.

Nurses' Notes, November 7. Demeanor and appetite much improved. No anxiety. Talked to volunteer, Kelsey Raye. Gave her medical records re Dr. Horgan's note.

Kelsey's Diary, November 8

Stuart was asleep when I got there today, around 5 P.M. Reginald, too. I knew they'd wake Stuart for dinner, so after holding his hand for awhile, I followed Samantha the nurse around, picking her brain. She knew Stuart's brother and sister, and said they were very different from him. She also hinted that I'd find some interesting things in the medical records.

I asked about Stuart's meds. He's getting Prozac, which helps with mood swings, and coenzyme Q. The jury's still out on that one, but I guess they figure it can't hurt. He hasn't needed Ativan too much yet, but he might soon, Samantha said. And ethyl-EPA and tetrabenazine are two drugs in clinical trials that he's taking, but they don't seem to be doing much. He's been on them for two years already.

Samantha said that she thought my visits were doing some good, but she wanted to warn me about what was to come. I've been just taking things day to day, without thinking about the future too much. It's hard to notice changes when you see someone so often. But Samantha can. She's been watching him much longer than I have, and she's seen his decline. A year ago he was able to chat with her!

I can't even imagine that.

She said it will be gradual. Choking will increase, swallowing ability decrease, and he'll keep losing weight. She showed me the panic button on the side of the bed, in case he ever starts to choke when I'm there. You're not supposed to help resuscitate a hospice patient, but I don't know… Eventually, even the occasional jerking movements will cease. His oxygen sats will drop, making him more tired, and his agitation will increase. He'll spike fevers. When things worsen, he'll get squirts of morphine in his mouth every few hours. I've seen the nurses giving that the few times I've come in the early evening.

I could barely listen to what she was saying.

I've known him such a short time, and I'm already so attached. I wonder if I should talk to Emily or even chaplain Timothy. I should probably just talk to Marsha, she thinks like I do. This isn't supposed to happen, is it? This bond? So fast?

10

AMES NURSING HOME, DAYROOM, NOVEMBER 10

It was lunchtime on D3, and Elvin was trying to keep up with the dropping food. Stuart's corner was especially messy, what with him sputtering and slobbering all that green crap. But he liked the poor guy. Everyone felt sorry for Stuart, being so young and all. A nursing home was pretty depressing for an old, sick person, but for such a young man? Elvin could tell, from when Stuart used to talk about the women, how much he'd lost. He mopped his way over to the ruckus in Stuart's general area, then looked up to see Nurse Smithies. She had green stuff dripping from her hair. Elvin suppressed a giggle.

"I give up," the nurse was telling Stuart. "I know you didn't get much, but we're not supposed to feed you when you're chokin' so bad. Well, maybe you'll do better at dinner. Or maybe your famous girlfriend can feed you." The nurse looked around the room. "Where the heck is she, anyways?"

Smithies took the food tray away and left to test blood sugars. Stuart looked longingly at the meal trays he could see, sniffed at those he couldn't. Trays with real food, he thought, not blended dog chow like they tried to shovel into him. People who ate solid food just couldn't appreciate the importance of flavors and textures. A hot dog on a roll with kraut and mustard was an entirely different experience from the mess that came out of a blender.

Stuart stared at the peanut butter and jelly sandwich on Cornelius' tray. His mouth watered, which made him choke again. When the spasms stopped, he shut his eyes to recover. Just then, Kelsey stepped out of the elevator. She walked over to the window of the dayroom and peered in, frowning, then hurried to the nurses' station.

"Is Stuart okay?" she asked. "Why isn't he being fed?"

Nurse Smithies scowled. "Forget it. I gave up. He spewed all over me." She wiped at the stains on her uniform, then looked up. "Aren't you dressed rather, er, not for here?"

"I'm just coming from Pilates. I don't understand. Why can't he eat?"

"Just following orders," the nurse replied. "Don't want him to choke. Could kill him, you know. I think you should put on that sweatshirt you're holding, before a breeze gets to your headlights, if you know what I mean. You don't wanna get the geezers in an uproar."

Ignoring the crabby nurse, Kelsey went over to the doorway to the dayroom, where she stood for a minute and watched Stuart gazing wistfully at his neighbor's meatloaf and peas. Then, knowing instinctively what she needed to do, she hurried to his side.

And so, when Stuart looked up to check on the status of the elevator door, his eyes instead met a pair of breasts straining beneath a thin and very tight tank top. His gaze slowly lowered to the leggings that clearly defined Kelsey's firm thighs. She heard his sharp intake of breath as his eyes finally rose to her face, which she could feel was quite red. He'd obviously forgotten all about the coveted meatloaf.

"Hey, Stuart. Time for a little brain music?" Kelsey asked.

Elvin, who'd sauntered over to the vicinity with eyes down as he pushed the mop, looked up. "What the fuck?"

Activity around the nurses' station halted as everyone watched. Nurse Smithies glared and picked up a phone.

Kelsey's Diary, November 11

Yesterday was awful. I was too embarrassed to want to show up today, but I went anyway. Fortunately, nobody said anything. But what was I supposed to do? Putting someone who can't move and can't eat anything but pureed shit, and yesterday not even that, right next to people eating a normal lunch? Stuart may be dying, but he isn't dead. Far from it. He thinks and feels like anyone else.

I felt better as soon as I saw him today. He hadn't been moved to the dayroom yet, so we watched TV. Since I force my musical tastes on him, I figured I should give his TV shows a chance. Actually, I think he likes my music. I can tell when he doesn't, because he either falls asleep, or slightly moves his head in a "no" direction. Maybe nobody else can tell, but I can. Anyway, he watches Jerry Springer religiously. Today's story was the same as when I've been forced to watch that show at the dentist's office. Two grotesque women fighting over an ugly, lowlife dude. They tackle each other, blubber bulging and jiggling. Stuart loves it.

I saw Emily from hospice at the supermarket. She asked how I was doing with Stuart, then mentioned that a nurse had called from his floor, and suggested that I dress more professionally. So I told her the whole story. She said not to worry. Not that I was.

Nurses' Notes, November 12. Stuart's oxygen sats were down a little tonight, but his appetite has improved markedly. He regularly eats two ice creams and drinks a lot of milk and Ensure. He's put on a pound since the start of the month. He is sleeping well, without agitation.

Kelsey's Diary, November 13

Today was fun. Stuart and I were sharing the new Coldplay CD when there was a fire drill. That place is so full of beeps and buzzes, I ignored it at first, but this noise was more persistent. So I got to wheel Stuart outdoors. He never goes outside. As part of his disease, his body can't control temperature. A little like a lizard. But today was spectacular, a last gasp of Indian summer. It was close to 70 degrees and sunny. The trees, with just a few straggling, orange leaves clinging to them, looked oddly out of season. We only stayed out for a short time, but it did Stuart a world of good to see something besides those same dreary walls.

Tomorrow I'm going to play him "Rocket Man" and "Space Oddity." I hope he doesn't see the songs as a metaphor for his situation, being stranded where no one can reach him.

I can reach him.

Kelsey's Diary, November 14

Something's not right. Stuart fell asleep listening to The Killers' new CD, which should be physiologically impossible. When I saw he was sleeping, I noticed that there was greenish crusty gunk at the corners of his eyes. So I told Smithies. She gave me a hard time, saying I'm not a nurse and don't know anything.

Nurses' Notes, November 15. Fever and conjunctivitis. Started antibiotics. Respiratory consult tomorrow.

◁∞▷

AMES NURSING HOME, NOVEMBER 17

Although the dayroom still had that telltale nursing home odor that the occupants don't notice the way a visitor does, the atmosphere was more festive than usual. Thanksgiving cut-outs brightened the drab green walls, and small baskets of gourds cheered up most of the rooms, all courtesy of the Girl Scouts. The remains of lunch hung like stalactites from the tables and trays. A semicircle of residents in wheelchairs shouted answers to a TV game show.

Stuart preferred Jerry Springer. And *Star Trek*. Just as he was about to nod off, he heard the telltale rumblings begin.

"Ahhh, ahhh, ahhh."

"Shuddup! Shuddup! Shuddup!"

The TV watchers turned around, the goings-on in the dayroom more entertaining than TV. And live.

"YOU shuddup, you moron! She can't help it!"

"Ahhh ahhh ahhh."

As annoying as the trio was, even worse was the Owl Lady. She suddenly began to chant "Hoo-hoo, hoo-hoo." As her voice rose in a crescendo, one at a time the other residents echoed her, until the whole room was hoo-hooing. Then Doc began reciting genetic code: A T G T A G C G T A.

But the trio didn't like to share the stage. And so the shuddup lady, Laverne, took her half-eaten, ossified hamburger and hurled it at the ahhh-ahhh lady. Her aim was off, though, and the airborne meat patty hit someone's glass of milk, sending it shattering to the floor. This initial volley signaled a food fight, and chaos ensued. Fries and peas flew everywhere.

Nurse Smithies rushed into the room, another nurse, Maria a step behind her. "Stop it, you retards! Whaddya think this is, a high school cafeteria?"

Elvin stood to the side laughing. As another glass shattered, the sound even louder than the first one, Stuart suddenly turned his head toward the noise and lifted his legs.

"Holy shit!" shouted Elvin. "He moved!"

As all eyes turned to Stuart, a grin broke out on his face.

◁◉▷

BIOTECH USA OFFICE

"Great job on the kinase inhibitor story!" Kelsey said as she leaned over the magazine layout with Tony.

"Thanks, but they're not really—"

Tony was interrupted by the meowing of Kelsey's cell phone. "Sorry," she said, "gotta get that. Could be hospice." She opened her phone.

"Oh, hi, Emily." Kelsey walked a few feet away from Tony. "He turned his head? How? Why? Thanks!"

She shut the phone and walked back to where Tony stood examining the layout.

"Good news, Kel?"

"Yeah, Stuart moved his head!"

"Am I supposed to be impressed? I can move my head. See? Who's

Stuart?"

"He's my hospice patient. Remember? I told you about him. Well, maybe I didn't mention his name. Anyway, he has HD."

Tony looked confused. "Hodgkin's disease? Or Huntington's?"

"Huntington's."

"Oh. That's too bad, he'd be better off with Hodgkin's." Tony looked puzzled. "Shouldn't he be moving all the time? Why's it a surprise he moved his head?"

"He's end-stage, when they sometimes stop moving. So this may mean something." Kelsey looked wistful.

"Like what?"

"Well, maybe," she didn't want to allow herself to express hope, "maybe he's getting a tiny bit better."

Tony looked skeptical. "Kel, that's a triplet repeat mutation in Huntington's, an expanding gene. It won't just shrink back to normal."

"I know," Kelsey said quietly.

"Anyway, what do you do over there, when you visit him? Is he in a home? A halfway house?"

"No, he's a hospice patient, but he's in a nursing home."

"Can he talk?"

"No. Although he grunts a little. In context." Kelsey smiled.

"What do you talk to him about?"

"Well, you know me, I never run out of things to say. That's where my iPod comes in. We share music. I make him playlists to tell stories."

"Great idea, Kel." He looked at his watch. "Hey, it's late. Wanna try that new Thai place on Walnut?"

"Another time, okay? I have to look up some stuff tonight."

"OK."

※

AMES NURSING HOME, NOVEMBER 21

As Kelsey got off the elevator, looking down at her iPod, she bumped into Elvin, who was busy eyeing the legs of an impossibly young nurse's aide.

"Oh good," muttered Nurse Smithies from her perch in the nurses' station. "Ms. Perfect is here. Slut." She went back to measuring out medications.

Kelsey overheard the meant-to-be-overheard comment and wondered if she should bother to tell the old fart that she should address her as *Dr.* Perfect. But she forgot about the nurse the second she entered the dayroom. Stuart was all spiffed up—shave, haircut, dress shirt.

Nurse Maria looked up in time to see the astonishment on Kelsey's face. "We thought it was time to make him a little more presentable," she said casually. She was painting Mrs. Onderdonk's fingernails a vibrant red. "As you can see, most of our ladies benefited from the skills of visiting beauty school students. Now we're polishing their nails to match their pretty faces."

Kelsey had to suppress a giggle as she looked at the happy faces like wizened apples painted with eye shadow, rouge, and lipstick.

She bent to hug Stuart, then plugged him into the iPod. They listened to all twenty-two minutes and twenty-three seconds of "Alice's Restaurant," Arlo Guthrie's ode to an arrest for littering on a long-ago Thanksgiving. Miraculously, Stuart's attention span held out. They looked at each other, smiling, the entire time, oblivious to the stares of everyone else in the room.

When the song ended, Kelsey leaned over to gently take out the earbud. In a burst of energy, Stuart suddenly wrapped his arms tightly around her and shouted "*KELSEY*"!

There was a moment of astonished silence in the dayroom. Then Laverne shouted, "Oh my!" Origami man gasped. Doc stopped reciting the periodic table. Cornelius quietly threw up. A new nurse's aide simply looked puzzled.

Elvin dropped his broom. "Well I'll be a motherfucker!"

11

AMES NURSING HOME, DAYROOM, NOVEMBER 25

Stuart didn't understand. Where was Kelsey? She hadn't been to see him in three days. That hadn't ever happened before. What had he done? Or not done? Had she gotten mad that time in the dayroom when she was practically naked, right in front of him? Her face had been bright red. Or was it that last day, when he'd grabbed her and yelled her name? She had burst into tears and run out of the room.

He hoped that religious dude who'd stopped in to see him for half a minute wasn't some sort of replacement for Kelsey. He was scared at how much he missed her. Before her visits, he had come to accept his fate, which he knew all too well from watching Livvie and Will. But now...well, he didn't like to think about why Kelsey had come to him to begin with. Who was she? Where was she? If she was visiting her family for the holiday, surely she would have told him. She'd mentioned having a sister somewhere out of town.

Pretty soon they'd come to hoist him out of bed and drag him to the dayroom, so he could watch everyone else's Thanksgiving Day visitors. Maybe Sheila or Jim would make it. But he really didn't care.

⋘∞⋙

TV shows were different on a holiday, and Stuart didn't like the change in routine. He missed Jerry and *The Price is Right* and even the soaps.

Instead, a bunch of kids visiting their grandparents sat around the dayroom TV, watching the Thanksgiving Day parade. He missed the regular staff, too. They were all off with their families.

So Stuart stared at the elevator, until, just after lunch, it delivered his family. Jim and Sheila, their spouses, Carol and Bill, and their respective kids all greeted the sentries in their wheelchairs parked along the hallway, and then walked into the dayroom.

"Stuart!" Sheila shouted as she ran over to him. "Sorry we're late, traffic was horrible. How are you?"

She embraced her brother as he grunted what passed for a reply.

"Hey, bro." Jim pushed forward. "Sorry I haven't been here in awhile, things are crazy at the store. You look kinda different. Carol, take a look at Stuart. Bro, did you put on a little weight?"

As Jim pushed his reluctant wife toward his brother, Stuart suddenly lurched forward. Carol stepped back, barely masking her revulsion.

"Kuh-kuh-kuh!"

"What?" Jim and Sheila asked in unison.

Stuart strained to speak, but had to give up. It was just too hard. He leaned back.

Sheila gave him her brightest smile. "Bill's here, too," she said, her voice as cheery as her smile, "but he's off keepin' the kids from dueling with the walkers."

Jim leaned down and sniffed Stuart's food. "Do you know what this is, Stu?" He grimaced. "I can't tell if the tan stuff's turkey or pie." He sniffed again. "Pie! Want some?" Jim scooped some up onto a spoon and put it in his brother's mouth. And back out it came, along with a violent sputter.

"Kel!"

"That's what he said before!" said Sheila, taking away the plate of food and wiping Stuart's face with a napkin. "Kel… Isn't Kelsey the volunteer who visits?"

Stuart's brows shot up.

"I guess it is!"

Stuart bolted forward. "Ya! Kellll. Seeee."

Sheila dropped Stuart's plate of pureed Thanksgiving dinner. His utensils clattered as they bounced on the floor.

❦

Kelsey had gotten back from Jen's too late on Sunday to stop in to see Stuart, but she'd called Chaplain Timothy ahead of time to make sure he'd visit her friend over the long Thanksgiving weekend. She made it to the nursing home before work on Monday, but when she walked down D3, stopping to greet the residents, she saw that Stuart's door was shut. The aides, she thought, probably hadn't finished dressing him yet.

While she waited for his door to open, Kelsey read the activities calendar posted on the bulletin board outside his room. All Christmas stuff. She noticed a newcomer out of the corner of her eye, a large black woman stuffed into a wheelchair. She was chattering away to Doc, Laverne, and Reginald, prisoners in their locked-into-place wheelchairs, her words not registering on them. Her face lit up when she saw Kelsey.

"Hey, you. Talk to me!"

Kelsey smiled. "OK. I'm Kelsey. Who are you? I've never seen you here before."

"Justina. Just got here, day after Thanksgivin'. I was livin' with my son and his family, but I started fallin' down 'bout a month ago. Fell straight into the closet last week, stark nekkid, an' they hadda call 9-1-1 to haul me out. So what with my oxygen tank and the diabetes and me fallin' all over the place, well, here I am." Justina adjusted the tubes in her nostrils and squinted at Kelsey's ID badge. "So who're you? A nurse?"

"No, I'm a volunteer. I visit Stuart, in 319."

"Oh, yeah. I seen him. The young guy, right? Pity. What's wrong with him? Why's he here with all us old folk?"

"I'm not allowed to say. But I keep him company."

"Ain't that nice. Now, lemme give you some advice, hon."

"Yes?"

"You need some help with your hair."

"What do you mean?" Kelsey patted the corkscrews emanating from her head.

"Well, you's a white girl, but you's got black hair!" Justina let out a loud laugh at her own joke. "You need to put some olive oil on that mess. Calm it down, girlfriend!"

"But I like my hair this way."

"Thaz alright. I likes it too. But it needs olive oil. Just trus' me. I knows hair, even whitey hair. I was once a beautician!"

"I'll take that into consideration. Thank you. Oh look, the door's open. Gotta go. It was nice meeting you!"

Kelsey gave Justina's arm a squeeze and headed into Stuart's room.

He was in bed, staring at the photograph in the corner of the mirror, ignoring Jerry Springer droning in the background. Kelsey walked over, stood briefly in his line of sight, then leaned over to hug him. But Stuart just lay there. He made no attempt at all to lift his arms, didn't smile, and, when Kelsey pulled back, she saw a single tear roll down his cheek.

"Oh, Stuart, what's wrong?"

Still no response.

"I know I haven't been here, but didn't you know I was going to visit Jen?"

Stuart moved his head back and forth in minuscule motions. *No.*

"Damn. I forgot to tell you that day you said my name. I was so shocked and excited, I just forgot! But I did remember on the train, so I called and asked Nurse Smithies to tell you where I was. I talked directly to her, didn't leave a message or anything. Didn't she tell you? Someone should have told you that night!"

No.

"Omigod, I'm so sorry, so sorry! Did you think I'd stopped coming to see you?"

Yes.

Kelsey was near tears. She leaned down to hug him again, and this time he raised his arms.

"Damn that bitch!" she muttered. "Well, I'm here now, my friend. Give me a hug. Do you want to hear music? How about a discography lesson?"

Stuart's brows lifted, his eyes riveted on Kelsey as she plugged both of them in. "Where the Streets Have No Name" came on. When it ended, Kelsey unplugged them and sat back.

"OK. Remember when I told you how I went to school to study genetics? Well, geneticists make charts of who's related to whom. I like to do that with bands. It's fun to find songs to show how they're all related. Like all that U2 we listen to? Sure, Coldplay and the Killers copy U2, but the roots of U2 can be traced to the Who. And the Who claim they were influenced by Elvis." She grinned at him. "But today I thought we'd start with the Yardbirds." As Stuart struggled to move his legs and flex his fingers, she called up the playlist she'd put together the night before.

"OK," she said. "The Yardbirds were Jeff Beck, Eric Clapton—you know who that is, right? —and Jimmy Page. Betcha know him, too. I've seen your Zeppelin shirt. So first, here's some Yardbirds. 'For Your Love.'" She plugged them both in again, and for the next three minutes, they listened, looking at each other and smiling.

"Great, right? Well, the Yardbirds begat Cream, which was Jack Bruce, Eric Clapton, and Ginger Baker. Before our time, but you probably know 'Sunshine of Your Love.'" Kelsey plugged them back in. A minute later, she jumped as Samantha tapped her on the shoulder.

"Hi Kelsey," said the young nurse, flicking back her heavy braid. "Is this a class? Can I listen, too?"

"Sure. Sorry I didn't hear you. Here, take the earbud."

Samantha put the white plug into her ear. "Omigod! I never used one of these things before. No wonder Stuart's so revved up right after you visit."

Kelsey clicked the button. "Next up is Blind Faith. Clapton and Baker left when Cream dissolved, and picked up Steve Winwood from Traffic, adding Rick Gretch on bass." She called up the next song. "Here's 'Can't Find My Way Back Home'". Kelsey sat back for a few minutes, watching the patient and the nurse listen together.

"Who's next?" Samantha asked. "I have five more minutes on my break. This is fun!"

"That won't be long enough for the next song," said Kelsey as she clicked the iPod again. "'Stairway to Heaven.' It's about seven minutes."

"What's the connection to these others?" Samantha asked. "Eric Clapton wasn't in Led Zeppelin, was he?"

"No. But Jimmy Page came from the Yardbirds. He replaced Clapton. He'd wanted to call them The New Yardbirds, but, as legend has it, Keith Moon said that that 'would go over like a lead zeppelin,' and the name was born. Only Page changed it to Led so people wouldn't pronounce it *leed*."

Samantha gave this history lesson some thought. "Keith Moon," she said. "Is that the guy who fell out of a coconut tree and landed on his head a few years ago?"

"No, that was Keith Richards, from the Stones. Keith Moon was the drummer for the Who. He drowned in his swimming pool back in the '70s. And Keith Moon brings us back to where we started. Right, Stuart? The Who's influence?"

Stuart gave them a lopsided grin.

Suddenly the ambiance was shattered by a familiar shrill voice. "Excuse me for breaking up this little joyfest, but just what is going on? Samantha, don't you have anything to do?"

"Yes, Myra. But I was on break."

"Well, time's up." Nurse Smithies looked at her watch.

"Hello to you, too," said Kelsey.

"So you decided to finally show up. How's the spazz doin' today?"

Kelsey whipped around to face her. "Shut up!"

"What's the problem, dearie? He can't hear me plugged into that idiot box."

"Oh, yes, he can!" As Samantha slunk out, Kelsey laid the iPod on the bed. "I want to talk to you. Outside. Now." She grabbed Smithies' arm and pulled her into the hallway, where Justina looked up, fascinated by this new drama.

"Don't you EVER talk in front of him like that!" She was nearly loud enough to be heard all over the floor. "He can *hear*! He can *understand*!"

The nurse shook her arm free and held out a clipboard. "Chill, honey. Look at his chart. He's not doin' so hot."

Kelsey grabbed the chart and began to read the most recent entries.

Nurses' Notes, November 27. Persistent low-grade fever. Conjunctivitis resolving. Diminished affect, listless, fatigued. Poor appetite.

Nurses' Notes, November 28. Spinal contortion limiting lung capacity. Oxygen sats 88. Supplemental oxygen. Ativan for anxiety.

Nurses' Notes, November 29. Difficulty swallowing. Liquids. Listless. Oxygen sats 87."

"That's yesterday." She forgot her anger. "What's wrong?"

The nurse gave a self-satisfied smile. "My guess is he missed you. Or your tits."

Justina's mouth dropped open.

12

AMES NURSING HOME, DECEMBER 1

Kelsey got off the elevator, noticing that the tired turkeys and horns-of-plenty had been replaced by a wintry wonderland. A train of reindeer had been tacked to the wall beneath the large window that looked into the dayroom, and a small fake plastic tree teetered on the ledge of the nurses' station, dripping candy canes that would be stale by the time the actual holiday rolled around. Somehow Christmas required an entire month.

"Hey, Kelsey," said Maria, coming out of the nurse's station. "Wait up."

Kelsey stopped. "What happened? Is he worse?"

"He ate two lunches! And not just ice cream and pudding. Real food."

"But he seemed so out of it when I was here yesterday."

"Check out the chart." The nurse handed it over.

"Ate whole breakfast," Kelsey read aloud. "Increased purposeful leg movements. Finger flexion. Vocalization." She broke into a huge smile.

Maria touched Kelsey's arm. "Hey. Did you ever think that maybe it's YOU that's healing him?"

At that moment, Nurse Smithies walked by, wheeling in the lunch trays. She overheard them, and scowled, but nothing could ruin

Kelsey's joy. As she entered the dayroom, she paused to look for Stuart and took out her iPod and stood for a moment, gazing at it.

"Get out of my way," Smithies bellowed.

⦅◦◦⦆

Kelsey headed back to her office, so distracted that she barely noticed the throngs of holiday shoppers on the suburban line. She entered the building, flew past Bruce at the desk, and ran up the stairs.

When Tony stepped out of his cubicle, Kelsey careened into him, then practically fell into her own work area.

"Hey, Kel," he said, rubbing one elbow, "slow down. I gotta run this by you. Can you look? It's my editorial on confidentiality at sperm banks."

"Not now, Tony."

"It'll just take a sec. It's important. About that website where kids hunt down their sperm donor daddies."

Kelsey ignored him, sat down, hit a computer key, and impatiently retrieved papers from her backpack. She then clicked on the "hospice diary—private" icon. The document opened, and she looked rapidly from it to the papers in her hands.

"What're you workin' on?" Tony squeezed into the cubicle and sat precariously on a stack of magazines.

Kelsey was typing furiously. "Comparing things."

"What things?"

"My diary. On Stuart. And the nurses' notes. Showing his improvement." She paused to read a page.

"Improvement? Isn't he supposed to croak?"

"Tony, please, not now. I'll explain just as soon as I see if what I'm thinking is really happening."

"OK." Not taking the hint, however, Tony flipped through the latest *Nature Biotechnology* as Kelsey compared playlists to nurses' notes. Suddenly she leaned back in her chair and shouted, "*that's it!*"

Tony, startled, fell off the magazines. "Yo, Kel, take it easy," he said. "What's got you so charged up?"

Kelsey pulled out a calendar. Looking from the diary to the nurses' notes, she scribbled on a pad (swiped from a reproductive medicine exhibition) that had an outline of a uterus and ovaries on it that looked curiously like a reindeer. As Tony watched from behind her, she took three Sharpies from her desk drawer and began marking the days.

"Care to translate?"

"Days when Stuart improved get red dots, days he declined get blue dots, and days he listened to music get green dots. I'm sure glad they told us in death class to keep a diary."

"Death class?"

"Hospice training."

"Oh. So what's the verdict, Dr. Kevorkian?"

Kelsey was about to object but laughed instead, then turned to her co-worker. "Well, Stuart's better days definitely followed my visits. And he backslid tremendously when I went to visit Jen around Thanksgiving. That's very clear."

"Well, duh! You've given him something to look forward to. Maybe even to live for."

"No," she said. "That's not it. Let's not get too sappy. It's not *me*. I'm just the surrogate marker, as the clinical trials folks might say."

"Then what is it, Kel? What's making him better?"

She was silent a moment. "I think I know."

"I know you think you know. Care to share?"

"It's the music."

"The music?"

"Look. The days that Stuart improved follow the days we listened to U2. Except for four times. And on those days, we heard either Coldplay or The Killers."

"OK." Tony gave this some thought. "So what?"

"They're the same, Tony. The same music. Almost."

He wasn't keeping up. "What do you mean?"

"Well, compare U2's 'Pride' to Coldplay's 'Moses.' I'll get it on my iTunes, wait a sec. The riff is superimposable. You'll see." Kelsey minimized the diary and nurses' notes and clicked on the iTunes icon.

"I still don't get it. I'm afraid I don't have your musical expertise. Please enlighten me."

"Listen a minute." Kelsey clicked on the U2 song, the Coldplay song, and then The Killers' "Somebody Told Me." "Let me start that last one again," she said, concentrating. "OK. What does the guitar remind you of?"

"U2."

"Exactly."

"So?"

"Tony, you might have me locked up if I told you what I'm thinking."

"You have a point there. When it makes sense, give me a call." Tony turned and headed back to his cubicle, shaking his head but smiling.

Kelsey clicked off her iTunes and sat back as the cover of the next issue of *Biotech USA* filled the screen with greenly-glowing, rotating neural stem cells giving new life to an injured brain.

13

"Hi, Marsha. Sorry I'm late." Kelsey slid into a booth at the rear of the Mediterranean restaurant on Juniper. "Did the store manager like the hats you selected?"

"Loved 'em. And I get to keep this one, like it?"

Kelsey admired the beret. "It looks great with your hair. Very Jennifer Aniston. My hair was once that straight for about eight minutes, I think."

"Thanks. But straight hair can get pretty boring. Hey, I'm glad you could come. Great column last weekend. I'll never think the same way about intestinal gas."

Kelsey grinned. "Well, it is fascinating how genomics can be used to identify the microbes in our colons, especially the ones that can't be cultured. We didn't even know they were there. Did you realize that, if you count the colon, ninety percent of the cells in a human body aren't even our own?"

"If you say so. As I said, I have a renewed respect for farts."

This time Kelsey gave her a dirty look. "Thanks, I think." She self-consciously tried to tamp down her mane. "So, Marsh. Tell me about *you*. How have your patients been?"

The other hospice volunteer could only sigh. "Still a parade of deaths. I haven't gotten to actually know any of them. But I think I'm helping the families."

"Yes, you are, just by being there. I'm sure you'll eventually get someone not so close to the end." Kelsey touched her friend's hand. "It's really too bad people wait so long to contact hospice." She thought a moment. "Hey, why don't you switch to home care? The nursing homes do get the sickest patients you know."

"That's for sure. Sometimes I feel like I'm bringing on the end for them. Do they even know I'm there?"

"Of course they do! The sense of hearing is the last to go. Remember from death class?" They both laughed.

"Funny how all us hospice people develop these weird senses of humor," Marsha said. "Or maybe it's just us. Anyway, that's not what's happening with you and...and Stephen?"

"Stuart."

"Right. Hey, what's with the smile? What aren't you telling me? How old is this guy?"

"My age. Exactly."

"How did you get him? Don't they stick to the same sex for the nursing home set? And why's he at Ames with all those geezers?"

"Questions, questions! I just got lucky, I guess. I was leaving the hospice office as his family came in, so Emily must've been thinking about me when she talked to them. Who knows, maybe she remembered I'm a geneticist. Or maybe it's fate?"

"Can he talk?"

"Not really."

"Not *really*?"

"Well, he couldn't when I first started visiting him. But now he can say my name. In a grunty sort of way."

"So you just yak away with him grunting now and then?"

Kelsey nodded. "I can't explain it, but we do communicate. And the music helps."

"What music?"

"We listen to my iPod. I make playlists that tell stories."

"I'll bet he loves that. I've been to that nursing home. Their activity schedule sounds like preschool. Kindergarten. Those patients are *not* all demented. I don't know how they can stand it. There's probably doctors and lawyers and teachers and who knows what behind those walkers and in those wheelchairs. About the most interesting thing to do at Ames is to take a crap. If you can even do that."

"Yeah, it can be pretty depressing. That's why it makes my day when his face lights up. I think I'm really making a difference."

"Well, he's obviously making a difference in *you*."

Kelsey drew closer and grabbed Marsha's hands. "Marsha, the most incredible thing is happening."

"Oh no. Don't tell me—"

"I think the music's helping him."

Marsha looked relieved. "Well, of course it is."

"No, I mean *really* helping him. Making him better."

"Whoa, Kel. Didn't you say that you don't get better from what he has? DH?"

"HD. Huntington's Disease. But he is. He *is* getting better."

"And you think this because…?"

"I'm not sure yet. But I think I know how it's happening, and I'm going to talk to someone about it. After work today."

"Who?"

"One of my stem cell sources. A cell biologist over at Franklin."

Marsha looked skeptical. "Stem cells?"

༺༻

Kelsey leaned back against the battered old couch at Java Jim's, a rare, non-Starbucks coffeehouse. Across from her sat Peter Holloway, a forty-ish cell biologist. With a blond ponytail tinged with gray and a single turquoise earring, he looked more biker than geek. He was flipping through Kelsey's diary and nurses' notes, arranged chronologically.

"So that's the evidence," Kelsey said. "Am I crazy? Can his brain be healing?"

"Um, I don't know," Peter replied in a carefully noncommittal voice. "It's certainly unprecedented." He reread a paragraph. "A reversal of symptoms in a neurodegenerative disease like HD. Plateau? Maybe. Reversal? No."

"But brains do have stem cells," Kelsey said. "Isn't that how birds learn songs? Remember those experiments where the researchers moved the food farther away, so the birds would have to learn more complex songs to signal each other where the food was? And they had more stem cells in their brains after learning the harder songs? Those cells are in rat and monkey brains, too, even in the brains of dead people. They *must* be there—in normal brains of living people, too."

Peter nodded. "Yes," he said, "but neural stem cells are exceedingly rare. They're tucked away only in a very restricted part of the brain, the subventricular zone. The good old SVZ."

"Sounds like a sports car."

"Yeah, it does. Anyway, something I just read might be relevant, now that I think about it. Makes your idea maybe not as out there as it might otherwise seem." He smiled and sipped his tea.

"I'm listening. *What?*"

"I got an online preprint from my friends at the McQueen Brain Institute in Tampa. It's near the university, the one with the alligators in the lake in the middle of campus."

"Yes, I've interviewed them. Even visited once. Interviewed the researchers, not the alligators. That's the campus with the tree that Tom Petty planted when he worked there as a kid."

Peter couldn't help but grin. "You certainly are in command of the important facts. Anyway, the work is incredible. They took brain cells from a sixteen-year-old with intractable temporal lobe epilepsy. We're talking dozens of seizures a day. The surgery was, of course, to help her, but instead of throwing away what they took out, they grew out some samples. From the SVZ, where the stem cells are, but also from the parts of the cortex that get zapped during the seizures. And from two other areas known to house stem cells in other species. So they grew the cells in culture, along with markers to tell the stem cells apart from the neurons and supportive glial cells."

"Which markers did they use?"

"A whole bunch. DAPI to mark the nuclei, BrdU to track the dividing cells with GFP so they'd glow green, GFAP to distinguish the glia from the neurons, and finally nestin and neurofilament markers to tell which cells were fated to become neurons."

"Sounds like a bunch of jargon, but I actually know what they all are. What was in the culture medium besides the markers?"

"Basically, a stem cell cocktail. Let's see," he started counting off on his fingers, "bovine pituitary extract, fetal calf serum, and growth factors. Of course."

"Of course. Wouldn't want to leave those out. What about special sauce?" She smiled.

"They let the cells divide about three hundred times, which of course most of them couldn't do, then splashed on some oxygenated artificial cerebrospinal fluid."

"To…'"

"To provide the ambiance of the subventricular zone." Peter paused to drink his tea.

"So what happened? Peter, don't keep me in suspense."

"Well, the surviving cells, the ones that kept dividing well past the normal fifty-division limit, looked like progenitors. The immediate daughters of stem cells. The markers indicated the neuronal lineage. Pretty clever experiments, eh?"

Kelsey was quiet for a moment. "Neural progenitors?" She was close to shouting, but didn't realize it. "And they didn't form tumors?" The students at the tables near them turned and gave her strange looks.

"No, Kelsey. And that's the amazing part. No tumors from the progenitors or from the glia. The progenitors apparently regained the capacity to divide, but they stayed specialized enough to resist seeding a tumor."

"Did they form neurospheres?"

"Yup. That shows they're neural progenitors." Peter took another sip of his tea. "Without question."

"Were all the experiments *in vitro*? When do we get to the inevitable mice?"

"Yes, the mice." Another maddeningly slow sip of tea. "When the cells were transplanted into nude mice," he said, "they gave rise to neurons. *Human neurons*. Human cells in a mouse are pretty easy to spot. They're gigantic. But they were also stained for human ribonuclear protein."

Kelsey nodded. "And the green fluorescent protein, the GFP, enabled the researchers to actually *see* the transplants of human brain cells, right? Green mouse brain parts? It still seems weird that a jellyfish protein is used in so many other organisms." She took a deep breath. "But what does this have to do with Stuart?"

"The Florida researchers pointed out that a single one of their cells—which they're calling adult human neural progenitors, or AHNPs—can generate enough material, theoretically, to supply about 40 million adult brains with cells that can give rise to neurons. They term a therapeutic application based on these cells 'restorative neurobiology.' Sort of a new twist on regenerative medicine. I like it. 'Restorative' shouldn't upset anyone worried about mangling embryos. After all, the cell source is just medical waste."

Kelsey shook her head. "Well, you can never say that. Every time someone comes up with a way to get around destroying embryos, the anti-science folks find something else to rant about. Remember the column I wrote about that Citizens Against Stem Cell Research group?"

"Yes. Well done, by the way."

"Thanks. And remember the first reports of using 8-celled embryos? Plucking off one cell to start an ES cell culture while salvaging the 7-celled remainder? It was a variation on what's been done since 1989, preimplantation genetic diagnosis. PGD's generated thousands of unused embryos that've been discarded or frozen. And most of the frozen ones eventually are discarded, too. But once a scientist associated *stem cells* with PGD, a congressman who'd obviously never heard of the procedure immediately called for PGD to be made risk-free before using it to derive stem cells." She snorted in disgust. "As if any medical procedure can be risk-free. It's a losing battle when the decision makers simply do not understand the science and are way behind on medical technology."

Peter smiled. "Kelsey, you're preaching to the choir here."

"I know. Don't get me started." She took a sip of her coffee, which was cold. "But getting back to Stuart," she said. "What's the connection?"

"Think about it. The donor had seizures, and her brain was able to grow new neurons, presumably from neural stem cells already there." Kelsey nodded as he continued. "So maybe the altered electricity that caused the seizures activated the stem cells, replenishing her brain tissue."

"And that could be happening to Stuart? Because his brain is stressed, too? Gobbed up with huntingtin protein?"

"You got it."

"But…but getting back to the initial stimulus. Would it have to be altered electrical activity?"

"That should be easy enough to monitor with an EEG. But," his voice held a note of caution, "something else might be stimulating stem or progenitor cells. Huntington's isn't associated with seizures."

"Signaling?"

"Right. Good old signal transduction."

Kelsey was quiet a moment and then leaned so far forward she nearly fell off the couch. "I've got it! Endorphins."

"And," Peter leaned forward with her, "what do endogenous opiates have to do with his response?"

"That's the connection to the music! The brain makes endorphins, and related molecules, when something makes you happy. That's a bit oversimplified, sure. Or to protect you from pain, as in childbirth or after a long run, the so-called runner's high. Our own opiates. Maybe Stuart's brain releases endorphins when he hears music. It may bring more joy to him, in that stultifying environment, than to a normal person listening to an iPod. We take it for granted."

"OK," Peter said. "But how would a flush of opioids stimulate cell division? If it did, we'd get cancer every time we got happy."

She thought for a second. "What if endorphins were somehow affecting growth factors? Maybe under certain conditions, endorphins or related molecules bind growth factor receptors on those adult neural human progenitor cells."

"That sounds a little crazed, Kelsey." He leaned back again. "I get the growth factor stimulation part, although I can't see how or why an opioid would bind a growth factor receptor, unless there's a somatic mutation thing going on. But what about the other end of the signaling pathway? What is it about the music that's making neurons secrete endorphins?"

She shrugged her shoulders. "I don't really know. The frequency of certain notes, I guess, because that's what the songs that correlate to days of Stuart's improvement have in common. But I don't know that much about music. What do you think it could be?"

"I'm stumped too. But I know who to ask."

"Who? Do you know any musicians?"

"I do. My grad student, Eliot, plays lead guitar in a band. He's always got his head in a *Guitar World*, at least when he's not reading *The Journal of Neuroscience*. He was babbling something the other day about a Malcolm Gladwell article in *The New Yorker* about software that analyzes the components of a hit song. I think he said he was going to get the software." Kelsey's eyebrows shot up in interest, a habit she'd subconsciously picked up from Stuart. "Maybe he can get a handle on what those songs have in common."

"Yes! And if whatever that is can trigger the mobilization of new brain cells in a way that counteracts that awful disease…" She could hardly bring herself to the apparently logical conclusion. "So. I'm not totally nuts?"

"Not *totally*," he said, "or else I am, too. The pieces of your hypothesis do make sense. And it's something we could test."

"How? It's not as if we could get a sample of Stuart's brain like from that epilepsy patient."

"I know. But maybe we can do something less invasive, yet still measurable."

"Like what?"

"First, we'll look at brain scans to see if anything macroscopic is going on with Stuart that we can correlate to his improvement."

"OK."

"Didn't you say the family was in the government study to find the Huntington's gene?"

"Yes. That's in the medical records, which I have permission to see. So?"

"Kelsey, my dear, this just may work. For a start, anyway. Come on." He stood up, tucked the papers under his arm, grabbed Kelsey's hand and pulled her up. "Let's go."

She downed the rest of her cold coffee and let herself be dragged away.

⚜

FRANKLIN MEDICAL COLLEGE, STEM CELL LAB

"Here! Aren't these neurospheres gorgeous?" Peter clicked through a series of images of bluish-green balls. "Pull up a chair, Kel. I've a lot to show you."

Kelsey sat next to him and watched as he tapped the keys and the neurospheres faded away, to be replaced by a large illustration of a human brain.

"See," he pointed at the screen with his pen, "the part of the brain that shrinks in HD is right next to the stem cells." He clicked an area next to a triangular space. "That's the caudate nucleus. It runs along the lateral ventricle, which as I'm sure you recall is a space filled with cerebrospinal fluid. This is a normal brain."

"Sounds like that old public service announcement. 'This is your brain on drugs.'"

Peter smiled. "And here's an HD brain."

He doubled clicked and the two brain images appeared side by side. "See the difference?"

Kelsey gasped. "The ventricles in the HD brain are *huge*."

"Yes. Can you guess why?"

"Apoptosis?"

"Right. Cell death. The neurons in the HD brain are dying, so the space expands. But all this is happening right near the subventricular zone, the natural repositories of neural stem cells."

"But this isn't Stuart's brain, is it? How do we know he has the same problem?"

"I'm a step ahead of you. We can look at Stuart's past scans, from the NIH studies, starting with the 1994 one. Then we'll do another to see what's going on right now."

"You mean we'll get Stuart in here?"

He nodded. "Sure. Why not?"

"Peter, I think you've been around cells and molecules too long. Moving an HD patient isn't trivial. But assuming we can figure that out——and I'm sure he'd *love* to get out of that place—what, exactly, are you thinking of doing?"

"I may be able to enroll him in an open clinical trial comparing the stem cell numbers in Alzheimer's, ALS, and Parkinson's brains. We do our cell counts the same way the McQueen group does, DAPI staining to mark the nuclei, then neuroimaging. We'll just add Huntington's to the protocol." He smiled as her eyes lit up. "If his brain's changing in response to the music, maybe we can quantify it. As long as he keeps improving. Or see something. Or maybe even find out if there's a DNA microarray out there to look at his endorphins. Maybe he's got a mutation in one of the genes. Or an altered expression pattern."

"You'll look at enkephalins and dynorphins, too? I think there've been about 120 endogenous opiates found in the human body. Tony did an article on it awhile back."

"I think so. At least 120. Microarrays would allow us to compare gene expression patterns, since the opiates may exist only transiently."

She thought for a minute. "But won't microarrays miss opiates that maybe aren't abundant, but exert powerful effects in tiny amounts?"

"Yes," he said, "that's always a limitation. But let's see what we can find."

"OK. I can do searches on available and customized microarrays. Some of those companies advertise with the magazine. Keep me posted and I promise not to write about it. Not yet, at least. Meanwhile, I'll also see if I can find out how the brain processes music."

《∞》

CHILDREN'S HOSPITAL OF PHILADELPHIA, AUDIOLOGY LAB, DECEMBER 5

Tuesday morning found Kelsey sitting before another split screen with another researcher. A sound wave pattern appeared on the right and a brain map on the left as U2's "Angel of Harlem" played. Kelsey had just explained her idea to Dr. Sarah Swetsky, a neurologist specializing in hearing.

"Sound waves stimulate neurons in the auditory cortex," the neurologist said, pointing at an area near the top of the brain. "Some of these neurons fire when they detect the same notes coming from different instruments. Others sense frequency and amplitude. If both types of these neurons are activated, or perhaps the same cells respond to both types of stimuli, they might detect the U2 signature."

"Would the signal be strong enough to stimulate receptive neurons to secrete neuropeptides?" Kelsey asked. "Such as endorphins?"

"Well, endorphins are made mostly in the hypothalamus. But I don't see why the auditory cells in the cortex couldn't secrete them, too. I don't think anybody's looked. What are you thinking?"

"That the music activates stem cells via opiates. But I haven't figured out the mechanism. That is, *how* the opiates do it," Kelsey said.

"There's certainly evidence that cells react to music," Dr. Swetsky told her. "Plants grow faster when they're exposed to music. And brain cells in Alzheimer's patients secrete more melatonin—not quite the same thing, I know—when they have music therapy."

"I don't know about the plants," Kelsey said, "or the Alzheimer's. Huntington's is pretty complicated, on both cellular and molecular levels."

"I'm not that familiar with Huntington's. Don't think I've ever even met anyone with it, or in their family. I work mostly with kids who have sensorineural hearing loss. What parts of the brain degenerate in HD? It's movement, so is it the basal ganglia?"

"Yes. And some cortical neurons. But that's part of the problem. Cells all over the brain build up the toxic mutant protein as the disease progresses, although only a relatively few cells actually die," Kelsey filled her in.

"I presume we don't know why and how they die," Dr. Swetsky said, "or we'd be able to do something to slow or stop the pathogenesis."

"Right," Kelsey said. "We know some of the steps, the things that go haywire, but not their order. So it's hard to tell causes from effects. I used Huntington's in an article recently as a prime example of how knowing a gene's sequence often isn't enough to reveal how the gene works—that was part of the human genome project hype, remember?"

"Yes, DNA sequences would solve all the mysteries of biology."

"Anyway, getting back to HD, the pathology seems to have something to do with trafficking of vesicles containing brain-derived neurotrophic factor. Without BDNF signaling, neurons die. But that still doesn't explain the specificity."

"That's all very interesting. But I guess I just prefer whole patients to molecules." Dr. Swetsky turned from the computer to face her visitor. "Anyway, is this man at an early stage? He's so young to have full blown Huntington's."

"Unfortunately, he's end-stage."

"Oh, my. That's just terrible. Well, I'm not sure what you're up to, but I hope it will do some good. If not in time for him, perhaps others. And maybe for other diseases, too. Please stay in touch!"

"Thank you! You've been very encouraging."

Kelsey got up and shook Dr. Swetsky's hand. She glanced at her watch. "Looks like I have time to squeeze in a short visit with Stuart."

※

AMES NURSING HOME, ROOM D317

Kelsey rounded the corner and passed the nurses' station, which, to her relief, was empty. She was too excited to deal with Smithies' evil stares and remarks today. She stopped briefly to watch a group of teens who had brought big, calming dogs to visit with the residents, half-listened to Justina's latest hair care advice, then turned into the half-open door of room 317. She was about to greet Stuart when she stopped short. Someone was already standing at his bedside. The woman was talking, but Stuart had his frozen non-listening expression on his face.

"Oh! Excuse me," Kelsey blurted. "I didn't expect anyone to be here."

When Stuart saw her, his blankness vanished instantly. He lurched forward, arms outstretched. "*KKKKKKKKKKKKKKKel…*"

"Kelsey," the woman said. "Of course. He was calling for you on Thanksgiving when we visited."

"Oh, you must be his sister. Sheila? I think I ran into you, literally, the first day you visited the hospice office."

"Yes. Well." She gestured toward her brother. "This is most astonishing. I must admit I'm a little jealous. He never reacts this way to *me*."

Kelsey had to smile. "Oh, it's not me. He looks forward to the music that I play for him. It breaks up the routine around here, I guess."

"Anyway, I'm glad you can come," Sheila replied. "Jim and I don't make it very often, not often enough, especially so close to Christmas and all." She took Kelsey's arm. "Stuart, do you mind if I borrow your friend for a moment?" She guided Kelsey out the door.

"I think I need to explain why we don't visit as often as we probably should," she whispered when they were standing in the hall.

"Sheila, you don't need to explain anything."

"No, I do. We keep saying it's because we're so busy with kids and jobs and such. But that's not really it."

"But you *are* busy with those things. Aren't you?"

Sheila was looking down at the floor. After blinking several times, she looked up again. "The real reason is that we've been through this before. Three times. Dad. Will. And Livvie. Aunts and uncles and cousins, too. We just can't stand to see anyone else go down this path, especially our little brother. You do understand, don't you?" When Kelsey nodded sympathetically, she continued. "But Stuart does seem to be different from the others."

"How so?"

"Well… How can I say this? They had to put Livvie in a rubber room. Those things really exist. She was moving constantly, you had to have seen it to understand what the disease is usually like. Some of the aides on B2 were here back then. They'd remember. Stuart seems so *upbeat*. More aware than Will and Livvie were, even though he can't talk. You know, Kelsey, I think the others had some of the dementia that mercifully comes with Huntington's." She shook her head. "But Stuart seems to know, and accept, what's happening."

"I can't imagine watching my sister go through something like this. I'll bet you and Jim are having some survivor guilt, too."

Sheila's eyes welled up. "I didn't think there was a name for that. You mean we feel bad that we're not sick, too?"

"Something like that. It's pretty common."

"How do you know that?"

"I'm actually a geneticist. I mean, that's what I went to school for. Survivor guilt happens in breast cancer families a lot. The inherited forms of breast cancer."

"Oh." Sheila wiped a tear from her cheek. "It helps a little to know that others feel this way. Anyway, Jim and I are grateful for your visits. I think Stuart prefers you to us these days. See how he's staring at you?"

Kelsey blushed. "He's looking at us both. Do you want to stay and listen to the music with him?"

Sheila glanced at the clock on the wall. "No, I really can't. And that's not just an excuse, I do have to be somewhere soon. But I hope I run into you again."

"OK. Bye!" They hugged briefly, and Sheila waved to her brother before walking down the hall. Kelsey pulled a chair up and sat down next to the bed, then leaned over and brushed strands of hair off Stuart's forehead.

"Hi! I'm back."

"Kel. Hi!"

"Let's hold off on the music a little," she said. "I want to discuss something with you."

He raised one eyebrow.

"I've been noticing something. You've been feeling better since I started visiting and playing music, right?"

"Yeah."

"The nurses see it too. And Sheila and Jim. They said you said my name at Thanksgiving."

He managed to say the word yet again. "*Kel.*"

"Well, I've got this idea ..."

14

FRANKLIN MEDICAL COLLEGE, STEM CELL LAB, DECEMBER 14

Kelsey and Peter leaned forward, staring intently at the four images on the computer screen. Superimposed on the grayish brains were swaths of yellow, orange, and red, indicating where increased blood flow marked neural activity. The ventricle spaces near the centers of the brains, as well as the highlighted areas, were clearly enlarging from left to right, the yellows giving way to the more intense colors as the scans captured key points in time.

"Can you see it?" Peter moved the mouse from left to right, from brain to brain.

"I think so. But walk me through it, Dr. H."

He moved the mouse again. "The ventricles house the stem cells. In the 1994 scan, here, when the predictive gene test came back positive, Stuart's ventricles looked normal. And he was still healthy."

"Right."

"In 1998, he started having symptoms. Stumbling, fidgeting, twitching. And see, the spaces are bigger."

"Cell death?"

"Correct." Peter clicked on the scan from October, 2007. "The spaces are even bigger right before you started playing music for him, which means that the rate of disease progression had actually been accelerating. And, presumably, his symptoms were worsening."

"That's why he was put on hospice, I suppose. I'll check my diary, but that sounds about right."

"Now look at last week's scan again." Peter clicked and an arrow appeared, which he used to measure the diameter of the same ventricle highlighted in the other scans. "Clearly, the ventricle has shrunk. And the colored area has grown."

"It must be filling. With cells? Are they…"

"We don't know yet. But all he'd need is one activated neural stem cell, or one of those adult human neural progenitors—the McQueen cells—to replenish that space." He glanced at her. "Anyway, we'd need to mark and stain brain slices to really see what's happening, and I don't think Stuart wants his brain cut up right now like they did to those mice in Florida. But new neurons might very well explain his improvement. And the changes on these fMRI scans."

"Isn't there a way to identify the cells non-invasively? To see more detail than those splotches of color?"

"I've been working on it. That's why Stuart's here now. Let me show you."

⁂

The lab setup was so simple, and so seemingly safe, that the proposal had breezed through the hastily assembled Institutional Review Board at Franklin. Jim, Sheila, and the various physicians had agreed to the experiment, too, and of course Stuart himself had agreed. Even the nursing home had been helpful in arranging the three-day transfer, especially when the Huntington's Disease Society of America made a nice donation to defray costs.

The ambulette had picked Stuart up on a bright Thursday morning, and Kelsey rode along, watching his expressions change as he saw the holiday decorations on the streets as they whizzed by. To other people, she knew, he appeared rather expressionless, a little like an aging celebrity who'd gone overboard on Botox, but she could read volumes in his eyebrow lifts, hints of smiles, and even in his skin tone. Stuart hadn't been outdoors since the freak warm day during the fire drill, and he was thrilled to be out, his eyes darting everywhere. Kelsey held his hand, for a moment seeing things as she thought he did.

She wanted desperately to report on the experiment for the magazine, but had so far managed to keep her mouth shut, even around Tony. She didn't want to risk any publicity that might attract anti-science freaks who might try to sabotage this special experiment, even though no embryos would be used. You just never knew with those types. Some people heard the words *stem cells* and just assumed embryos would be destroyed.

Now a team of Peter's technicians, students, and post-docs were meeting the ambulette. Samantha directed them in transporting Stuart into the lab's testing area. A Hoyer lift was brought over to place him in a reclining chair near an oscilloscope. Kelsey leaned over him and smoothed his hair as a blood sample was taken, as well as a few hairs, a bit of skin from his forearm, and a swish of cells from inside his cheek, all for baseline DNA analysis. She'd never seen his eyes so bright.

"That's Peter over there," she said in a soft voice, "talking to his students. Dr. Holloway, I mean. He's the stem cell researcher I told you about."

Stuart gave a lopsided grin.

"I met him a year ago at a conference. Nice to have him so close by. Okay, here he comes."

When Peter strode over to Kelsey and put one arm around her, Kelsey noticed a brief shadow clouding Stuart's face. Or maybe it was just her imagination.

Peter promptly took Stuart's hand. "Well, hello, experimental subject! Are you ready to rock 'n' roll?"

"Yah!" When Peter smiled, Stuart relaxed a little.

A technician placed electrodes on Stuart's head as his eyebrows shifted up. In an instant, brain waves appeared on a nearby EEG screen. In the corner near the Larson cartoon-covered refrigerator, a figure with masses of black curly hair sat with his head down over a guitar, from which came the unmistakable riff of "Stairway to Heaven." The electric guitar was connected to a screen showing cycling sound waves.

"Hey, Eliot," Peter called over, "don't you know this is a No Stairway to Heaven Zone? Like in Wayne's World?" He laughed at his own joke. "Earth to Eliot, beam down. This is Kelsey," he said when the guitarist's head finally came up. "And Stuart. I've gotta duck out. Be right back."

Eyes and a nose appeared from beneath the forest of black frizz, which ran continuously into a mustache and a beard. Eliot, post-doc and rock musician, put the guitar aside and came over to shake hands. "Hi. Peter talks so much about you. Both of you."

"You, too," Kelsey replied. "Hey, can you tell me about that software that deconstructs hit songs? Peter mentioned that you'd gotten ahold of it. Can we use it? Did Peter tell you about U2, Coldplay, and the Killers?"

Eliot grinned. "I'm way ahead of you."

Kelsey was excited at Eliot's excitement at combining his two loves—music and stem cells. "You've actually used the software already to explore our little hypothesis?"

"Just got it last week. Let me show you."

Eliot led Kelsey over to the computer screen that had been showing the "Stairway to Heaven" sound waves, hit a key, and the screen suddenly filled with a universe of white dots against a dark blue backdrop. Their distribution wasn't even; some were clustered, like constellations.

"What's that?" she asked. "It looks celestial."

"Hit song signatures. There's sixty of them."

"The clusters? What do they mean?"

"Each dot is a song," he explained. "Its location is determined by twelve quantitative parameters. This field displays 10,000 dots. That's 10,000 songs."

"And they fall into sixty groups, based on the parameters?"

"Right."

"I'm impressed," she said, "but I still don't quite get it. Why do we need this? Can't we just tell if songs sound alike?"

"Not really. Your ears aren't sensitive enough. An artificial neural network runs along with the spectral deconvolution program, so similarities as they appear to the human ear are considered. But the program goes well beyond that. The songs within the clusters are mathematically similar."

"What does the deconvolution do? How does it work?" She gave a modest smile. "I'm afraid I didn't get very much out of calculus and statistics in college." She noticed that the technicians and other grad students had crowded around them.

"The software analyzes mathematical descriptors of the song. Physics, basically. And adds that to the neural network scanning."

"What sorts of parameters? Frequency and amplitude?"

"Yes, and it turns out, as you suspected, that those are the two key characteristics in terms of the songs that are apparently jumpstarting Stuart's brain cells. We hope. And those songs you told Peter about? 'Pride,' 'Moses,' and 'Somebody Told Me'? You're dead on right. They end up in the same cluster. But it turns out they share more than the frequency."

"What?" asked another student, a lanky blond who stood about a foot taller than Eliot.

"Things like melody and harmony, beat and tempo, rhythm, analysis of the octaves, pitch and cadence. I've added to the program sequences and subsequences—"

"Like the riff in 'Pride' and 'Moses'?" Kelsey interrupted.

"Right again."

She spontaneously gave Eliot a hug. "It sounds just like comparative genomics, searching for similarities in DNA sequence to infer how modern species are related. This is incredible!"

"If you say so. Take a look at my playlist, Kelsey. We'll use yours, of course, because it obviously works, but other songs match the putative stem cell signature." Eliot clicked again and a new list appeared. "We can create a stem cell symphony, if you like. Hell, maybe different diseases will respond to different symphonies. This could be huge!"

Kelsey looked over the new playlist. "'Come To My Window'? 'Livin' on a Prayer'? 'Don't Fear the Reaper'? Who would have thought—"

Peter came striding into the lab. "OK, guys, MTV time's over. Eliot, start the first playlist."

"We have to plug Stuart in," Kelsey said. "It's important that he hears the music through the earbuds."

"Why can't he hear it played through the air, with the rest of us?" Peter asked. The students all started to talk at once.

"You don't have an iPod, do you Dr. H.?" asked Nils, the tall blond. "It separates the tracks. You hear totally different instruments and vocals in each ear. We want to exactly replicate what Stuart has been listening to."

"KKKKKel!"

"I guess Stuart agrees." With a smile, Eliot started the playlist, placed the earbuds in Stuart's ears, and connected the iPod to a computer linked to the oscilloscope. The screen displayed a rapid frequency pattern.

Facing his lab group, Peter went into professor mode. "Stuart's the first part of the experiment," he said, "the *in vivo* part. The BrdU analog that he's getting replaces the thymines in replicating DNA, so only new cells take up the dye and are thus marked. Older neurons would have been sitting around for years post-mitosis. They don't take up the BrdU. So if stem cells or progenitors are being activated, we'll see some blue when we scan his brain in a few days."

"What's the second part?" asked Kelsey.

"That's the *in vitro* part. C'mere." He led her to three flasks filled with amber cell culture medium, the lab crew right behind them. A probe in each flask led to the computer, where a monitor displayed a graph with the Y-axis labeled *cell #* and the X-axis labeled *time*. Three lines were beginning to track from the lower left corner. The computer was also connected to a fluorescence microscope.

"This whole setup is a parallel experiment," Peter explained, "a control of sorts, to see if we can replicate in cultured cells what may be happening in Stuart's brain. Natalie, care to explain? Natalie's a postdoc with a magic touch."

Natalie, a dark beauty who looked like her namesake actress Natalie Wood, took over the impromptu seminar. "Flask A has human neural progenitor cells, courtesy of the McQueen team. Flasks B and C are mouse cells. The cells in flask B are from the Huntington's model, and the cells in C are wild-type, normal."

"Are the human progenitors normal?" Kelsey asked.

"Yes, they'll eventually serve as a control as soon as we can add the human HD cell line. The Boston group has those cells. They had enough private funding to use SCNT on patient's cells, so the cell culture could represent the earliest stages of the disease in humans. Which of course we wouldn't be able to see otherwise. They're just waiting for validation studies to send them to us," Natalie said.

"What markers are you using?" asked Kelsey.

"The usual. DAPI for the nuclei, which tracks cell number and, by inference, cell division rate. And the BrdU analog intensity indicates the number of cell doublings as a check. The software monitors the markers," the young researcher replied, smoothing back her dark shiny mane that contrasted sharply against her white labcoat.

Kelsey walked over to Stuart and took his hand. "How long will we have to wait to see results?" she asked, turning back to Natalie and her entourage.

"We'll try four-hour shifts over the next three days. Take blood and the other tissues at various points for the microarrays to track gene expression. We can even run a few whole genome chips to see if we can spot anything other than endorphins being activated. Or suppressed. Maybe we'll even find a gene not annotated yet."

"I plan to stick around all weekend," said Eliot. "Anyone care to join me? It'll be quieter around here, that'll help."

"Sure!" said Kelsey, and Stuart grinned.

15

AMES NURSING HOME, DECEMBER 18

Kelsey glanced into the dayroom, then checked room 317, puzzled. She came back out to the nurses' station where, fortunately, Maria was on duty.

"Where's Stuart?" she asked.

"Catholic services. Why don't you go, too?"

"Catholic services? Oh, God! He's an atheist! Didn't anyone read his chart?"

Too impatient to wait for the elevator, Kelsey took the stairs to the cafeteria, but she was too late. The place was dripping in Christmas decorations. Two women in Santa hats sat at a piano singing about Jesus' blood, trilling like Edith Bunker on the *All in the Family* reruns. A priest stood beside the piano, holding an acoustic guitar. Dozens of residents, most in wheelchairs, were parked in concentric circles around the piano, about seventy percent of them dozing, some quite audibly. Most of the other thirty percent were attempting to join in the song. Stationed among the singing and snoring ladies was Stuart, awake and looking extremely uncomfortable. Squeezing in, Kelsey knelt next to him and took his hand.

"Hi," she said in a loud whisper. "How did you end up here? At least it's almost over." She looked around, and suddenly her gaze riveted on a familiar face.

Connie, the newly-minted nurse from death class who had tried to save Kelsey, was sitting beside a drooling woman. It took Kelsey a moment to recognize her because she didn't have the ponytail she'd worn at hospice training – just dull brown frizz emanating from her head. She met Kelsey's stare, nodded cordially, and waved. Kelsey waved back, less cordially, then whispered to Stuart how Connie had tried to save her soul.

Aarrghhhhaw, he yowled, which set Kelsey giggling. She rubbed his hands until they both calmed down. The Edith Bunkers were now bellowing a new hymn, a slower one. Kelsey yawned and Stuart drifted off, and within a minute she fell asleep with her head on his scrawny thigh. Stuart began to gently snore. And then, quietly at first but clearly building, began a familiar crescendo. "Ahhh, ahhh, ahhh." "Shuddup! shuddup! shuddup!" And "YOU shuddup, you moron! She can't help it!"

Just as Kelsey and then Stuart were jolted awake, the tiny woman next to Stuart, a snot stalactite swinging back and forth in the cavern of her nostril as she breathed, started to laugh hysterically. Then the owl lady started to hoot, and one by one, the members of the captive audience all picked up the "hoo hoo" signal, until everyone was awake and the room erupted into a familiar cacophony. Two nurses' aides, zeroing in on the bickering trio, tried desperately to shush them, but their efforts proved futile as the other residents replaced the squabbling and hooting with more random babbles and moans.

The Edith Bunkers and the priest gave up. Unable to hide her smirk, Kelsey quickly wheeled Stuart out of the cafeteria to join a line of wheelchairs waiting for the elevator. And then she saw another familiar face, this one more welcome.

"Marsha!"

"Kelsey!"

As Stuart looked on, the friends squealed and hugged. Connie wheeled her patient by and glared at them.

Marsha stared. "Was that Connie?"

"Yup."

"At the service?"

"Yup."

"Well, did she help you find Jesus in there?"

"I think she would have tried, but things got a little crazy." Kelsey laughed again. "This is a tough crowd."

"I can imagine. My patients are too far gone to make it to services. Hey, are you going to introduce me to your handsome friend here?"

"Of course. Marsha, I'd like you to meet Stuart."

"Kelsey's told me all about you." Marsha took Stuart's hand and he smiled.

"Marsha buys clothing for a store in Philly that has lots of retro gear," Kelsey told him. "Urban Outfitters and Anthropologie. She gets to go to garage sales and thrift shops and sift through old stuff to invent new combinations of things, which people pay a lot of money for. That's why she has such cool clothing." Kelsey tugged at the purple feather boa around Marsha's neck. "Much more exciting than anything I do."

Marsha pressed the elevator button impatiently. "Damn this thing. I've been waiting forever. I think I'll just take the stairs."

"Remember to punch the code in," Kelsey told her. "You don't want the alarms going off."

"What alarms?"

"You know. To stop potential escapees."

"You're kidding."

"No, I'm not. About six months ago, an old demented lady was found wandering the grounds. At 3 A.M. She'd just waltzed out of here, probably right after bedtime. Nobody noticed."

"So what's the code?"

"It's idiotic. 1-2-3-4-5."

"Thanks. I have to get to Edna on B2 before her loudmouth son gets here. Good luck with that elevator." Marsha turned toward the stairs, then turned back. "Hey, Kel, call me. We'll catch up. Maybe spend Christmas together? The boringest day of the year."

"Great idea. But why don't you come up to Stuart's room after you see your patient? Then we can ride back together. He's in D317."

"Sure. See you in a few. Here goes: 1-2-3-4-5!"

The door clicked, and Marsha ducked into the stairwell. Just then, the elevator doors opened and Kelsey wheeled Stuart in.

《∞》

Kelsey waited outside Stuart's room, admiring Justina's new nail polish as Samantha and an aide finished transferring Stuart back to his bed. Kelsey wondered how the nurse got her work done with that crazy long braid whiplashing into everything, but somehow she'd managed to make Stuart comfortable. Stuart really liked Sam, who squeezed Kelsey's arm as she and the aide left the room. Kelsey went over to Stuart, took one of his hands and began rubbing it. "You really do have the most beautiful eyes," she told him. "Any woman would kill for those lashes."

Stuart answered, not exactly in words, but with sounds that had a cadence that had become familiar to Kelsey.

"That Christmas service sure was fun, wasn't it? Are Catholic services always that lively?" Stuart's response was staccato, a laugh. "Guess not. Would you like to hear some music? Other than a hymn about Jesus' blood? Or are you too tired?"

"Ya."

"OK. This will be fitting, I think." Kelsey put one earbud in Stuart's ear, one in her own, and clicked on a playlist that began with Peter Gabriel's *"In Your Eyes"*.

Kelsey sang the intensely romantic and intimate song softly as she leaned closer and closer to Stuart. They were only inches apart, staring into each other's eyes as if caught in a Vulcan mind meld, Kelsey oblivious to the approaching footsteps. Just outside Stuart's door, Marsha peeked in to see Kelsey drawing ever closer to Stuart. She quietly retreated.

《∞》

Stuart's mind was racing, his senses surely playing tricks on him. He was on his back, as he usually was, but there was a weight that was at the same time strange yet also familiar. He felt it all over. The feeling was so remote, as if conjured from the distant past, that he had difficulty identifying, let alone believing, what was happening to him.

It was overwhelming, as if he were more than himself. He could smell her, see her, breathe her. And parts of him were responding. His mouth was, and down below, that was, too, although it seemed she was doing all the work. The music and the sensations enveloped him until he felt utterly transported to a place he had thought he would never visit again. He was trying to savor every second, every sensation, yet even as he hoped it would go on forever, he could feel something building. An unnamed pressure, an increasingly frenzied race, finally led to an explosive release. And then…oblivion.

Some time later, Samantha peeked in to check on Stuart and caught the scene. She silently left, closing the door, and told the aides not to disturb him for dinner. He needed rest.

When Stuart was next awake and aware, hours had passed. He sensed Kelsey's lingering presence, but when he finally opened his eyes, hers wasn't the face he saw.

"That must've been some helluva dream you had," Nurse Smithies growled. "We've gotta change you!"

16

AMES NURSING HOME, DECEMBER 20

Kelsey leaned on the door to the dayroom, trying hard not to laugh. It was the dementia residents again. The ones who wandered were hooked up to cushion alarms, so that if they tried to get up, a shrill sound went off. With so many staff taking end-of-year vacation time to do their holiday shopping, the demented residents greatly outnumbered the aides, who just couldn't keep up. So up and down the mostly old people went, like a series of jack-in-the-boxes.

Looking across the room, Kelsey could see Stuart enjoying the scene, too. Funny, she thought, how alike they were. Someone had put a Santa hat on him that would have been demeaning if the aides weren't also wearing them. She walked over and kissed him on the cheek, then grabbed a nearby washcloth and wiped the remains of lunch from his chin.

"Stuart," she said, "I've got that podcast I told you about, the one about the whales. Okay?" Just as she was leaning over to place the earbuds in his ears, her cell phone meowed. Kelsey flipped it open and looked at the screen.

"Hey, Stuart," she said. "It's Dr. H. Let me take this, okay? We'll do the whale podcast in a minute. This could be important."

She pressed a key on the phone. "Hi, Peter. What's up? Wait, I can't hear you. Let me move closer to the window." She walked over to the low window that overlooked the snow-covered evergreens that ringed the nursing home. Out of the corner of her eyes, she could see Nurse Smithies, cleaning up a quasi-digested turkey sandwich that had been projectile-vomited at the heating ducts and had dripped slowly in, the chunks remaining to slowly bake.

"That's better," she said, turning her back on the nurse. "I can hear you now without the buzz. Did you get any results?" Keeping an eye on Stuart, she listened intently.

"Really? And you're sure what's growing in Stuart's brain are stem cells? Not a tumor?" Kelsey began to twirl her hair around a finger.

"OK," she said. "And what about the music?" She was growing more and more excited as she listened to Peter's lengthy reply.

"So the cells in the culture dish and in his brain are reawakening?" She was now speaking so loudly that Nurse Smithies looked over at her, but Kelsey was facing the window and oblivious to the nurse's sudden keen interest. "In response to U2? Coldplay? Eliot's playlists too? Wow. And that's why he's improving?"

She checked her watch.

"Right. Damn, I'm on deadline, I can't get there until morning. Is it okay even though it's the weekend?" She turned back towards Stuart. "I thought so. Franklin 334, the office next to the stem cell lab. Okay. I'll be there. Thanks Dr. Holloway!"

Kelsey snapped the phone shut and went over to Stuart, then plugged them both in to hear the podcast.

In the corner, Nurse Smithies quickly averted her eyes, towards the TV. And on the screen an advertisement flashed:

"HAVE A STORY IDEA?
WANT $10,000 FAST?
CALL 1-800-555-TELL
WORLD MEDICAL MYSTERIES"

As the nurse put down the sponge, a grin spread slowly across her face, momentarily stretching her three chins into one.

17

FRANKLIN MEDICAL COLLEGE, STEM CELL LAB. DECEMBER 23

Kelsey could barely sleep, but she must have, because she awoke at 5:30 A.M., filled with anxiety about her meeting at Franklin. Starbucks was empty this early on a Saturday. She sat there nursing a latte for the better part of an hour, staring at the same *Philadelphia Reporter* article. Finally, it was time to meet Peter.

Now she stood beside him in his office. His desk was covered with brain scans, cell counts, electron micrographs, colorful DNA microarray data, and EEG wave tracings. Peter shoved the papers aside and they sat down at the computer screen.

"The results are quite striking," he began.

"I don't know what to look at first," Kelsey said, eyes wide. "I'm glad you can make some sense of it all. Can we start with the cell cultures? That seems straightforward."

Peter clicked on a view of Petri dishes coated with cells, then opened a second window that showed a field of round and star-shaped cells, each harboring dark red areas. "See the nestin staining? That indicates that the cells are from a neural lineage. Of course we're validating that with the gene expression microarrays. Gotta be sure they're what we think they are."

Kelsey looked more closely at the screen. "So the microarrays selectively highlight the genes that are active only in neural stem or progenitor cells? Do we even know what all of those genes are? What they do?"

"Well, we can't know what we don't know," Peter replied dryly, back in professor mode. "That's a limitation of these gene expression studies. We don't quite know what it is we're looking for. But, really only a few genes seem, so far, to be uniquely expressed in stem cells. Several studies have implicated fewer than a dozen. Most of the genes that turn on in stem cells also work in other cell types. But it's the combination, the expression pattern of all eighty or so of these genes, some unique to stem cells and some not, that forms the overall 'stemness' signature."

"Like fashion."

Peter looked at her quizzically.

"Like what my friend Marsha does. She creates outfits and displays at Urban Outfitters, you know, those funky retro things. Any one outfit doesn't have very many unique features. Maybe a distinguishing belt or buttons. It's the *assemblage*, the *combination* that makes the outfit, the details added to a basic skirt or pants. Like a neuron is an embellishment of its progenitor. Marsha arranges other peoples' junk into something that somehow makes sense."

Peter smiled. "Spoken like a true XX, and unfathomable to this stylistically clueless XY." Peter pointed to his jeans and flannel shirt. "But a stem cell doesn't just use random cast-off genes. There's an underlying program to it all. Not that Marsha—hell, I don't know much about outfits, I don't quite follow. Anyway, whatever these cells in your friend Stuart's brain are listening to, they're definitely responding by dividing. And they are maintaining their *neuralness*, if that's a word."

Peter clicked and replaced the cells displayed on the screen with three cell-count charts. "And we can track the division. Look at all the new cells."

Kelsey studied them for a moment. "Too bad we don't have the human HD cell line yet. But these preliminary counts do show that the mouse HD cells divided in response to the stimulation. But the healthy ones didn't. That supports our hypothesis, doesn't it?"

"It sure does."

Kelsey leaned in to study the screen more intently. "Why is the pattern so regular like that?" she asked, pointing to the neat peaks building across the graph. "No bumps. It looks like they're marching to the beat of the same drummer. Literally?"

Peter smiled and nodded. "That's what I think, too. I'd say that the cell cycle has synchronized to the music. The damn things actually divide in response to U2."

"This is great, so far. But what about Stuart? What did the EEG show?"

"That was interesting, too." Peter leaned away from the computer and picked up several brain tracings, then swiveled back and touched a few keys. "I superimposed these EEG tracings against the data from Eliot's deconvolution/neural network thing. Take a look."

Kelsey sat bolt upright. "They correspond!"

"They sure do. And I did EEGs on Eliot, as a control brain." He grinned. "Assuming a grad student's brain is normal. What do you think?"

Kelsey squinted at the screen. "Let's see. He isn't having the same response as Stuart?"

"Right. And why not?"

"Because his brain isn't sick or injured."

"Or buzzed with seizures."

"So do you think Stuart's Huntington's somehow made his brain sensitive to the musical stimulus? Is this response unique to Huntington's? Could this work for someone with a spinal cord injury? Or maybe Alzheimer's or Parkinson's or ALS? And, of course, seizures?"

Peter smiled and laid one hand on Kelsey's arm.

"Kelsey, this is just one case. We can't draw any conclusions. Not yet."

She smiled at him. "I know. Hey, what about the mechanism? The gene expression profiles? You left them out."

"No I didn't. I'm still mulling over the results."

"Care to share?"

"Yes, but not now." Peter got up, faced Kelsey, and put his hands on her shoulders.

"When?"

"Are you busy tomorrow night and the next day?"

"That would be Christmas Eve and Christmas day. I promised Marsha I'd meet her for coffee sometime, but that's all I've got going on. But aren't *you* busy?"

"No. I hate this time of year. Don't you, too? I remember when you were called away from the stem cell conference when your dad died…something about not having been in a church in years. So I thought we might celebrate the holidays together in the sacred tradition of the non-believer."

"Chinese take-out and *Twilight Zone* reruns?"

"You got it. But I thought maybe we'd go see the new Woody Allen film first."

"Deal."

Kelsey and Peter had gone to a late afternoon showing, saving nightfall for Rod Serling. The film had been a disappointment, the twenty-something star making Kelsey wish for Woody's old films with Diane Keaton and Mia Farrow. Seeing Woody lust after the young actress du jour, whether as actor or director or both, made her squirm. And feel ancient.

But it had been a fun day. They'd taken the take-out to her apartment and settled into the annual *Twilight Zone* marathon. The frazzled businessman had already escaped to the fictional town of Willoughby, and nervous airline passenger William Shatner to the wing of his plane. Talking Tina, the doll from hell, had just murdered a young Telly Savalas, and now they were watching Billy Mumy zap people he didn't like into the cornfield. He'd just turned an outspoken neighbor into a jack-in-the-box.

"You know," said Peter, "when I was a kid that used to scare the crap out of me."

Kelsey chuckled. "I thought little boys weren't afraid of anything."

"Well, that did it for me. Things in the wrong place, like in *The Fly*, when Jeff Goldblum's head is on the fly at the end. Did you see that? I forget who was in the original."

"Things in the wrong places," she replied. "Did you know that I worked with homeotic mutations in *Drosophila* for my Ph.D.? Flies with legs in place of antennae? So, nope, that doesn't scare me, although Jeff Goldblum's head is scary even on him, like in *Jurassic Park*." She stopped to slurp up noodles. "You know what scared me as a kid?"

"Someone else's head?"

"No. *Feet*. In the *Wizard of Oz*, when the house dropped on the Wicked Witch of the East, and her feet shriveled up in the ruby slippers."

"The feet scared you? What about the lit broomstick her sister threw at the scarecrow?"

"The broomstick scared me, too, but not in that scene. It was when Miss Gulch riding her bike turns into the witch on the broomstick as the house flies up in the tornado. Right after Dorothy wakes up."

He considered that for a moment. "I guess that was a pretty intense film for a little kid. It spooked me, too." He moved closer and Kelsey nestled into him.

"I used to hide in the bathroom as soon as the house started to rise," she confessed.

They were silent for a few moments as Billy Mumy sent someone else to the cornfield.

"Kelsey," he suddenly said, "what scares you now?"

She thought for a moment. "Things that I can't control."

"Like what?"

"Like Stuart. With hospice, there's a feeling that we come in when people give up. But with Stuart, I don't *want* to give up. Maybe it's because he's so much younger than our typical patients. I want to fight his disease, not just comfort and distract him. I want to understand what's going on in his brain and reverse it. I want to *control* it."

"Well, maybe you are doing that."

She sighed. "But sometimes I want to do the impossible. I want to turn back time, so that I can have a real conversation with him. So I can be sure that what I think he's feeling is what he truly is feeling."

"I think about that a lot, too." Peter stretched and sighed.

"About what?"

"Turning back time."

"That sounds heavy. Is there something that you want to go back to? Someone?"

"Yes." His voice was barely above a whisper.

"Want to talk about it?" she asked. "Is that why you dislike the holidays? Did something happen around this time of year?"

"You're pretty perceptive. This is only the third year since the accident."

"Uh oh. What happened? Can you tell me?" She reached over and grabbed the remote and shut off the TV, then turned her full attention to Peter.

"It was this very day, December 24. An ice storm. My wife was driving …"

"Your wife?"

Peter nodded. "Stacey was just going out to pick up some milk. She has to have a latte every morning, can't make coffee with water."

"Like me."

"Yeah, I noticed. Anyway, it hadn't even been a storm, really, just a light coating of ice in some places, and since rush hour had passed, neither of us thought the roads would be bad. But she skidded going downhill a mile from our house. Black ice. Couldn't stop at the stop sign."

"Omigod."

"A truck was coming. She was gone by the time the EMTs arrived." Peter was silent for several minutes. "And she was four months pregnant."

"Oh, Peter. I'm so sorry. Tell me about her?"

He took a deep breath and collected himself. "Well, Stacey actually looked a little like you, only her curls were dark blonde. She was very athletic, liked to ski. We used to run together. She was an R.N. Worked in spinal cord rehab, often with teenagers. And that's actually how she died." He shook his head. "A spinal cord injury. The only good thing, if you can call it that, is that she died instantly, because if she hadn't, she'd have known too much of what she was in for."

Kelsey reached out for him. "Now I understand a little better your love for those neurospheres. We're going to make it happen. For Stacey. And for Stuart."

"And for us."

※

AMES NURSING HOME, DECEMBER 26

Stuart lay flat, his arms restrained under tightly pulled sheets. Dried blood stained the pillowcase, and several small band-aids dotted his face.

"Omigod, Stuart!" Kelsey shouted as she came into his room. "What happened?"

He groaned as Samantha pushed past Kelsey with cleaning equipment, braid swinging in her wake. "Hi, Kelsey," she said. "I was just about to call you."

"What the hell happened? Did someone attack him? It can't be his roommate, he's half dead."

Samantha checked the bandages. "No. Actually Stuart did it."

"To himself?"

"Yeah. Amy the new aide was in here. She'd set up the food tray at a position where he can't reach it. But he leaned forward and moved his arms. Or rather he was unable to prevent his arms from moving, and the tray went crashing to the floor. His hands then flung up and he scratched himself."

"I didn't realize that could happen."

"You didn't know him before he grew still. It used to happen all the time. And, of course, Will and Livvie were constantly injuring themselves when they were here."

Kelsey was thoughtful a moment. "Does that mean…"

"It could. Looks like he's got that ability back. If too *much* movement is an improvement over too *little*."

Stuart made a gurgling sound.

"Oh, Stuart, I'm sorry," said Samantha. "I didn't mean to talk about you as if you're not here. What I meant was that this could be a good sign, even though it doesn't look like it, with those bandages."

Elvin stuck his head in the door. "Hey, Sam, whazzup?"

"Kelsey, will you excuse us? We have to change the sheets. Can you call hospice and tell them what's happened? About the self-inflicted injuries?"

"Sure."

Kelsey saw Justina wheeling her way over and ducked into a storage closet to make the call on her cell phone, positioning herself between two pillars of Depends packages until she got service. When Justina had passed and Samantha and Elvin had finished, she went to Stuart and leaned over, stroking his hair. They smiled at each other.

He opened his mouth. "Kel. Hurt."

"Shh. It's okay. No music today, I'm not in the mood. I'll just put the TV on low and sit with you awhile, okay?"

"Yah."

The chattering of the women on *The View* soon lulled Stuart to sleep. Kelsey sat with him, holding his hand, as the morning bustle of the nursing home faded into the background. No one disturbed them.

The buzz of the intercom jolted Kelsey awake. For an instant, she didn't know where she was, then she looked up at the clock and realized she'd already missed an editorial meeting. After a quick goodbye to Stuart, she headed directly back to the office. She stopped to sign in and greeted Bruce, whose face was hidden behind *World Medical Mysteries*.

"Mornin' Bruce. How are you?"

He slowly lowered the tabloid.

"I'm fine. But how are you?"

"OK. What do you mean?"

"Have you seen this?" he asked. He raised the tabloid.

"Should I have? Sorry, but that isn't on my reading list."

"I think maybe it should be. Here, keep this. You might wanna frame it."

"What? Thanks, I think."

Kelsey took the paper, folded it face in, and shoved it under her arm as she disappeared into the elevator. Glancing at her watch, she burst into the offices of Biotech USA, where Tony was joking with

Miranda, the administrative assistant.

"Hi, Kel. You're late, but not to worry, the meeting got postponed until four."

"Great. Thanks, Tony." She rushed past him and turned into her cubicle, where she put down her bag, then fumbled and dropped the tabloid onto the keyboard. It opened to where Bruce had folded it, page 3.

Kelsey stared at the headline, shocked into a moment of silence, and then screamed out "oh, shit!"

Tony came rushing in.

"I'd know that *oh, shit* anywhere. What's the matter?" He looked down at the tabloid. "Kel, so Britney's preggers again, who gives a—"

"No! Look at that headline!"

"OK. But I'm beginning to question—"

"Just read it. Then go to the article and please please please tell me my name isn't in there."

"OK. *iPod turns on stem cells, turns off deadly brain disease, in nursing home resident.*"

"I can't bear to look. Tony, why are you so quiet? It's not like you. Say something!"

"Well," he finally said, "*oh, shit* was an appropriate response."

"Give me that!"

"I thought you didn't—"

She grabbed the paper out of his hands and read aloud:

> *While debate over stem cell research continues, Kelsey Raye, a science writer at Philadelphia-based Biotech USA, has come up with her own, rather unconventional experiment, with the help of Dr. Peter Holloway, chair of cell biology at Franklin Medical College—*

—Christ, here it comes—

> *—She is using her iPod to activate stem cells in the brain of a young man who lives in a nursing home. And it's curing him of*

a horrific inherited, incurable disease. But it's not just any music, said Myra Smithies, a devoted nurse where this apparent miracle of science is taking place. It's U2.

"I'll kill that bitch!"

18

BIOTECH USA OFFICES, DECEMBER 27

Kelsey arrived at the office very early the next day, hoping to avoid as many people as she could. Or she tried to. If her office phone was any indication, *World Medical Mysteries* was more widely read than she'd thought. She'd started sending calls to voice mail after an hour, but now, since her concentration was shot for the day anyway, curiosity won out. She picked up.

"Yes, that's me." She checked her e-mail as she listened to a tale familiar from responses to many of her articles over the years.

"I'm very sorry about your mother," she told the caller. "Yes, Lewy body dementia is horrible. But I'm not a doctor. I'm sorry, I can't help you."

Kelsey hung up, but the phone immediately rang again.

"Maybe you shouldn't answer that," Tony said as he came around the divider. But she picked up the phone.

"Kelsey Raye, Biotech USA. Can I help you? Excuse me?"

Kelsey covered the receiver. "Tony, I've got a lunatic here. Wanna listen in?" Tony picked up a phone out in the hallway. Kelsey was letting the caller rant, and when he finally paused, she answered with crisp, cold anger.

"No one's killing embryos. The stem cells, if that's what they really are, are right in his brain. Yours, too. *Assuming you have one.*" She slammed down the phone.

Tony gave her a sympathetic look. "Want me to field your calls for awhile? You should really record them. Might be material for a column."

"That's what I'm thinking, too. When shit happens, I can almost always eventually use it somehow. Thanks." She gave him a quick hug, then opened her cell phone and scrolled down to Peter's number. "Hi, voicemail. Peter, meet me at the coffee place Thursday after work? I forgot. It's never after work for you. Five o'clock? Something's up. Call me to confirm. See you then. Thanks." She snapped the phone shut.

"Calling Dr. Frankenstein?" Tony smirked.

✺

JITTERY JIM'S, DECEMBER 28

Kelsey was nursing a double mocha when Peter strode into the cafe.

"Sorry I'm late," he said, pulling out a chair across the tiny table from her. "Forgive the cliché, but the shit has really hit the fan."

"You saw the article."

"I was *shown* the article. By PR. They gave me exactly two hours to come up with a statement describing the experiments. Sorry I didn't get a chance to call you, but it was a rush job. And then I had a disturbing call…"

"Me too."

"From a Dr. Benjamin. Of the Neurodegenerative Disease Foundation."

"What did he want?"

"She. Victoria. She was alarmed."

"About what?"

"Just a second, I need caffeine." Peter got a mug of coffee from the bar and came back.

"Well, for starters, she thinks the tabloid is raising false hopes. The foundation's already flooded with requests for information." He took a long drink and sighed.

"What else? I sense a *what else* here."

"She's worried that we don't know enough to control Stuart's stem cells. *If* we've actually activated them."

Kelsey considered this and nodded slowly. "I wonder if that's why he's been hurting himself when his arms flail. After all, we don't know if the new cells are working the same as the ones that degenerated. Poor Stuart, he had cuts the last time I saw him, did I tell you?"

"No, that's awful. But even worse, Dr. Benjamin is afraid the activated cells could divide to form a tumor."

"But the Florida work suggests otherwise."

"True," he replied, "but we can't rule it out. Stuart isn't a mouse, and the experiments done so far might not have gone on long enough for cancer to develop. Anyway, maybe we should write up a case report. I know its premature, but—"

"Do we have enough data?"

"For a case report, yes. But that's all. A sample size of one doesn't mean much. But it would mark our territory, so to speak."

"Our territory?"

"We're in this together, Kelsey. Time to put the old scientist hat back on."

"Now *that's* a cliché." She smiled uneasily, then thought a moment. "Territoriality makes me think of wolf pee."

"You would." Peter smiled.

"But seriously, maybe we should file a patent application, too," she said. "After all, dozens of stem cell companies are inventing catheters and implants and who knows what to yank out peoples' stem cells, grow them, get them to specialize, then stick them back into the body. Invasively. We may have stumbled upon a way to do that noninvasively." She thought back to the last biotech conference she'd attended. "One company's coaxing heart attack victims' fat cells to give rise to cardiac muscle patches, another's restoring damaged bladders, another's fashioning dental implants from stem cells in tooth pulp. But these cell therapies have to be painfully delivered."

"It's not dozens of companies, Kelsey, it's hundreds. And that's probably a good idea, filing a patent claim," he said. "I'll contact the IP office at Franklin. Getting back to writing up a case report, if we pursue it, maybe we'd hear from others who've made similar observations, like the music therapy folks. And maybe our case would inspire a pilot study."

"Or private funding?"

"Sure."

She grinned. "I assume no blogs. We'd just sound like two nuts if we go that route. But which journal?"

"Let's aim high," he said. "How about *The Lancet*? Or the *British Medical Journal*? The Brits have been much more open-minded toward stem cells than the Bush-era U.S., even though we're talking about the so-called adult variety. I'd rather steer clear of *Science* since they screwed up big time with the Korean fiasco a few years back. And *Nature*'s too picky, they'd probably just shove our paper into one of their spin-offs. You know, *Nature Biotech*, *Nature Medicine*, or *Nature Leftovers*. We need to distinguish ourselves. Should I get Eliot working on it?"

"On what, the paper? No, even if his brain scan wasn't empty." She finished her mocha. "Just kidding. Actually, I'd like to give it a try. After all, if you can write the PR statement, which is more my job, I can write the scientific article."

Peter smiled and took her hand. "But do you think you can write like a boring old scientist again? It's been awhile since grad school, hasn't it?"

"Sure. But I remember the style. Dry passive voice, acronyms and jargon, qualifiers throughout, repetition, repetition, repetition, obfuscation, and lengthen all words, sentences, and paragraphs." She gave his ponytail a yank. "Sure I can do it."

"Have you ever noticed that we tend to complete each other's…"

"…sentences? No. And you do sometimes talk in clichés." Kelsey got up. "Anyway, I have to drop by the office, and then I'm off to visit Stuart."

"Have fun!"

※

BIOTECH USA OFFICES, DECEMBER 29

"Hey Kel, quit abusing that delete button. I can't focus," said Tony from his side of the divider.

"Sorry. I don't believe all this e-mail. Just from overnight."

"Didja see the phone messages I took while you were cavorting with your partner in crime? Triaged by degree of mental impairment, of course."

"Thank you, but I haven't gotten to them yet."

Tony came over to her side and pointed to her shelf. "Here. I put them into three piles: stem cell groupies, disease families, and anti-science folks."

"Here comes another e-mail. Let's see which group it falls into." They both read the message: *Rock music is evil. You've let a demon loose in that man's brain.*

"Tony, this is from that group of wackos I wrote about, Citizens Against Stem Cell Research. Well, at least we know they read the finest scientific literature."

As Kelsey and Tony laughed, her cell phone meowed. "Hi, Peter. Yes, come over tonight. I need the data for the *Lancet* article. And the microarray stuff, you never did explain what that showed." Kelsey listened while moving the three piles of papers nearer her computer. "No, don't. If you e-mail all those scans my computer will throw up. And bring a pizza, white with broccoli. Thanks!"

Head down, Tony quietly returned to his cubicle.

⟪∞⟫

Kelsey had finally unplugged her phone and turned off her e-mail so that she could do the preliminary research for an article on gene expression in acne. Comparing the DNA microarrays for whiteheads, blackheads, and unblemished skin samples, she thought, would get her used to looking at the columns of red and green spots that made sense to molecular biologists.

She'd printed out some articles to read on the train out to Ames, and had become so engrossed that she looked up with a start to make sure she was on the correct suburban line and hadn't missed the stop. Head down again, she began wondering if the microarrays for the gene expression in Stuart's blood after he listened to the music would differ in any meaningful way from the control microarrays done without the stimulation. The ideal experiments, of course, would be on people who'd inherited the Huntington's mutation but didn't yet have symptoms. Then maybe something could be done to at least slow the progression of the disease with an earlier intervention.

She knew something wasn't right on D3 the minute she stepped off the elevator. It was silent. Even the bad '80s music that always played in the background was missing. Stopping at the nurses' station, she learned that Mrs. Rinehart, the dementia patient known for her resounding belches, had died that morning. Kelsey supposed that deaths were a normal part of life in a nursing home, but still, no matter how old someone was, how many deaths one had witnessed, it was hard to comprehend that someone could be sitting there at lunch one day, but gone forever the next. Even Stuart was difficult to cheer up, so she just sat with him, holding his hand and watching CNN.

Kelsey picked up Stuart's sadness and was a little down when she got home. Peter was due any minute, but she was too tired to clean up, so quickly shoved all the clutter into drawers and under furniture. She tripped over Foghat and broke her fall by grabbing the small table that held the phone. She happened to glance at the caller ID. So many calls! She just couldn't cope with them right now. Just then, the doorbell rang. She opened the door to a man standing behind a large, white box with a paper bag on top.

"Thank God, it's you," she said to Peter. "The pizza smells great, let me take it." She took the box and peeked into the paper bag. A bottle of decent wine.

"Thanks," he said. "I was afraid I'd drop it. I'm a little frazzled. What a day!"

"You, too?" she asked. "What's up? Any more repercussions from the tabloid?"

Peter laughed. "Well, PR made my intentionally vague and meaningless statement even more so, then sprinkled in the requisite numbers of 'breakthroughs,' 'cures,' and 'scientific proofs' before they released it."

Kelsey groaned. "Why must everything be a *breakthrough*?"

"Because that's what the public thinks science is," he said. "And here I'd thought the medical center would want to hush it all up, but no, they love the attention. So we'd better get moving on that report. They want something to send out that's more legit than that rag."

"Did you bring the data?"

Peter cleared the cats off the coffee table, pulled papers from his briefcase, and arranged them into piles. He then sat on the couch and patted the cushion for Kelsey to join him. "Here it is. All yours."

Kelsey sat down and thumbed through the papers. "Do you have suggestions on how to organize the report? Remember, I'm used to writing newspaper columns and biotech articles."

"Relax," he said. "You don't have to go through it all right this minute. You seem a little hyper. And you look beat."

"Thanks."

"No, seriously, is something the matter? How'd the nursing home go? Stuart isn't sicker, is he?"

"No, he's okay. Well, about the same. Bad day at the nursing home, though. Someone died."

"Oh. I guess that happens a lot, but it still must be tough. How's Stuart taking that? Was it a friend?"

"Not really. But it's strange there, the people and staff become like family. They all watch out for each other. This lady had been there as long as Stuart has, longer I suspect. Everyone was pretty down. But she died in her sleep, and she had dementia. It mustn't have been easy for her family, but for her, it was peaceful."

"I've often thought about dementia. How it can be a blessing not to know everything."

Kelsey twirled a lock of hair. "Marsha had a dementia patient who would forget at least once a day that she had cancer, until she retreated into her past and forgot altogether. This lady at Ames, Mrs. Rinehart, thought that each time she met me was the very first time. I must have introduced myself a dozen times. But she was sweet. The residents will miss her. The staff, too."

"Come here." Peter reached over, pulled her to him, and gave her a long hug. "OK," he finally said. "Writing the report. Since it's short, a chronological approach might work. Describe Stuart's status when you met him. Maybe a timecourse showing his decline when you went away and recovery when the music resumed. A table comparing the different types of data. Show those constellation things that indicate the cluster 29 song signature, or whatever it is that Eliot calls it. Oh, and we should include him on the paper."

"That's right. Cluster 29. What order should I present the data in? They were acquired at the same time."

He shrugged and yawned. "That doesn't really matter. Maybe *in vitro* first, the cell culture counts. Then *in vivo*. The EEGs and brain imaging?"

"Sounds good," she said. "What about the microarray data? Now will you finally tell me what you think they show?"

"Ok. But I'm not really sure what's going on. It's just a hypothesis at this point, and a shaky one."

"That's fine. Explain, please."

"Well," he began, "I ran Stuart's blood from the check-up he had about the time he went on hospice, roughly a week before you started seeing him."

"Right, when I was still in training."

"Then I ran the blood samples taken during the experiments against a microarray that had probes to all 121 currently known endogenous opiate genes. Endorphins, dynorphins, and enkephalins."

"So what showed up?"

"Beta endorphin lit up on all the arrays."

"OK. I guess that confirms that he's basically a happy guy, with or without U2. Odd, considering his circumstances. Was there anything distinguishing about the arrays from during the experiments?"

Peter broke out in a grin. "Yes! Two spots lit up, an enkephalin and a dynorphin, neither of which have been well characterized. Expression peaked in the sample taken just before Eliot turned the music off. And those genes weren't expressed at all in the blood samples from October."

Kelsey thought a moment. "Nice. What about the degree of expression?"

"Well, the fluorescence was equivalent for both spots. That's highly unusual, they're two different molecules. Why would the cell produce equal amounts of them? I'll bet it's not a coincidence. The equivalence *could* mean that transcripts representing the exons from each gene fused, so the protein products are present, and detectable, in equal amounts. Because the genetic instructions are essentially stuck together, at the RNA level."

"In other words," she said, "the stimulated stem or progenitor cells make a novel, combination endogenous opiate? Creating a new feel-good molecule from old parts? And you laughed at my fashion analogy. I was right!"

Peter looked momentarily puzzled. "I don't know about the fashion industry, but evolution has done exactly what I think we are seeing, over and over again. Teaming the exons that provide the non-junk parts of genes. In novel ways. Just look at all the gene families that we share with the other primates, only we've mixed and matched genes from the past to create new ones, the ones that make us human. That's why our genome sequence is so similar to those of chimps, orangutans, and gorillas, our great ape brethren. It's the number of exons and their organization that primarily differ."

"Among primates. Very funny. Getting back to the here and now, Peter, how can you tell if Stuart's gene *expression* is being altered, or if he has a *mutation* that brought the two gene parts together? A fusion gene? Those are completely different scenarios."

"I know. Eliot's probing Stuart's DNA as we speak to figure that out. If it's a fusion gene, it would probably be in DNA from all the different sources—the white blood cells, hair roots, fibroblasts in the skin and the cheek cells. And then the response would be unique to him – a mutation enables him to have the stem cell response to music. That's what we *don't* want. But fortunately for our hypothesis, the preliminary results suggest the combining of gene parts is at the level of RNA transcription. Not a mutation. That's one reason why our observations on Stuart must be validated with a trial."

"This is unbelievable! It all makes so much sense!" Kelsey grabbed an unsuspecting Nirvana and squeezed him.

Peter leaned forward. "Well, you won't believe this either."

"There's more?"

"Much more. I used some of Natalie's computational software to come up with all possible combinations of exon sequences from the two genes, and then predict the corresponding protein conformation."

"And?" Kelsey released the panicked feline, who bolted.

"I ran the predicted structure from the putative fusion protein against a conformational database. To see what it would fit. Like trying a key in different locks. And guess what it pulled out?"

"No idea. This better be good."

"None other than a neural growth factor receptor."

Kelsey actually felt chills at the sudden implication. She gaped. "The pieces are beginning to fit. Please tell me it's the receptor for BDNF?"

"Yes." Peter sat back with a huge smile on his face.

Kelsey was speechless, but not for long. "Omigod! Have we discovered a BDNF receptor agonist? A molecule that turns on a growth factor in the brain—selectively?" Kelsey suddenly jumped up, scattering the papers.

"*Yes*," Peter repeated. "The novel opiate, induced by the music, indeed seems to turn on brain-derived neurotrophic factor."

Kelsey continued their brainstorming. "BDNF, the Holy Grail, the linchpin in the pathogenesis. It's true that HD neurons are, to put it bluntly, totally fucked up, but basically they die because they run out of BDNF."

"That's right," Peter said, clearly enjoying her excitement.

"I wonder if we should call it Bono-BDNF," she said, only half jokingly. "After all, without U2 we never would have stumbled on this."

"*You* never would have stumbled on it. And give yourself some credit. Remember Pasteur: chance favors the prepared mind. It's really *your* hypothesis, Kelsey."

But she was still running through the molecular choreography in her mind. "That's the connection! It's almost too perfect, too logical, to be true. Stuart hears music, he gets happy, his brain cells ooze a weird hybrid opiate that is uniquely responsive to the U2 signature, and in addition to binding opiate receptors, the Bono-BDNF also binds uh, care to finish, Dr. H.?"

"Growth factor receptors on sleeping neural progenitor cells. Not blocking them, but activating them. The signal to divide is sent, received, transduced, and the very cells uniquely capable of healing a sick brain wake up and snap into action. The missing brain tissue fills in. *Holy shit.* The grant proposals are already writing themselves in my head."

"And the articles! There's so many more experiments to do, too." As Peter smiled, Kelsey switched into scientist mode, pouring out ideas. "We should do what the McQueen people did," she said. "Synthesize a human fusion opiate gene like what happens in Stuart and stick it into the mouse model of Huntington's and see if the beasts get better. Try the music therapy on other patients. Other diseases—"

"Whoa, hold on." Peter put up his hands. "Let's get this case report out, and see what the Huntington's community thinks. And let's get to that pizza."

Kelsey found the box and opened it. "Oh, yuck. The pizza's cold. Nothing worse than cold broccoli and cheese. I'll stick it in the oven. Can you get some beers from the fridge? We can have the wine later."

A half hour later, pizza demolished, they sat back.

"Kelsey, I almost forgot. PR's getting media calls. Local radio. Even national TV."

She couldn't help but laugh. "In response to the *World Medical Mysteries* article? Do those shows employ morons to read the tabloids?"

"No. Morons have IQs of 51 to 70. The talk shows use imbeciles, with IQs of 26 to 50. Or idiots, with even lower IQs."

Kelsey laughed as she picked at the pizza crumbs in the box. "How on earth do you remember that from psych 101?"

"Actually, I'm talking *20/20* and *Oprah*. So I don't think we should underestimate who's reading that paper. Or the blogs that're popping up. They're not all morons."

She gave it some thought. "Media coverage might not all be bad, Peter. If *20/20* and *Oprah* do a decent job, which they usually do, they'll fill in statistics on neurodegenerative diseases a lot more common than Huntington's. Alzheimer's. Parkinson's. And of course spinal cord injury. People still remember Chris Reeve. Things people can relate to."

"You have a point. I wonder if the TV shows'll mention Smithies. I'd like to meet the old girl. After all, you've spoken so highly of her. But being ignored would serve her right for eavesdropping and blabbing."

"Not to mention selling out. I could shoot myself for talking so loud to you on the phone when she was so close by. I just wasn't paying enough attention to her, even after I turned my back. But who thought she'd actually call that stupid number from the TV?"

Peter reached over and took Kelsey's hands. They were smiling at each other as the apartment phone suddenly rang. Kelsey reluctantly let go and answered it. She listened, paled, and slammed it down.

"He called me Ms. Hitler! I wish they'd leave me…us…alone."

Peter came over and took her into his arms. "You know they won't. And it's going to get worse. Why do you even have that phone, anyway? Turn it off. No one can get your cell number."

"Good idea."

"Hey, Kelsey, why don't we spend New Year's Eve together, too? I don't want to go anywhere. We can watch old *Planet of the Apes* movies or something." He paused. "Unless you have plans?"

Kelsey looked up at him. "No. No plans. *Apes* would be great, or *Star Wars*. I'll make dinner."

"Wonderful. Oh, before I forget. Do you know if Stuart's ready for Thursday's session?"

"I think so. But I'll tell him again tomorrow. I don't think he absorbed much last time because of Mrs. Rinehart."

They quickly kissed, and Peter left.

19

FRANKLIN MEDICAL CENTER, JANUARY 2

A small knot of protestors lined the street in front of Franklin Medical Center. They were earnest people, mostly older, temporarily diverted from their usual stint at Planned Parenthood. A tall, fifty-ish man with salt-and-pepper hair who seemed to be the ringleader held a sign with the standard mutilated fetus photos and STEM CELL RESEARCH KILLS BABIES in six-inch letters.

Wearing a baseball cap that hid his ponytail and trying to approach the center quickly and quietly, Peter tripped and bumped into the protestor with the sign. When he looked up briefly, he noticed something unusual about the man's face, but before he could figure out what it was, he spotted a clearer route to a side entrance and made his move. In the elevator, he kept his head down, listening to the nurses' aides chattering about the protestors. He got out at his floor and strode toward his office door, coming up short when he saw three official-looking men in suits blocking the way. Judging by their dress, he thought, they had to be sales reps or editors, not reporters.

"Gentlemen," he said, relief evident in his voice, "may I help you?" Office key in hand, he tried to push past them to open his door.

Just then, director of public information Judy Devereaux and grants administrator Tyler Jackson burst out of the stairwell door, breathless. They had also escaped from the protestors. Judy, a sleek thirty-ish blonde, was carrying her high heels because she'd been unable to run up the stairs, and now put them back on.

The tallest of the three visitors, a man with an acne-scarred, long face and greasy black hair, stepped in Peter's way. "Are you Dr. Peter Holloway, chair of cell biology?" he asked.

Peter stopped. "Yes. What is this about?"

"We're from the NIH," said another of the visitors, who looked like Robert Redford in his Butch Cassidy days. "We've learned that you are using NIH funds to conduct experiments using human stem cells. Since this is against government policy, we are temporarily closing this laboratory pending an investigation."

Peter turned to face him. "Wait a minute. Those charges are untrue. In more ways than one. The funding for the stem cell—progenitor cell, actually—research comes from the Juvenile Diabetes Research Foundation."

"Yes," said the NIH man, "but not the DAPI stain, some of the cell culture plates, and the microarrays."

"But those are generic reagents and tools, not specific to particular experiments. If we purchase them in bulk, they're cheaper. Do you have any idea how difficult it is to maintain NIH and NIH-free zones?"

"That's irrelevant," the first man said. "If you use NIH-funded materials on any human stem cell experiments, you are in violation." He took a step closer to Peter. "You are well aware of the restrictions, I'm sure."

Peter was trying to keep his anger in check. "I was not aware that the NIH used *World Medical Mysteries* as a scientific resource."

"Someone with access to your laboratory informed the NIH," said the third visitor, a gnome-like man with dark hair.

Judy, who had been listening to the encounter, now stepped forward. "Peter," she said in a professional voice, "take it easy now."

He nodded at her, then turned back to the man with the acne-scarred face. "OK. Which stem cells, as you call them, are you referring to?"

The gnome answered. "The ones in cell culture. And the ones in the man's brain."

"Let me repeat myself," Peter said. "The JDRF funds the cell culture work. Those cells came from neurospheres that have been growing in the lab for years. If I've been violating regulations, where have you been all this time? We've published on the neurospheres several times. And not in a tabloid."

"That's true," Tyler, the grants administrator, said unhelpfully.

"And Mr. Matheson's stem cells?" asked Scarface.

"They're in his brain!"

"Yes. And how did they get there?"

"He was born with them! Don't the stem cell police have to take basic biology somewhere along the line? Like in the tenth grade?"

"Peter ..." Judy's voice was quieter but strained.

"Are you manipulating his stem cells?" asked the Robert Redford look-alike.

"That's what we're trying to find out. Using an external stimulus. Music."

"You can't do it with U.S. government funds," Scarface said, "and we have to follow up on all reports. Professor, you are in violation."

"But isn't it *embryos* the anti-science camp is so concerned with? We're not working with embryos. The only thing being destroyed, if this research is restricted, is hope—for millions. Do any of you have a relative with Alzheimer's? Or ALS? That's Lou Gehrig's disease. Or a spinal cord injury? A kid with diabetes? Why would you deny research that could help them when you don't even understand what it entails? Why—"

Judy grabbed Peter's arm. "Let's go to my office. I think it's time to work on another statement. Tyler will see about getting your lab up and running. And better separating the various experiments."

Peter let himself be led away. While walking he took out his cell phone, made a call, and waited.

⋘∞⋙

Kelsey got the message and at noon headed over to the Liberty Bell, looking for Peter among the tourists. She finally spotted him. When she tapped him on the shoulder, he whirled around.

"Sorry," she said. "I didn't mean to scare you. Why are we meeting here?"

"I was afraid someone might recognize us at the coffee place."

"A little paranoid, are we?"

"Maybe," he admitted, "but after Nurse Ratshit was on the local news this morning, and they ran our photos, who knows?"

Kelsey groaned. "Oh no. I didn't know about that. No wonder the people in the lobby stared at me."

"Next time you see that damn nurse, stick a Depends down her throat."

"Yeah, a used one. But what else is going on?"

He led her away from the tourists to a park bench. "The NIH sent three goons to shut down the lab. Using the 'no national funds for stem cells' mantra."

"But you aren't even using embryonic stem cells," she replied, "presidentially-sanctioned or not. What about the diabetes foundation funding? Did you mention that?"

"Didn't seem to matter. If you so much as share a pipette between government-funded and privately-funded stem cell research, well… you know."

"So what can you do?" she asked. "We can't stop the work."

"Tyler Jackson from grants can get a partial lab up and running to keep the cultures going. But I'm screwed as far as the work on Stuart goes. At least for now."

"But why? His family's taken part in NIH-funded research for a decade."

"Yes, but that was an entirely different project, long done. And the informed consent wasn't enough. The document the goons left at Franklin said the family was misled into thinking our work is an extension of their previous participation in the NIH trial that led to discovery of the Huntington's gene." Peter sighed and put an arm around Kelsey. "It's all my fault. Stuart's response fit so perfectly with the ongoing Parkinson's and Alzheimer's work. Adding him to the protocol was a no-brainer."

"Very funny. Peter, none of this is your fault. We'll find a way to keep it going."

Back in her office, Kelsey was finding it difficult to concentrate on her report on the joys of working with zebrafish. Her mind was on Stuart, on his response to the experiments. On the maddening government intervention. As she sat staring at her computer screen, she noticed Tony's head appearing over the divider. She'd forgotten that he was still fielding her calls. What a sweetheart he was.

"Hi, Kel," he said. "Check it out." He handed her a list. "The usual wackos. A few interesting ones. And, oh yeah, some government guy called a few times."

Kelsey looked up. "What's his name? I didn't call any government researchers for my zebrafish article."

"Probably nothin'. Wanna get dinner?"

Waving him away, she returned the call. "Not now, Tony, I can't think about food." When someone answered, she said, "Yes, this is Kelsey Raye from Biotech USA. I'm returning a call to Earl Wexler." Kelsey mouthed a goodbye to Tony as she listened. "He's a congressional staffer?"

Peter and Kelsey were on their second bottle of wine. Her cats were sitting with them on the couch, staring as only devoted felines can do.

Peter hoisted his empty glass. "It's the senate subcommittee on stem cell research, Kelsey. We might have to go to one of their meetings."

"Omigod. When? And to do what?"

"Probably not for a few months. These things take forever, but I know they're planning to ask several researchers to testify."

"What exactly will we have to do? Will I need a suit and a haircut?"

Peter laughed. "Answer questions, yes, and yes. They pay the most attention to the testifying celebrities anyway. They'll listen more to Michael J. Fox or Julia Roberts than you or me. An actor trumps a Ph.D. any day."

"Yeah, like politicians and rock stars suddenly becoming experts on global warming." She emptied her glass. "Will Smithies be there?"

"I doubt it. All she did was overhear something that she blurted verbatim to that rag. Why do you care?"

"She hates me. After she outed us, I started remembering all the snide comments and nasty looks she'd been making every time I visited Stuart." She laughed and reached for the bottle of wine. "At least she can afford some decent clothes now. About $10,000 worth, I'd guess."

"Has she said anything to you since the tabloid thing?"

"As little as possible. She stares. Calls me Stuart's girlfriend."

"What does she look like?" he asked.

"Why?"

"Just curious."

"Well, she's not exactly fashion model material. Out of shape. Dumpy. Could use Botox and a dye job. Need any more clichés?"

"I get the picture."

"I don't."

Peter took Kelsey's hands. "I do. You trot in, glowing from the gym, and Stuart, who formerly could not respond at all, worships you. Ignores her. Starts to feel better. She does the scut work, you get the glory. The old cow is jealous."

Kelsey blushed. "I don't think so. But the hypothetical insecurities of a nurse aren't what's important." She put the wine bottle back on the coffee table. "OK, let's get back on track. Why do I have to go to Washington? What could I possibly tell them that isn't in the medical records?"

"You know about Stuart's condition over time, albeit a short time, in a way that the measurements and notes in the record don't. Aren't you the one who spotted the conjunctivitis? They might look at your diary, for example."

"But I'm not a doctor," she said. "And that diary is not only personal, but it's not a continuous record. I just write in it sporadically. When I get busy on articles, I let days go by."

"Still," he said, "you know Stuart best. And you're writing the *Lancet* report. Did you forget you have a Ph.D.?"

She smiled. "Sometimes I do, being away from the lab and all. The people I interview know so much more than I do that I really do forget that I have a degree in genetics." She sighed, got up, took Peter's wineglass, and walked into the kitchen. Peter freed himself from the cats and followed, and could see her gripping the sink. He turned her around and seeing her tears, pulled her close. They separated for an instant, looked into each other's eyes, and kissed. Then, tripping over cats and stacks of papers, they stumbled into the bedroom and collapsed onto the bed.

Maybe it was the wine, maybe it was the excitement of the work. More likely, it was that it had been a long time since Kelsey had been with anyone. After they had made love, Kelsey sat up and stared into Peter's blue eyes. Just fleetingly, they became brown and his face seemed to morph into Stuart's. She pulled back, not sure, for a second, who she was with, then buried her head in Peter's shoulder until the disturbing image faded. She finally fell asleep, her head on Peter's chest, his arms securely around her, both of them surrounded by furry balls of cats, as snowflakes and Christmas lights twinkled outside the window.

The next morning, the sun streaming in woke Kelsey. She groggily noted the time, then shook Peter awake.

"Damn," she said, "it's 6:30. I have an editorial meeting at eight, then phone interviews all morning."

"Well, so much for the rosy afterglow," he muttered as he slid out of bed. Kelsey leaned over and kissed him, then headed for the bathroom.

"Sorry," she said. She closed the door, then opened it again and stuck her head out. "Last night was wonderful. And unexpected."

"Was it really?"

Kelsey blushed. "Omigod, I just remembered. Can you get into your lab today?"

"I think I can get into the lab long enough to start sorting things out."

"OK," she said, "you take the first shower then. I'll get my e-mail done here. You have more hair to deal with than I do, anyway!"

20

BIOTECH USA OFFICES, JANUARY 8

"So," Kelsey propped the phone to her ear as she typed, "how do you measure a hormone in rat pee…er, urine?" She typed faster. "Is it a model for the incontinence you get when you laugh and leak?"

She sat back and listened for awhile without typing. "And the stem cells you use are human?" she asked. "What's the source?" More typing. Finally, "Thank you Dr. Cho. I'll call back if I have further questions."

Just as she hung up, Tony appeared in her cubicle with a powdered donut and a bottle of lemonade. "Yo, Kel. What's with the rat pee?" He gulped the yellow liquid.

"Stem cells again."

He polished off the donut. "Speaking of stem cells, how's your pal, Stuart? I feel like I know him."

"Stuart! I lost track of the time. Thanks, Tony! If I leave now, I can get to him before lunch."

❦

Approaching the entrance to the nursing home, Kelsey was surprised to see people milling about. She didn't have to wonder long, however, as several reporters ran up and shoved microphones in her face, screaming questions. She brushed past the reporters and the crowd behind them, hearing people calling about sick relatives, yelling at others who carried anti-stem cell research signs. A strange-looking man held up a large sign that read CITIZENS AGAINST STEM CELL RESEARCH. She was about to talk to him, then decided against it and forced her way inside. Aware that she was being watched through the windows in the foyer, she entered the stairwell code on the keypad and ducked in as soon as the lock in the door clicked, being certain to shut it behind her. She was afraid to wait at the elevator.

She sprinted up the three flights, then made her way down the hallway toward the nurses' station. She skirted the origami boats, stopped to compliment Mrs. Onderdonk on her nail color, only to be shown her matching toenails peeking out of the special nursing home shoes designed for very swollen feet. She heard Doc listing oncogenes as she went by, then saw Elvin, who looked up and smiled at her and then went back to scraping something unrecognizable off the floor, his dreads shaking back and forth as he scrubbed. A minute later she heard a familiar voice.

"Girl, you gonna frizz your hair out to Neptune if you take the stairs like that."

"Hey, Justina. I told you, I can't help what my hair does."

"Sure you can. You ain't using the right stuff on it. Get yourself some olive oil, like I told ya."

"Ick. I'm not a salad!" Kelsey laughed as she approached Stuart's room and knocked lightly before slowly opening the door. As she leaned down to give him a hug, he wrapped his arms tightly around her and smiled.

"Wow! Some greeting," she said. "Did you miss me?"

"Yesssssss."

"Another improvement. Ya to yes."

"Yessssss!" He grinned.

Kelsey backed away slowly, then turned off the TV. "Enough with Judge Judy," she said. "Eliot gave me some of that music cluster signature 29 software stuff, so I made some great new playlists. This one's all Radiohead. Maybe we'll have you dancing soon."

They both listened to the music, oblivious to the nurses' aides peeking in. After awhile Stuart's eyes started to droop. Kelsey gently took out his earbud and started to kiss him on the cheek, but suddenly, he swiveled his head so that the kiss made a more direct hit. Locked at the lips the kiss went on and on, until their eyes opened, Kelsey's shocked, Stuart's not. They finally pulled apart.

She picked up the iPod and wound the wires around her hand. "I think I'd better go now." She shoved the iPod in her purse, getting her hand more tangled, then tripped over the chair leg. She broke her fall by reaching out for the mirror, dislodging the time-worn photograph of young Stuart on the playground with his brothers and sisters.

•••

"Hold up, Kelsey," said Maria from the nurses' station.

"What? I mean, excuse me?"

"What's wrong? You seem frazzled. Is Stuart okay? I saw you go in."

"He's more than okay. He moved his head!"

"Yes," the nurse said. "It's startling, isn't it? The first time was during the food fight a few weeks ago. But I don't think he can control it."

"Oh, yes," Kelsey said, "he can control it. Sometimes, anyway. I just saw movement a lot more purposeful than his response to a flying burger in the dayroom."

Maria looked puzzled, but shrugged in agreement. "That's good. Isn't it? Every movement, especially a normal one, is an improvement, right?"

Kelsey chuckled. "This might've been a bit *too* normal. But, hey, what did you need to see me about?"

"I hate to do this, but we have to confiscate your music thingy."

"My iPod? Why? The music isn't hurting him. It's helping!"

"Oh, we agree. Most of us. But some government men came in yesterday. They said that's what we have to do. We also have to look in Stuart's room to be sure you don't try to use another one. We had to sign some papers. Wanna see them?"

"No. But this is totally idiotic!" Kelsey took the iPod out of her bag and handed it to the nurse. "Keep it here. And I want it back. Don't give it to those assholes from the government until I contact my lawyer."

Just then, Nurse Smithies emerged from the back office. "An attorney? Ever hear of freedom of speech, Ms. Reporter?"

"What? I wasn't talking about you."

"I can talk to any magazine or TV show I want," Smithies said. "Maybe it'll get you to stop messing with that poor man's brain."

"I'm doing no such thing. And even if I was, so what? Stem cells may be able to help millions. As a nurse you should care about that."

"What I care about is not making a patient a guinea pig, and not swiping cells from embryos, then dumping them down the drain. That's what the *Citizens Against Stem Cell Research* stands for."

Kelsey looked confused for a moment. "Excuse me, but—"

Suddenly shrieks came from the dayroom. Kelsey and the two nurses ran in. Two of the residents who required neither walker nor wheelchair had hopped up onto a table. Most of the others were pointing to a corner, where a tiny white mouse with red eyes cowered.

"Damn that Elvin," said Smithies. "Get the rat poison!"

Kelsey bent down. "But it's just a tiny mousie! What's the fuss?" She picked the frightened creature up by the base of the tail, dropped it into her other hand, then gently closed her fingers to cradle it. When the animal had calmed somewhat, she began to gently stroke its back with a finger. Some of the braver residents drew closer and stared. "See? He's more scared than you are!" She held the animal out in her palm.

A few more of the residents tapped forward in their walkers, curious to see the mouse, but Smithies paid no attention. "I told him weeks ago to order more poison. We hadn't had a rat—"

"—mouse—"

"—whatever ... in so long that he probably didn't bother. Lazy ass."

Kelsey gently tucked the mouse into her purse. "I have a new pet now. Thanks!" And she walked over to the opening elevator and got in.

21

PETER'S APARTMENT, JANUARY 9

Peter and Kelsey were curled up on the futon, watching CNN and sipping drinks. A small tank on the coffee table housed the mouse.

"So you think the great and powerful Nurse Smithies was actually afraid of our new friend, Darwin?" Peter asked.

"Yeah. It's odd, though. Field mice get inside sometimes, but they're brownish. This little guy's albino. The kind used in labs, like the ones you get neurospheres from. Where do you think he came from?"

"Who knows," Peter said. "Maybe someone planted him. But I'll keep him. Your felines would have him for dessert."

"I'm sure Darwin will be very happy here. Two bachelors."

Peter put their glasses next to Darwin and moved in closer to Kelsey. He kissed her, but after a few seconds, she froze and abruptly pushed him away.

"Peter," she stammered, "I'm sorry. I have to go."

"What's wrong? What did I do?"

"It isn't you," she said. "It's me."

"Well, that's a line I've heard before…"

"No, really. I've just got something on my mind, that's all."

"So suddenly? What is it? Can I help?"

"No, not now. I have to go home."

"Kelsey, wait."

But she had already picked up her jacket and purse and was heading toward the door.

〰

The next day, Kelsey was typing furiously in her cubicle when Marsha walked in.

"Hi, Kelsey," she said. "Nice office. A little cramped, though. Ready for lunch?"

Tony appeared as if by magic right outside the cubicle. "Yo, Kel. Gonna introduce us?"

The two women grinned. "Marsha, this is Tony; Tony, this is Marsha, my friend from hospice."

Tony held out his hand. "Hi. Glad to meetcha. Sorry I can't make it to lunch. Thanks, Kelsey, for asking, but I've got an interview in a few minutes. Ciao!"

"He's cute," Marsha whispered to Kelsey.

"I suppose he has his endearing qualities," she replied. "He's actually a terrific writer, but don't tell him I said that. Let's go." She steered Marsha through the warren of cubicles.

〰

The two women were sitting at a table near a window at Cosi, sharing a cheese and fruit plate.

"So, what's up?" Marsha asked, spearing a chunk of pineapple. "You sounded upset. Is it Peter? Or Stuart?"

"Actually both."

"OK. Explain."

"I think Stuart and I are getting too attached. Emotionally, I mean."

"I could have told you that weeks ago."

Kelsey looked up. "What do you mean?"

"Remember that day we met at the nursing home? After Catholic services?"

"Yeah."

"Well, I was going to come up to Stuart's room to meet you. Remember?"

"Yes. I wondered what had happened to you."

"I did come up. But when I saw you two looking at each other, using that music thing, well, I felt as if I was invading a private moment. So I just left."

Kelsey looked thoughtful. "Oh, yeah. I remember. We were listening to 'In Your Eyes.'"

"Well, whatever. Kelsey, remember class? We were cautioned about getting too close. And you and ... hey, did something happen?"

Kelsey hesitated before she answered. "Sort of. Two days ago, as I bent to kiss Stuart on the cheek, he suddenly moved his head."

"What? You mean ..."

Kelsey nodded. "Yes. It wasn't quite platonic. And it went on for awhile."

"Kelsey, that's more than a sort of."

"It gets worse."

"No!" Marsha dropped the pineapple.

"No, not that! My God ... I didn't *flunk* death class, you know."

"Then what happened?"

"As I was leaving, the dayroom erupted because of a mouse on the loose. With the distraction, I never processed what had happened with Stuart."

"And when you did?"

"It was when I was with Peter. We were ... well, you know. Suddenly I just jumped up and ran out. I don't know how he will forgive me."

"I didn't know you and Peter .. wait a minute. Which one don't you think will forgive you?"

"Peter, of course."

"Can't you just tell him? I'm sure Peter realizes Stuart has normal feelings. And you didn't start it."

"But I didn't exactly finish it, either."

"But you did, after a bit. Just tell him. And soon."

Kelsey sat back and pushed the food away. "Well, maybe you're right." She sighed. "I do feel like I can talk to Peter about anything."

Marsha took Kelsey's hands. "They didn't prepare us for everything in hospice training, after all, did they? But I'm here to talk to, any time. And you can tell *me* anything."

"Thanks, Marsha." They stood up and hugged.

"Where are you off to now?" Marsha asked. "Got an interview?"

"Nah. Back to the office to crank out that piece on direct-to-consumer nutrigenetics testing. I was going to visit Stuart, but I'm still feeling weird from that kiss. I'll wait a day. Let him calm down."

"You mean let *you* calm down!"

Kelsey laughed. "Right. But I can miss a day, he's doing okay. Physically, I mean." She blushed.

"Well, good luck. Let's get together again soon."

The next morning, looking at a *Rolling Stone* as she exited the nursing home elevator, Kelsey tripped over a man in a janitor's uniform on his knees cleaning a spill that was coming from the supply closet. She noticed the skull and crossbones on the container of overturned rat poison, then made eye contact with the janitor. It wasn't Elvin, but he looked oddly familiar. And he seemed nervous.

"Oh," she said. "I see Smithies finally got her rat poison. Where's Elvin?"

"He got moved to Building A. Cleans up after bingo and church and whatever else they have down there."

"Oh. Well, hi, I'm Kelsey. I'm here a lot. I visit."

The janitor wiped his hands on his pants as he stood up. "Name's Damon. I'd offer my hand but it's been in some nasty places today."

"That's okay. Welcome. We'll miss your predecessor. But you look familiar. Have I seen you around here before?"

"Don't think so."

"Well, nice to meet you." In a hurry, she sprinted past the empty nurses' station and looked into the dayroom. Same as usual. The demented black lady cradled her black doll, the demented white lady, her white doll. A snoring man had his head down on his plate, and Doc was reciting the steps of a signal transduction pathway. Two students were helping three women decorate their walkers. Not seeing Stuart in his usual spot, Kelsey wove her way past the parade of walkers towards his room.

Reginald was sound asleep, a trail of iridescent green snot slowing meandering down his pillow, surging slightly and bubbling every time he exhaled. Repulsed, Kelsey turned away, catching sight of herself in the mirror. Something wasn't quite right, she thought, something was missing. Then she glimpsed Stuart in the reflection, propped up in bed. She turned and went over to him.

A white foamy substance ringed Stuart's mouth. Clues to its composition lay in the pushed-aside tray table that held the remains of lunch, including a telltale can of Ensure. The TV blared an inane talk show, not Stuart's usual fare, and he was staring dully at the screen.

"Hi, Stuart!" She bent to kiss him on the cheek, then went to get a wet paper towel and came back. "Here, let me clean you up. Someone oughta mop up old Reggie's snot faucet, too. Hey, what's that smell?" Kelsey sniffed near Stuart's head. "Nuts of some kind? Must be the Ensure." She picked up the can and read the ingredients. "Vanilla almond. I hope that's not all you had to eat."

Stuart pointed to the TV and grunted. Kelsey watched for a minute.

"Oh, gross. How many facelifts can one actress have? Let me see what else's on. Anything's better than this." Kelsey picked up the remote and flipped through the channels, thinking fleetingly that such a routine movement was completely beyond the capability of someone with Huntington's disease. She thought often about the things that Stuart could no longer do, things everyone takes for granted.

"Maybe we can find a *Star Trek* or *Law and Order* rerun," she said. "Isn't *Law and Order* on 24/7?"

"Mew ... sik."

"Music? Oh, Stuart. I can't play you any more music."

"Waa ...

"Remember I told you how Dr. Holloway's in trouble for taking you to his lab?"

Stuart nodded and raised his eyebrows.

"Well, the guys who closed his lab also took my iPod. Just to be sure it isn't hurting you, I think. So instead I brought a *Rolling Stone*. I can read it to you. You'll like it. It's about music. See the great cover?"

Stuart nodded, and Kelsey began to flip through the magazine.

"OK. This is from last month, when they ran the usual remembrance of John Lennon's death. We were just little kids when he was shot. Here goes:

> *The story is as familiar this time of year as that of Santa. Earlier that day, John and Yoko had posed for photographer Annie Leibovitz. It was a little after 10 o'clock, and they had just left the studio. John and Yoko were rushing home to 5-year-old Sean, the inspiration for the new music...*

Kelsey read on for about fifteen minutes, finishing the story, then put the magazine down.

"Stuart, you're so quiet. Am I boring you?" She looked down at him. He rarely fell into such a deep sleep when she was there, except for the day they went to church services. But this wasn't sleep.

Something was very wrong. Stuart was staring blankly at her, his face flushed a deep red. He didn't blink. Of course, he was normally quite still, but Kelsey knew instantly and instinctively that this was different.

Slowly, her gaze turned from his eyes to his neck, to the snake tattoo over his carotid. To her horror, although gleaming with a thin film of sweat, the serpent was perfectly still.

22

One hand on the pulseless serpent, Kelsey frantically pushed the panic button at the side of Stuart's bed, then bolted from the room, colliding with staff in Santa hats running towards her in well-practiced response to the signal. As she was pushed aside, she glimpsed Damon running down the hall and slipping into the elevator. Her attention quickly returned to the activity around Stuart's bed, and she stood just outside his door, unseen. Despite the race to his room, everyone was surprisingly calm once they got there. Had they been in a hospital, Kelsey knew, there'd be monitors beeping and crash carts careening and people pummeling and shocking Stuart's chest. But hospice care meant do-not-resuscitate, and so instead of the final violence that is never as neat as depicted on TV medical dramas, his vital signs were checked and, one by one, the nurses stepped back in astonished silence.

Maria was the first to find her voice. "But he wasn't even actively dying."

One of the nurse's aides spoke up. "He was improving, wasn't he?" she asked. "Did he push the panic button? How could he have reached it?"

"What happened?" Samantha asked, a tear sliding down her cheek.

"Well," said Nurse Smithies, "given all the publicity, I'm sure there'll be an autopsy. Samantha, call hospice. Get the team here."

"Shouldn't I call Kelsey? Or find her? Isn't she here?" Samantha started to look around and inadvertently swung her braid into Smithies.

"We can't call her," said Smithies, wiping the area on her face where the braid had touched. "Hospice's supposed to do that."

Kelsey stepped into the room. The nurses and aides moved to let her through, except for Smithies, who stood in front of Stuart's bed and tried to block her. Samantha took the head nurse firmly by the arm and pulled her away. Kelsey knelt beside Stuart and gently brushed a strand of hair from his forehead. Then she threw herself atop him and cradled his lifeless body, trying helplessly to cover as much of him as she could. As the staff slowly and somberly left the room, she began shaking uncontrollably.

❦

About a half hour later, Samantha came back into Stuart's room. She briefly checked the slumbering Reginald, then put an arm around Kelsey and told her that Sheila and Jim were on their way. Kelsey looked up, her face red and wet.

"Kelsey," the nurse said gently, "maybe I should call someone to come and get you. I don't think you should be alone. Do you have a friend from hospice? A relative I can call?"

She wiped her eyes with the heels of her hands, smearing her mascara. "Oh, thanks, Samantha. No, I'll be okay. It's not like I didn't know he would die. It was just so sudden. And I guess I never imagined the actual moment. I thought I'd have some sort of a warning. But you knew him longer than I did. How are you holding up?"

"I'm okay. But you're right. He didn't show any signs of this happening anytime soon."

"You know," Kelsey said, "he wasn't quite right during my visit. Subdued. But I thought he was just tired."

"Well, the disease does seem to have affected him differently than his siblings. Are you sure you'll be okay?"

"I think so. Thanks. I'll just walk over to the train. The cold air will help. I must look awful."

"No you don't," Samantha lied. "Look, here's my number." She wrote it on a paper napkin. "Call if you want to talk."

"OK, thanks."

Not even feeling the biting cold, Kelsey didn't go straight to the train station. Instead, she walked the grounds of the nursing home in a stupor, circling the building at least three times, snowflakes mixing with her tears. She made one brief phone call, to Peter, before walking slowly to the train.

※

DAVIS FUNERAL HOME, JANUARY 14

About thirty people filled the pews in the chapel. Sheila and Jim, their spouses and children, and various cousins occupied the first rows. During Sheila's eulogy, which shared memories from their childhood, Kelsey looked around. It seemed to her that at least two of the extended Matheson clan showed early signs of Huntington's, maybe a few more if you counted the fidgeting cousins. She'd read studies that tracked people in HD families who were healthy and hadn't had the gene test, and those individuals who developed minor uncontrolled fidgeting were much more likely to go on to develop the disease.

Tony had his arm around Kelsey, and Emily, Marsha, and Lydia from hospice sat next to him. Samantha, Maria, and some of the other nursing home staff sat behind them, scooting over as Myra Smithies arrived. Kelsey was surprised at how devastated she looked. A few other hospice volunteers were also there.

Up front, Chaplain Timothy was finishing up his few words about Stuart. As he returned to the pew, Jim stood and helped Sheila walk up to the casket, signaling the end of the ceremony. Everyone rose, Kelsey holding onto Tony as she slid from the pew and walked up the aisle. To her surprise, Connie reached out and patted her arm. Kelsey searched the back of the church and finally spotted Peter in the back row. She hadn't recognized him earlier because he was wearing a suit. She made her way to him and he wrapped her in his arms.

"That was a nice service," he murmured. "How're you holding up?"

"Oh, I'm okay. I'm glad you could come."

"Sorry I didn't get here sooner. Traffic."

"I'm just glad you're here now. And thanks for staying with me the past few nights."

"Anytime." Peter looked around. "A lot of people showed up. Too bad his friends from Ames couldn't come."

"I think the nursing home holds memorial services once a month, so Stuart's friends will get to say goodbye then." Kelsey pulled back and smiled. "Hey, let's go somewhere. I need a change of scene. And mood."

"Sounds good. Where?"

"Anywhere. Let's grab Marsha and Tony and get some hot chocolate."

"Chocolate is the answer to everything, isn't it?"

Kelsey smiled. "I'll go round them up."

⋘∞⋙

HOSPICE OFFICE, JANUARY 18

Kelsey sat at the long table at the final team meeting for Stuart with Chaplain Timothy, Dr. Pram, Kate the social worker, and Ellen the nurse. She'd missed past meetings due to deadlines, choosing to spend whatever time she could spare at the nursing home.

Losing a younger patient had a different effect on the hospice team than the more typical, older patients, many of whom had faced pain that even the drugs couldn't dampen. They usually died from cancer, emphysema, stroke, or heart disease, and for them death was, in a way, a relief. Not so for Stuart, however. Still, it was the habit of hospice people who deal with death daily to have a different attitude than most people. A patient's passing was often met with upbeat remembrances, rather than gloom. That's what was happening now.

Emily had just handed Kelsey's iPod back to her, and Kelsey was telling the others about the Christmas service she'd attended with Stuart. Even the chaplain was laughing at her description of its banal religiosity. Just then, Jim and Sheila came to the doorway. They stopped cold. The members of the team gradually saw them, and the room grew silent. Emily got up and walked over to them, taking their hands and leading them to chairs at the head of the table.

"Jim, Sheila, we're all so sorry," Emily said as Stuart's siblings took off their coats and hats.

"That didn't sound like sadness."

"I'm sorry, Sheila," Lydia said. "We like to remember some of our times with our patients and, well, sometimes funny things do happen."

"I was telling them about the time Stuart and I went to the Catholic Christmas service," Kelsey said, "and how much fun we had."

"Church? Stuart?" asked Jim. "We aren't religious people."

"I wondered the same thing," she replied. "But he was there when I arrived. I think a well-meaning aide must've brought him down. They hold services where they play bingo and have holiday parties."

"Well, we're glad you rescued him," said Sheila. "I guess."

An awkward silence settled around the room. Then Jim blurted, "Well, what the hell happened? Isn't that what we're here to discuss?"

"Yes, what about the 'active dying' you said would take a few days, that we'd get to say goodbye. We didn't." Sheila paused to wipe her eyes. "But *she* did." She pointed at Kelsey.

"Huntington's doesn't end like this." Jim laid one hand on his sister's arm. "We know that. We saw it with our brother and sister. Something else went wrong."

"Why don't you ask Kelsey?" Sheila was still angry. "After all, she was there."

Dr. Pram cleared his throat. "You're correct, Jim. Stuart's passing was a surprise. His death wasn't what usually happens with Huntington's. What's especially puzzling is that he seemed to have been improving. And that's unprecedented."

"Well, what good did it do? Just got our hopes up."

Jim reached for Sheila's hand.

"Once the autopsy results are in, we'll know more," the doctor replied. "The official cause of death was Huntington's. But the immediate cause was that he stopped breathing. And we don't know why."

"Wouldn't Kelsey have noticed if he was having trouble breathing?" Jim continued in a lower voice. "Seemed like she was awfully close to him."

The doctor cleared his throat again. "I hope you aren't implying that Kelsey had anything to do with…"

"No, I didn't notice anything," Kelsey said quietly. "But I may know what happened."

Everyone turned to look at her.

"It may have been a brain tumor."

Eight pairs of eyebrows shot up.

23

FRANKLIN MEDICAL COLLEGE, JANUARY 20

Sitting in front of an enormous computer screen, Peter was staring at images of Stuart's brain from the four previous dates, and, now, on autopsy. He was so lost in thought that he didn't hear Kelsey knock lightly, walk in, and touch his shoulder. He jumped.

"Oh, sorry," she said. "I didn't mean to startle you."

He swiveled around. "No, I'm sorry. I was spaced out. I didn't expect you."

"Well, I was downtown anyway so I thought I'd stop by, see what you're working on."

"How did things go at hospice the other day? You didn't mention it on the phone."

"Actually, not so hot."

"What do you mean?"

"Well, I sensed a bit of hostility."

"From who? Not the hospice folks?"

"No. They're all great. It's Sheila and Jim, Stuart's sister and brother. They practically blamed me for letting him slip away on my watch. Not that they were there often enough to even have had a watch."

He stood up and kissed her on the cheek. "Kelsey, maybe they just feel guilty. Remember how you felt after your dad died?"

"You mean about my not being there? Yeah. But I didn't blame Jen!

I blamed myself."

"Give them some time. Maybe they'll come around and realize how much you did for their brother."

"I hope so."

"Not to totally change the subject," he said, "but can you handle seeing preliminary autopsy results?"

"Maybe in a day or so. That's why I stopped by, I thought I'd be up to seeing them. But the sadness seems to just strike me at unpredictable times. And I think I'm afraid to know what made him stop breathing."

"Me, too. It can wait. Where are you off to now?"

"I don't know. Just for a walk."

Peter looked out the window. "Well, don't freeze. The snow's picking up. And make sure you get home before dark."

"Yes, sir."

※

She walked down deserted streets littered with the corpses of Christmas trees and entered the Penn campus. She strolled past the Wharton school to her favorite spot, the Benjamin Franklin bench, the bronze statue a gift from a long-ago class. Sitting down, she took out her iPod and stared at the screen, her eyes welling up.

Just wanting to see the names of the songs that had connected them, she called up Stuart's favorite playlists. She clicked on the U2 lists, then the ones that also had Coldplay and the Killers. But nothing appeared on the display. She checked out the "artists who died at 26" and the "marooned in space" lists, but they, too, were gone. Even Eliot's carefully compiled recent lists had vanished.

Growing frantic, tears dripping down onto the iPod and freezing on its surface, Kelsey fumbled clumsily with the controls, scrolling and scrolling to try to access Stuart's songs from the library. They, too, were missing. She turned it completely off and then back on, toggled everything toggable, then held down pairs of keys. Still nothing.

In despair, she finally hurled the iPod into a snowdrift and buried her head in her hands. After a few minutes, shivering, she got up, retrieved the iPod, and started to walk toward the dorms. Then she ran. For blocks. Winded and shaking, she finally stopped, looked up, and realized she was in front of an open church.

She went in.

※

She made it through the night with the help of a Xanax, and after her latte the next morning was back in Peter's office, looking over his shoulder at the screen.

"OK," she'd told him, "I'm ready now. What've you got?"

"Good news, I think."

"That would be nice. Did the scans show anything?"

"Well, yes and no."

"What do you mean?"

Peter pointed from one brain image to another. "It looks like the area that was depleted in Huntington's was clearly being repopulated. New cells were growing."

"So he really was getting better?"

"I think so. It's too bad that the experiment was cut off."

Kelsey stiffened and drew back. "Peter, Stuart wasn't an experiment."

"Sorry. Sometimes the scientist part of my brain blocks out the sensitivity center."

"I think your Y chromosome does that. Anyway, do you think the stem cell serenade could have killed him?"

"I was afraid so, at first."

"Me too."

"But take a look at the autopsy scan." Peter clicked a few keys, pointed the mouse at a tiny area down near the brainstem, and enlarged it. "Look at the medulla oblongata."

"The breathing center? What am I seeing?"

"It's enlarged."

"Do you think—"

"Well, I did think," he said. "I thought the stem cells seeded a tumor there, and when it got big enough, he just stopped breathing."

"Like those embryonic stem cells implanted into Parkinson's rats," she said, recalling some earlier research. "They gave rise to neural progenitors, but then those turned cancerous."

"Right. But before jumping to that conclusion, I tried to think of what else could have been going on."

"And?"

"So I checked the earlier scans, enlarged the same area."

"Please tell me the growth was there, too."

"It was! So it may have been a tangle of vessels he was born with. Maybe the blood vessels were stimulated to grow if the stem cells spewed vascular endothelial growth factor. And then bled. It's possible."

"That makes sense," she said. "A VEGF bath might do that. But how can you tell for sure if that's what happened?"

"I don't know that we can from the scan, the resolution isn't so hot. But I'll stain some sections to see if there's a tumor, and if so, what type."

Kelsey blanched. "Sections? Of his brain? Oh, Peter, this is...was... a *man*. My friend. His brain isn't a goddamn salami!" She started to tear up, and Peter turned and reached for her hand.

"Kelsey, I'm really sorry about all this. But don't you want to know how many glutamine repeats were in his Huntington's protein? To see if it's consistent with the gene test he had back in '94, that foretold the disease? We can directly measure that now. In brain tissue. It's possible that the activated progenitor cells underwent a somatic mutation that trimmed the number of repeats down into the normal range, what you geneticists call a reversion, and maybe that's how he was improving. We have to find that out. Don't you see? What we learn will help others."

"You're right." She shook her head to clear the emotion away. "I know. I guess when I'm less upset I can think about those details. And I'm sure Stuart would have wanted you to learn as much as you can from him. But I just can't—"

Suddenly the desk phone rang so shrilly that they both jumped, accustomed as they were to mellower cell phone ringtones. Peter picked up.

"Yes, this is Dr. Holloway." He listened intently. "The medical examiner? Are you an M.D. or a forensic scientist? Both? Oh, yes. I remember your talk last spring, about staging larvae in pig carcasses. Can I help you?"

A few minutes passed. Kelsey watched Peter's face change as he listened. "OK. We'll be right down." He paused. "Oh, that's Kelsey. Kelsey Raye. She was with the patient when he died. Thanks!" Peter hung up, grabbed Kelsey, and led her out.

"Whoa, what's happening? Forensic scientist? Is CSI on location here?"

"That was Patrice Donovan, M.E. They have results of a tox screen."

"On Stuart? But why? He took the same meds every day."

"No idea. Maybe it's routine. Or someone who knew something about Huntington's had the presence of mind to recognize that something was amiss and ordered it."

One advantage of having a basic research lab in a medical center was the easy access to corpses, and their tissues, from the morgue. Patrice Donovan's office was just two buildings over, in the basement. Entering the morgue that led to her office, Peter pulled Kelsey along between two lines of metal tables that each held a draped body, trying not to look at the drawers that lined the walls. Soon they reached the door at the rear. Just as Peter was about to knock, a regally beautiful woman with startling black eyes and a halo of gray-tinged frizz opened the door and held out her hand. Her white coat was in stark contrast to her ebony skin.

"Hi, I'm Patrice. Nice to meet you officially. I've seen you about. In the cafeteria, I think."

"Yes," Peter replied, shaking her hand. "I know you, too. The salad bar. Beets and celery, right?"

The M.E. smiled. "Right, Dr. olives and feta."

"Thanks for calling, I think. What did the tox screen show? Oh, forgive me, this is Kelsey Raye. She writes for Biotech USA and is a geneticist by training. She was the patient's hospice volunteer and was with him when he died."

"Hi," Patrice and Kelsey said together as they shook hands. They went into Patrice's office.

"Can we close the door?" Kelsey asked. "This place is giving me the creeps."

"Sure." Patrice gently shut the door as Kelsey and Peter sat close together on the small couch.

"Can I ask something?" Kelsey said.

"Certainly."

"Why did you do a tox screen? The chart would've indicated his meds."

"Yes, but any time the circumstances of a death are mysterious, or unexpected—"

"—or involve a tabloid story and Big Brother government nutcases," Peter interjected.

"Well, that too," said Patrice, smiling. "Anyway, it was routine. We didn't expect to pick up anything."

"But?"

The medical examiner looked from Peter to Kelsey. "You won't believe this," she said, "but we found cyanide."

Peter reached for Kelsey's hand as she gasped.

"And a dose that would kill a man of a healthy weight," Patrice added, "let alone this guy's skinny behind. Someone meant business. Given the dose and the patient's emaciation, he would have stopped breathing within about twenty minutes of being poisoned. Maybe even sooner."

Kelsey seemed to close in on herself, as Peter leaned forward. She put a hand on his back. "Peter, none of this is making any sense."

"Kelsey," said Patrice, "what might Stuart have been doing twenty minutes before he stopped breathing?"

"Doing? Stuart couldn't *do* anything."

"But people did things for him. *To* him. What do you think happened before you got there? Can you figure out what might have happened? I know you weren't trying to do that then, but think about it now. The details. What was in the room? Was he on oxygen? Had he had Ativan or Roxinol recently? Was there evidence that he'd been choking? Who'd been there? Where was his roommate, and if he was there, might he have seen anything?"

"That's too many questions." Kelsey could hardly breathe, much less think.

"Sorry. I'm just trying to jog your memory."

Kelsey blinked and collected her thoughts. "Well, Reginald was there in body, but he wasn't awake or aware. Just dripping snot everywhere," she began. "Stuart had just had lunch. He usually eats in the dayroom, but that day he had it in his room." She paused. "That was odd."

"Can you remember what he ate?"

"Hmmm. A sandwich, I think. He could sometimes gum the mushy ones. And pudding. Ensure. That was weird, too. He usually has chocolate Ensure. This time it was vanilla. With nuts of some kind."

Patrice suddenly sat bolt upright. "Nuts of some kind? What do you mean?"

"I looked at the can. I could smell it. It was vanilla almond, I think. And it was smeared all over Stuart's face. I remember getting a paper towel to wash it off."

"What did it smell like?"

"Like I said. Nuts. Almonds."

Kelsey remained slumped for a long moment, then gasped and jumped up. "Omigod! *Almonds*. Cyanide smells like almonds." She suddenly burst into tears.

"Well," Peter blurted out, "at least it wasn't the stem cells."

Kelsey turned on him. "Who cares? This means that somebody *killed* Stuart. Shit! I'd almost rather it be the stem cells."

She pushed herself off the couch and headed towards the door but tripped on a stack of journals. When Peter jumped forward to catch her, she pushed him away and ran out, banging her hip against one of the autopsy tables and sending it crashing into the others, like a macabre game of bumper cars. Peter snaked through the moving tables after her, with Patrice close behind.

PHILADELPHIA POLICE HEADQUARTERS, JANUARY 22

Kelsey and Peter sat close together, with M.E. Donovan next to Peter, listening to Captain Bigelow, a large man sitting behind a large desk. He'd explained the evidence and the procedures that would follow, and was now leading Kelsey through the events of January 11. Also in attendance were two detectives, two uniformed police officers, and an assistant district attorney. Peter and Kelsey were definitely on unfamiliar turf.

"So where would someone get cyanide, Captain?" Kelsey asked, nervously twirling a strand of her hair.

"I can answer that," said Patrice. "It has a lot of uses. Photography, the old-fashioned kind, and to remove artificial nails. Cyanide's also used in metal cleaning, ore refining, and in rodenticides."

"What?" Kelsey practically leapt out of her chair.

"Rodenticides. Rat poison."

"Yikes! Darwin."

Wendy Coleridge, a detective with short dark hair and a wiry but strong build, looked up from her notes. "What's any of this got to do with evolution?"

"Darwin's a mouse," Kelsey said. "He was in the dayroom. At the nursing home. On Stuart's floor. Smithies told Elvin to order some rat poison. I heard her."

"Slow down, Kelsey," said ADA Mitch Esposito, a very attractive forty-ish man with a handlebar mustache. "Who's Smithies? Elvin? When did this happen? And did you actually see any rat poison?"

"Hold on. Let me think. My head feel's like it's going to explode."

"Wait a minute," said the captain. "I want to record this. And I think we'd better start tracking dates on the blackboard, archaic as that may be. And names." Bigelow turned to the young, very blonde police officer. "Can you do that, Officer Post?" When she nodded, he turned to Kelsey again. "OK. Kelsey, please continue."

"This all happened during my next to last visit," she said. "Let me check my datebook." She pulled the tattered notebook out of her purse. "It was the eighth."

"Did anything unusual happen that day?"

Kelsey thought a moment. "Yes. Actually, a few things were different. The janitors changed. There was a new guy. His name was Damon. He replaced Elvin. But, wait, no, that wasn't until three days later, the eleventh, the day Stuart died. Damn. Now I'm all confused."

"So are we," said Detective Coleridge. "Damon, Darwin. Why don't you just slow down a little, Kelsey, take your time remembering. It sounds like you're onto something. Take us through the last two visits you had with Stuart. Moment by moment, if you can."

"OK, I'll try. On the next to last visit, there were protestors in front of the nursing home. I got around them. That was January eighth."

"Protestors against what?" asked Jie Zhang, the other detective. "A nursing home doesn't exactly sound like a place for demonstrations."

"I thought so too," Kelsey said. "It was anti-science. They had big signs: *Citizens Against Stem Cell Research.* I've written about that group, in the magazine and for a newspaper column. They're a so-called "vocal minority" against using human embryos in research or treatments. Most people are, in fact, for it." Captain Bigelow began taking notes, as did Officer Post on the blackboard. Meanwhile, Kelsey became visibly relaxed as the conversation took a more familiar turn, towards the scientific issue, but the questioning quickly returned to the details of the crime.

"Can you remember what any of the protestors looked like?" prompted Detective Zhang.

"Well, there were a few college kids. Some older women. And a very tall man, with salt and pepper hair. It was hard to tell his age. He could've been a lot younger than his hair color suggested, maybe in his late thirties. He had weird eyes, too." She frowned, trying to see them in her mind. "A strange color, I think."

Captain Bigelow looked up from his notes.

"Kelsey," said Detective Coleridge, "do you remember anything unusual happening *inside* the nursing home that day?"

"No. Elvin—the janitor—was mopping up barf on the floor. That's not unusual. Someone peed in the hallway while he was being wheeled from the shower room. Aides were doing what aides do."

"Sounds like the squad room." Bigelow chuckled.

"Who else was around?" continued Detective Coleridge. "You mentioned a Smithies? Who's that?"

"She's the evil nurse. Ever seen *One Flew Over the Cuckoo's Nest*? She's Nurse Ratshit."

"No, but was there anything unusual about Stuart that day? Anything at all?"

Kelsey blushed. "Well, sort of, Detective. Stuart was better."

"What do you mean?"

Kelsey turned even redder and spoke more quietly, focusing in on the pretty brunette detective to help her stay calm. "He was much better."

"How so?" Detective Coleridge leaned towards Kelsey as the others backed off a bit.

Kelsey glanced over at Peter uneasily. "I got a big hug. Then he said *yes*. Not *ya*, like he usually does. Did. And then he kissed me."

Peter straightened.

"I mean, it wasn't like it usually is." Everyone looked up.

"And how is it usually?" asked Peter, carefully enunciating each word.

Kelsey twirled her hair and then spoke with a rush, as if to get it over with. "I bent down to kiss him on the cheek, but he moved his head. So it was different. And it sort of went on awhile."

"And what did you do?" Peter continued, as Kelsey locked eyes with Wendy Coleridge, wishing she could be anywhere else.

"Like I said, I froze. It went on. Awhile. Then I left. I was upset."

"Because of the kiss?" asked Peter.

Kelsey ignored that question and plowed on. "Then I got distracted at the nurses' station."

"By what?" ADA Esposito asked. The two police officers seemed to be trying to suppress smiles.

"I couldn't think straight after the kiss. Then my iPod got taken away, then Smithies hassled me, then they trapped Darwin in a corner."

Bigelow stopped writing and looked up. "Kelsey, you've lost me again. Could you repeat all that and try to fill in the blanks? First off, what's an iPod got to do with any of this?"

"Oh, sorry. That's a long story. I'd been playing music for Stuart on my iPod, and he seemed to be getting better, and—"

Officer Post turned away from the blackboard. "I know about that, I heard it on the news. Or read it somewhere. You two are the reporter and the researcher using rock music to turn on stem cells in the guy's brain, right?"

"Right." Peter and Kelsey finally looked at each other.

"Can we please beam down to planet Earth for a moment," said Captain Bigelow. "Fill an old cop in? Kelsey, pretend you're on the witness stand and you've just been asked to recount the events following the kiss, as they happened, to the best of your memory. Take a deep breath."

She did. And a second deep breath. "Sorry. Government guys shut down Peter's lab because he was supposedly working with stem cells not in an NIH-free zone."

"English, please."

"He was in trouble because the government isn't supposed to fund human embryonic stem cell research, and even though the Juvenile Diabetes Research Foundation funds Peter's stem cell work, he does NIH-funded work, too."

The captain's eyes started to glaze over. "OK, maybe we can skip this part, after all. I take it, considering Officer Post's contribution concerning your recent notoriety, that the government confiscated your iPod for fear it was doing something to Stuart's stem cells? Yeah, I heard that story, too."

"Right. Anyway, after Maria took my iPod, Nurse Smithies started yelling at me because she'd overheard something, I forget what, and misunderstood. She's always looking for an excuse to rag on me."

"What does the rat have to do with it?" asked the other uniformed officer, Clayton Reynolds.

"Mouse. Darwin's a mouse. He ran out from somewhere and some of the residents screamed. That distracted Smithies. I remember thinking it was weird that the mouse was white, like a lab animal, rather than the cute little brown field mice that you usually see. I rescued him.

Peter kept him as a pet." She looked over at Peter, who was staring at his feet.

The captain stopped writing and looked up. "OK. I think we finally understand who all the main characters were on the next to last visit, including the infamous rodent. Thank you, Kelsey. Let's take an hour's break before we go over what happened to the unfortunate Mr. Matheson on his last day."

At the signal to break, everyone pulled out their cell phones and blackberries and checked messages, but the captain motioned for attention and stood up. "Hold on. I've got some assignments. Kelsey, call your office and have someone e-mail your online diary to Detective Coleridge. Coleridge, print out copies of it upstairs." Kelsey started to say something about privacy, but the captain was barking out more orders.

"Dr. Holloway, later on, send some of your new pet's blood or droppings or whatever to a lab that does mouse genealogy from DNA profiles, if there is such a thing. Maybe we can trace him to a specific breeding facility, then trace where he was sent and who ordered him. Zhang, call the nursing home and see if you can get that janitor, Elvin, over here. Pronto. The new janitor, too. Post and Reynolds, after we finish going over the last day, head out to the nursing home and find the Ensure can. Go through the trash. Maybe it's got prints."

Detective Coleridge led Kelsey out the door. "Let's go to Starbucks first," she said. "I think you need to recover a little. I can tell how tough this is on you."

"Thank you," Kelsey whispered, "but I have to talk to Peter." But he just brushed past her, so she turned back to the detective. "Guess that'll have to wait. Let's go."

"Try not to worry about him," the detective said. "He'll get over it. And we *will* find out who did this to Stuart."

"Thanks. I hope so." Kelsey wiped away a tear.

⦅◌⦆

An hour later, Captain Bigelow was checking over his notes, and one of the officers and ADA Esposito were chatting, when Elvin and the two detectives walked in. M.E. Donovan was already back, reading over notes.

"Kelsey and Peter, I mean Dr. Holloway, are involved in a…discussion," said Detective Coleridge. "They'll be along in a little while. Captain, can we start interviewing Elvin before they return? He has to get back. Bingo night."

"Sure. I don't see why not." The captain turned the recorder back on.

"Great. Well, this is Elvin Gray. He works as a janitor at the Ames nursing home."

Elvin walked up to the captain and held out his hand. "Nice to meet you. You all, too," he said, turning to face the others. "Anything I can do to help, just ask."

"Thanks, Mr. Gray," said the captain.

"Call me Elvin."

"OK, Elvin. We just have a few questions."

"Fire away."

Detective Coleridge cleared her throat. "I guess I'll start. How long have you been working at Ames, and how long were you on D3?"

"Comin' on six years, ma'am. Two on D3. It's a good floor, not too many screamers. And it don't smell too bad, if you keep on top of the barfin' and the aides gets the Depends changed on time."

The detective grimaced. "That's lovely. How well did you know Stuart Matheson?"

"'Bout as well as anyone, I 'spect. When you see a dude day in and day out, you get to know 'im pretty well. And I knew him when he could talk. Quite a funny guy. Liked to tease the ladies, even the old 'n' ugly ones. He made them feel good, like he was admirin' them. Pity what he had to go through, 'specially after seein' his brother and sister in the same place."

"Can you think back to the day that Smithies told you to order rat poison?" asked Detective Zhang.

"Which time? She asked a few times."

"Right after a white mouse turned up in the dayroom around lunchtime."

Elvin let out a whoop. "That was funnier'n hell. Seein' all those geezers hollerin' about a scared little furball ain't hurt nobody. And ol' Smithies got her fat ass in an uproar."

"What happened that day?" prompted Detective Coleridge. "Can you take us step by step through it?"

"She jus' freaked. Looked like a lab mouse, not one of those field critters. I really do keep them floors spotless, and it'd been so long since we had mouse turds or a roach or anything that the poison'd gotten rotten or something and was throwed out. So I got more from storage, used a bit after hours, then put it in the closet, in case mousie had some friends come 'round." Elvin sat back and smiled, enjoying the attention.

"Do you know what happened to the rest of the poison?" ADA Esposito leaned forward. "After you'd put it in the closet?"

"Well, I dunno. That's about when I got moved off the floor. Nice raise, too."

"How did that come about?" asked the captain.

"Ain't got no idea. It was strange. The mornin' after I'd stored the poison, some weird-ass dude stopped by the floor. Said I'd been transferred. He looked official, so's I just went over and reported to B2 instead of D3."

"What did this man look like?" asked the ADA.

"White guy. Like the mouse." Elvin grinned and looked around, but nobody was laughing except that foxy black lady in the lab coat that said M.E., so he continued. "Pretty regular lookin'. 'Cept he had one blue eye and one brown. Like them Eskimo dogs. Grayish hair with white parts, whaddaya call that? But he weren't too wrinkled, couldn'ta been too old."

"Do you remember the date when the mouse was found?" asked Zhang.

"I gotta think. It was a bingo day, otherwise, there woulda been more hollerin'. Must've been a Tuesday, then. Anyone got a calendar?"

The captain pointed to the wall behind his head. Elvin stood up and squinted at it. "January 8. That was it."

"Where, exactly, did you sprinkle the rat poison?"

"In the corner of the dayroom, only where the mouse was. That shit's nasty!" Elvin looked around and clamped a hand over his mouth. "I mean, that stuff's nasty."

Patrice stifled a giggle as Detective Coleridge picked up the questioning. "Elvin, about how far is where you sprinkled the poison from Stuart's room?"

"Pretty far. He's near the end of the hallway."

"Was it near where he sits for meals?"

"Not really. I sorta put it near them ladies that fights all the time, cos one of them upchucks a lot. I knows this is gross, but I think the mouse was eatin' the dried barf. So's that's where I put it, figgering he'd eat the poison. Only I sorta liked the mouse. Glad Kelsey rescued him."

"Are you and Kelsey friends?" the captain asked.

"I jus' see her a lot. She's there almost every day. I imagine she 'bout fell apart when ole Stuart passed on."

"So, getting back to the poison," said Coleridge, "it was only used in one place in the dayroom? And only in the dayroom?"

"Yeah. And usually we air the place out for a day or two after. That helps with the barf and diaper smell, too."

"Well, at least no one's thinking about breaking for lunch. I think that's it for now. Thank you, Elvin," said Captain Bigelow.

"Glad to help. Stuart was one cool dude, man. Didn't even seem all that sick, neither. You find that fucker—sorry … the guy that did this."

Elvin turned to walk out just as Peter and Kelsey came back in. Wordlessly, Elvin and Kelsey hugged, Peter looking on awkwardly. Finally he cleared his throat, and Elvin winked at Kelsey and walked away. Peter helped Kelsey out of her coat as the door closed.

"Welcome back," said the captain. "Thanks for the diary, Kelsey." She smiled uneasily. "Ready to continue? Elvin was very helpful in reconstructing events."

"I'll try."

"OK. On to January 11. Were the protesters outside?"

"Yes, but not very many. Nobody really bothered me."

"And you were a little uneasy about this visit, given the, er, kiss of the time before?"

Peter repeatedly crossed and uncrossed his legs.

"Yes, I was. I was also a little at odds because I didn't have my iPod. So I brought along something to read to Stuart instead."

"What was that?"

"The December *Rolling Stone*. I figured I'd read him the annual story about John Lennon, you know, the anniversary of his death and all that."

"Do you remember if you encountered anyone in the hallway when you got off the elevator on D3?" asked Detective Coleridge.

"I collided with the janitor because I was reading. But it wasn't Elvin, it was Damon."

"And can you describe Damon?" The detective had taken over the questioning, by silent agreement, since Kelsey seemed the most comfortable with her.

"White. Tall. Nice hair. He creeped me out, though, I think because he had one blue eye and one brown. Like those dogs."

Glances were exchanged throughout the room, and Peter looked puzzled.

"What?" Kelsey looked around. "Did I say something?"

Detective Coleridge started to speak, but the captain interrupted her, sitting forward. "Kelsey, what did this new janitor, Damon, say?"

"Well, I said that he looked familiar. But I couldn't place him." Peter was beginning to look agitated. "Wait!" Kelsey stood up. "I know. He was the man outside. The anti-stem cell guy holding the sign. That's what was weird about his eyes, they were different colors."

"Can I interrupt?" Peter asked, not waiting for an answer. "I saw him, too. He was protesting at the medical center. I also noticed his eyes."

The desk phone rang. The ADA picked up, listened, nodded, then hung up.

"Captain, can I continue the questioning?" asked Patrice Donovan.

"Yes, I was going to ask you to. We need to get at some of the medical details. Thank you."

"OK. Kelsey, you usually shared the iPod, right? And you and Stuart would be looking at each other?"

"Yes."

"But when you were reading to him, your eyes would mostly be down on the page, right?"

"What are you getting at?"

"Would you say that maybe you weren't quite as attentive as you normally were? Because you were reading to him?"

Kelsey's eyes started to well up. Peter looked at her.

"Oh. I hadn't thought about that. But, yes, when we share—shared—the iPod, I'm—I was—very tuned into his breathing. Maybe if I'd been paying more attention." She looked miserable. "But it wasn't my fault I didn't have the iPod."

"I didn't mean to imply anything," the M.E. said. "And you couldn't have stopped it. With cyanide poisoning, the body runs out of ATP, out of energy. Do you remember anything about what he looked like when you noticed he wasn't breathing?"

"What do you mean?" Kelsey sniffled.

"Did he have any facial expression? Was he blue?"

"Would that mean cyanide? Actually, he was red."

"In cyanide poisoning, when cellular respiration shuts down, oxygen is trapped in the bloodstream. And that turns the skin a rosy red."

"Excuse me," said ADA Esposito. "That was officer Clayton. Detective Zhang sent him over to the nursing home when he couldn't get the new janitor on the phone. Clayton says Damon's not there. And a can of rat poison was found in the janitor's closet on D3, lying on its side. He's also bringing thirty-seven cans of vanilla Ensure back. They were crushed and saved for recycling. Maybe the lab can pick up traces of cyanide. And, if we get lucky, some prints."

25

BIOTECH USA OFFICE, FEBRUARY 2

Kelsey stared at the blank screen. She'd never felt such an overwhelming and profound fatigue before, and now it was getting to be a constant. She just didn't want to do anything. At night, she was watching a few Seinfeld reruns, then falling asleep early instead of plowing through journals in search of article ideas, as she always used to do. She was awakening at odd times, her heart beating fast, and then she'd have trouble drifting back to sleep, only to awaken again with a caffeine-resistant grogginess. She was forcing herself to work out every other day (usually), but that didn't really matter because she wasn't eating very much. She'd met Marsha once for lunch and talked to her briefly a few times on the phone.

And things with Peter were still strained. She knew he was upset about the kiss, not to mention the way he'd found out about it at police headquarters and in front of strangers. But they'd had no chance to really discuss it—not that she'd even know what to say. She was still thinking things over, which was probably one reason why she'd been dragging so much. Peter was also busy, of course, traveling to various meetings and preparing for the upcoming senate hearing. It had been moved up due to Stuart's death.

But what really told Kelsey something was wrong was her writing. Or lack of it. She'd made no diary entries since Stuart's death, especially since she'd had to turn over her most private thoughts to the police. Nor had she made any progress on the *Lancet* report. Her problem was usually too many words, not too few.

Marsha had gently suggested that maybe Kelsey should see someone, a therapist of some sort, who could put her on anti-depressants. But Kelsey had written enough articles on depression to know that what she was feeling was situational, not endogenous. Her serotonin and norepinephrine supplies were just fine. She didn't have a disease. She was grieving, seriously grieving. She'd get over it, she knew, but it would take time. She just wanted everyone to leave her alone so that she could sort out her feelings.

She was staring morosely at the computer screen when out of the corner of her eye she saw Tony's head slowly appear over the divider. The look on his face was so out of character—fearful—that for the first time in weeks she cracked a smile, albeit a fleeting one.

"Hey, Kel," he finally said, but only after he'd seen her smile, "you've been sitting there for hours. Couldja maybe yell once in awhile? Like you usually do, so I know you haven't passed out or anything?"

"Oh, hi, Tony. Where have you been?"

"Right here. You're so out of it, you didn't even say hi when you came in." His head disappeared, then he came around and stood in her doorway. "Everything okay?"

"I don't know. Maybe it's just that it's February. So dreary. And I just can't get interested in detection of Ebola virus in fruit bat excrement," she shook her head and gave another brief smile, "although some part of my brain is registering that this is important stuff. The reservoir for Ebola. But I just don't care. And I can usually get myself interested in anything that involves a body fluid."

"Yeah. Normally you'd be all excited about a disease that makes 90 percent of your blood flow out of your orifices." He laughed. "Well, just be thankful that we're not at a regular newspaper and stuck writing about groundhogs seeing their shadows."

Kelsey's half-smile returned. "I did manage to write my newspaper column," she said, "but only because it was a great story."

"What's it on?"

"Wait and see. It'll be out tomorrow."

"Hey, is that teasing tone a sign of life I detect?" When she failed to respond, he went on. "Hey, seriously, I know you're still upset about Stuart. Wanna talk about it?"

"No, Tony, but thanks. I'm just not ready yet."

"Well, why don't you leave the viral shit and go shopping? That always works. And it looks like maybe you could use some new clothes. No offense."

Kelsey looked down at the sweater that she'd had on for three days. "Yeah. I guess I am getting a little ratty looking. But I have to start researching that piece on the cucumber genome soon."

"Kel, that's not exactly breaking news. Well, it is, but I just can't think of who would care. I'll talk to Richard about getting it postponed. I'm sure it won't affect anyone's salads for awhile."

Kelsey's eyes showed a trace of their customary gleam. "OK, thanks. If I can't get interested in Ebola," she said, "I'm sure I won't be able to work up much enthusiasm for the cuke genome. Oh, shit, what the heck is that buzzing?"

"Now that's the old Kel. You're either having an attack, or you left your cell on vibrate."

"Hold on a sec, Tony. I hope it's not Peter, I can't handle an XY ego today." Tony put a properly blank look on his face as Kelsey flipped open her cell phone. She listened a few seconds and then her face brightened.

"Hi, Emily. Yeah, I'm okay. Just a little writer's block. What's up?"

When Kelsey mouthed a "thank you" to Tony and motioned him that she'd be on the phone for a bit, he slunk back to his cubicle, smiling.

"Another patient? Isn't it too soon? Oh, maybe you're right. It'll distract me." Kelsey killed her blank document and put her computer to sleep as she listened. "No, don't mail it. I'll just stop by the office tomorrow to pick up the background info. It'll be nice to see you and catch up. Thanks."

She shut the phone, grabbed her coat, and walked around to Tony's cubicle. When he stood up, she flung herself at him and gave him a huge hug. "You're right, Tony. Retail therapy it is. I'm off to Urban Outfitters, then to rent a movie. Maybe *Outbreak* so I can get in the mood for Ebola and bleeding out."

"Good for you. Call if you need anything. And don't worry about the cucumbers."

≪∞≫

HOSPICE OFFICE, FEBRUARY 3

Kelsey sat in Emily's office, waiting for her to finish setting up a vigil. Once again, she marveled at the volunteer coordinator's style, her uncanny "whole is greater than the sum of the parts" approach to fashion. Today she had on a pinstriped pantsuit, clunky shoes, yet a frilly white blouse – and it worked. Beautifully.

"Phew, sorry. I think we've got most of the shifts covered now," Emily said as she hung up. "This woman has no family and can't afford private hire, so we're trying to get volunteers to her home 'round the clock. Her friends can't do it all anymore. But it shouldn't be long. Ovarian cancer."

Kelsey was silent a moment – she still had difficulty with the cancer patients. "I'm sorry. I don't think I'm up for a vigil just yet."

"No, of course not. How are you doing?" Emily stood up to give Kelsey a hug.

"OK, I guess."

"We all saw your latest column. So sad. How did you hear about the case? It hasn't been in the news."

"It hasn't been in the news for a reason," Kelsey replied. "Remember Jesse Gelsinger? He was the nineteen-year-old who died from a gene therapy experiment at Penn. Canceling gene therapy for two little boys at Children's Hospital and watching them backslide isn't exactly cheery news. Gene therapy is hardly enjoying breakthrough status right now."

Emily frowned. "What do the boys have? I'd never heard of it. Battle disease?"

"Batten disease. Only about 600 kids in the U.S. have it, and that's part of the problem. It's what we call an orphan disease. No big bucks.

So big pharma just isn't interested. But the parents of these two boys raised the funds to start the clinical trial. Only they couldn't raise enough to continue it." She shook her head. "That's why it's so tragic."

"Yes. I can't even imagine being told 'your child has a fatal disease and there is no treatment,' then to have it happen again with a second child. And then to have a possible treatment discontinued because of money."

"Well, it wasn't the first time that's happened. There was a Parkinson's disease trial, too, with a similar outcome – discontinued treatment and return of symptoms. But with children … " Kelsey couldn't keep the anger out of her voice. "The older boy, Graham, was getting better. Well, actually, he wasn't getting worse, which for Batten disease is sort of the same thing. But now he's lost his developmental skills. Can't run. Barely speaks. Seizures came back. He's blind." She looked down.

"Well," Emily tried to make her voice sound hopeful, "maybe your article will inspire donations and they can get back on track. Anyway, back to you. How are you handling Stuart's death? I heard it was likely not natural. That is, not due directly to the Huntington's. I guess we didn't prepare you to deal with foul play. How's the investigation going?"

"It apparently isn't."

"What do you mean?"

"Well, the prints on the rat poison can were too smudged to help. I haven't heard anything about the Ensure can, but I don't think anyone actually saw Damon poison it. And Darwin indeed came from a lab. One of Peter's grad students did some genotyping and traced it to the Jackson lab in Bar Harbor, no surprise there, and then back to a pet store in the King of Prussia mall here. But no one saw anyone set the mouse loose. I'm afraid unless someone can connect the dots the case'll be closed."

"Yes, I thought that, too. The folks at Ames filled me in. They all feel terrible. Even that Smithies woman."

"Really?" Kelsey paused to think about this news. "Well," she said slowly, "she did know Stuart for years, and did seem to care about him."

Emily touched Kelsey's hand. "Maybe you should see Rita over in bereavement services. That isn't just for the families, you know. It's for the staff and volunteers, too."

"I know."

"You know what I think? All of this intrigue and mystery hasn't given you a chance to process the fact that Stuart is gone. He might not have gone the way we all expected, but this is a major change in your expectations. And your routine."

"It sure is. I find myself looking forward to going to the nursing home, then suddenly remembering what happened. I just can't get used to it. I got in the habit of spending a little time every night thinking up new playlists for him."

"I'm so sorry. What you had with Stuart was really extraordinary."

"It wasn't just him. I got to know the other patients, too. And in a way, I visited them, too."

"I know. That's why I thought it might be good for you to see this new patient. She's at Ames. Same floor."

"Tell me about her."

"Her name is Henrietta. She's seventy-eight and has COPD and multiple myeloma. Her friend was taking care of her at home, but Henrietta's become so frail that she was starting to fall, and there were toileting issues. But she's very chatty and upbeat and should be fun to visit."

"Sounds good. I can go over there tomorrow, maybe catch her before lunch."

The two women stood up and Emily handed Kelsey the paperwork, then hugged her. "Thank you again, Kelsey."

《☙》

AMES NURSING HOME, FEBRUARY 4

Kelsey felt strange heading out to Ames once again. The beauty of the rare snowfall was distracting, coating the branches and quieting the city. In a few hours, of course, it would all turn yellow or brown and then disappear.

She took the familiar elevator up to D3 and walked slowly over to the nurses' station. It was a busy morning, and everyone's head was buried in a chart. She'd seen a few ambulettes out front, dropping off new admits and taking residents to the hospital.

February was a tough time in nursing homes. Even though all the staff had gotten their flu shots back in October, and all the elevators and hallways were festooned with signs warning visitors with the sniffles to stay home, inevitably somebody incubating a cold or flu would visit, silently spewing viruses. If anyone got the flu, the whole floor would be quarantined.

Kelsey could see Elvin's dreads in the distance, hanging upside down, as he stretched over a table, scrubbing at the underside. Maybe he had anosmia, she thought, an inherited lack of the sense of smell that could make life pretty unpleasant, but could be a help if you worked in a nursing home. Or maybe he was just used to the various stinks and stenches of old age and illness. She also saw Chaplain Timothy talking to Doc in a corner of the dayroom. Kelsey leaned her elbows on the counter of the nursing station.

"Hi," she called out. No response. "Hi, everyone," she called again, much louder. Nurse Smithies, not even looking up, grumbled something about waiting her turn. Then, one by one, they looked up: nurses Ellen, Maria, and Samantha, social worker Kate, a few aides, and finally Smithies herself. After a moment of startled silence, they all tried to rush around to hug her at once.

After a minute, she stepped back. "Can anyone tell me which room Henrietta Perkins is in?"

"She's in 308," said Maria. "But I think some folks in the dayroom want to see you first!"

Kelsey turned to look through the large window into the D3 community. Tears welling up, she walked around the window, and paused in the entryway. Slowly, then more earnestly, the clanking walkers and the wheelchairs approached and surrounded her.

Cornelius dropped the boat he was working on. "It's Kelsey!"

"It sure is!" bellowed Justina.

Now crying unashamedly, Kelsey bent to hug them one by one. Toward the back of the room, the three old ladies who were always at each others' throats were watching. But they were mysteriously silent. Kelsey approached them, curious. And then she heard an unusually low "Ahhh, ahhh, ahhh".

But the responding chorus, Laverne and Shirley, was oddly quiet. Had they gone deaf? Maybe they had. They were each wearing what looked like a hearing aide. Kelsey didn't recall having noticed the devices before, but nowadays the things were small and flesh-colored. She could easily have missed them before. Betty, the ahhh-ahhh lady, didn't have one.

"Hey," she asked Maria, who had followed her into the dayroom, "what's going on with the Greek chorus here? What happened to the shuddups and the anti-shuddups?"

"That's Doc's invention. He's over there, telling the chaplain all about it. And we thought the guy'd been a doctor way back when. Take a closer look."

So Kelsey looked, and much to her astonishment, the devices weren't hearing aides at all. They were the newest, tiniest, iPods, altered to look just like hearing aides.

"But what about Betty's?"

"Follow the oxygen line."

And there it was, hooked onto the tank holder, the earbuds snaking along the oxygen leads.

"That's positively ingenious! But why the disguise as medical devices?"

"Well, when Doc suggested plugging the old ladies in—he'd been watching you and Stuart more than you might've thought—I remembered how that government guy made me take yours away. We didn't know if there'd be any follow-up to the poisoning." Maria grinned. "So we set Doc to figuring out how to disguise the things. And we got them donated, too. Cool, huh?"

"The best! Is it just to distract them from each other, or to help heal them? Like Stuart?"

"Who knows? But it can't hurt them, they like it, and it keeps down the bickering."

Laughing, Kelsey leaned over and took the earbuds out of the three sets of ears. "Hello, girls! I see you've found the cure!" Their faces lit up.

After a few minutes of catching up on D3 gossip, Kelsey set off down the hallway in the opposite direction from Stuart's old room, checking the names on the doors. Coming to 308, she knocked lightly on the open door, peered in, then walked over to the bed near the window. A tiny, withered woman tethered to an oxygen tank was staring into space.

"Hello Mrs. Perkins," she said. "I'm Kelsey." She pulled up a chair, and sat down, and smiled at her. "I'm a new friend. I can come visit you a few times a week."

The woman smiled and reached out to touch Kelsey's arm. "Oh, that's so nice, dear."

"How are you feeling?" Kelsey asked her. "Is it okay if I hold your hand?" When the woman nodded, Kelsey took her small, gnarled hand.

"Please call me Henrietta," the old woman said. "We're not very formal here."

"OK, Henrietta. Maria the nurse said you arrived just a week ago. Must be a big change. Where'd you live before?"

"I was in a nice apartment," she replied. "My best friend was taking care of me, most of the time. I don't have any family. Sadie and I lived together since my husband died twelve years ago. We knew each other from high school."

"What a great friend to have."

"When you get older, and you see people get sick and die, and your kids leave or you don't have any, friends become more important. Sometimes all-important."

"Can Sadie visit you here?"

"She comes every few days," Henrietta said. "But it tires her out. I wish I didn't have to come here. But Sadie couldn't take care of me when I started to fall so much. Once she had to call 9-1-1 because she couldn't get me up." She smiled engagingly. "Little as I am, I still weigh more than her. And going to the bathroom was getting hard. So I came here. Can't afford that assisted living stuff, you know. That's for rich folks."

"I understand," Kelsey said, "but you might like it here. The people are really nice."

"I hope so. They all seem nice, although some of the nurses mutter a bit. Did you have a relative here?"

"No. I used to visit a man who lived down the other hall. That's how I got to know some of your neighbors. They're quite a colorful bunch."

"But it's so different, living in half a room. And the walls are so dull. It just doesn't feel like *home*."

"I'd be happy to help you brighten up the room. Half room. Can I see that pile of cards on your dresser? I can get a bulletin board and some pushpins and hang them up for you. Maybe next time? I'll bring some pictures, too. What would you like to look at?"

"How about *National Geographic*? Can you find that?"

"Sure."

"I wish I had something to look at other than the walls. I don't have a TV yet, either, not that there's anything much to watch."

"I have an idea." Kelsey walked around to the drawn curtains, peeked behind them, smiled, and then drew them wide apart.

The room lit up with the sparkling white of a tangle of snow-covered oak branches, filling the view from Room 308.

"Henrietta, meet your tree." She bent to give the smiling woman a hug. "I'll see you soon."

Kelsey was watching the elevator doors close when suddenly a hand reached out to stop them and Connie, the nurse from death class, got on. A hat was keeping her brown frizz under control.

"Hi, Kelsey," she said. "I'm so sorry about your patient. Stuart, I mean. I saw you with him at services that time, remember?"

"Yes, thanks. It was nice of you to come to the funeral. How've you been?"

"OK. I was just transferred here from the medical center. Quite a change of pace."

The elevator doors opened. They got off and stood still, not quite knowing what else to say.

"You looked pretty upset at the funeral. How are you holding up?" the nurse asked.

"Not great," Kelsey admitted. "I miss him. But I also miss being here. Today's my first time back. I'm seeing a new patient. A lady with COPD."

Connie touched her arm. "Kelsey, you look so sad. Are you sure you're okay?"

"Well...no, not really. Being here again is weird."

"Would you like to talk? We can duck into the chapel for a little bit. If you'd like."

Kelsey hesitated a moment. "Okay. Where is it? I'm not quite the chapel type, you know." She tried to smile.

Connie blushed as she took off her hat and her hair sprung out in all directions. "Hey. I'm sorry if I came on too strong back during hospice training."

Kelsey looked puzzled.

"You know? The 'A' word?"

"Oh, that." Kelsey shrugged her shoulders. "I forgot all about it. Well, I'm still an atheist, but I've come a long way since then."

"Hospice does that. You become a great listener. And then you start to notice things, to link things, even if you're not aware of it."

"I think I know what you mean."

"So come on. Tell me what's been going through your mind, what doesn't make sense." Connie took Kelsey's hand and led her into the chapel. "And maybe," she added, "maybe you should think about talking to Chaplain Timothy."

"We'll see." Kelsey was still skeptical.

26

Kelsey's Diary, February 13

I'm embarrassed at how long it's been since I updated this diary. So much has happened! First thing, though, I'm moving to a flash drive and deleting everything from the hard drive. No one will read this, at least no one whom I don't want to read it.

And I won't record the minutiae of the past two months. As if I could ever forget any of it. Stuart died, suddenly, before his time, and not of HD. *He was poisoned.* Peter and I suspect an anti-science, anti-stem cell group, or an individual with an agenda, perhaps confused over what the research really entails. But the investigation has stalled, and I have no idea what to do. I have to find out what happened to him.

Then there's this problem with Peter, and I feel too strange about it to ask him to help me get to the bottom of Stuart's murder. I blurted something about Stuart's not kissing me the way he usually did – I can't believe I said that – and Peter was not thrilled, especially since this happened at police headquarters. We haven't had a personal discussion ever since. Everything has become awkward and stilted. So now I'm thinking back to the dirty look Stuart gave Peter when they met, and how when I was with Peter I was thinking of Stuart, and I'm just so mixed up.

What was I feeling for Stuart? Was it just pity? No. There was more of a connection than that. It couldn't have been any physical attraction, because he was really just a shell of a man, unless I was responding to his need for me, a need that I encouraged. I keep thinking back to the first time we met, that spark. Were we both thinking of what might have been, had an errant gene not clogged his brain and destroyed his body?

Could Connie be right? Should I talk to someone???

◦◦◦

HOSPICE OFFICE, FEBRUARY 19

"Kelsey, that's quite a story." Chaplain Timothy folded his lanky body back into the armchair and ran a hand through his thinning hair. "I hardly know where to start. You know, I was pretty surprised when you called yesterday and asked to meet with me."

"I know what you mean," Kelsey replied. "The 'A' word and all. Actually, Connie suggested I talk to you."

"The nurse? The one you tangled with in training?"

"The one and only. I ran into her at the nursing home. She means well, I guess I knew that even then. It's just that the 'helping me find Jesus' stuff drives me crazy. But she was very nice when I saw her the other day. So, here I am."

Kelsey had run into the chaplain at the nursing home a few times. He usually visited Stuart on Friday mornings, right around when Kelsey left for work. But he had never witnessed their connection, not the way that Marsha had. But since Kelsey had stood beside him as he read the last rites to a woman who had refused treatment and calmly succumbed to her cancer in a mere week, she had come to feel she could tell him anything.

"The situation is so unusual," he said in a gentle voice. "Maybe we need to step back first and dissect just what you're feeling."

"I can't quite wrap my head around it," she admitted. "I'm used to being able to figure things out." She paused to gather her thoughts. "This is so frustrating. I mean, I think…at some level I was ready for Stuart to decline, maybe to start dying. Eventually. Maybe even soon. Although he *was* doing better. And so maybe I got my hopes up. But murder?" She couldn't help it. She started to tear up. She rose a bit shakily and walked over to a table that held hospice pamphlets and a coffeepot and refilled her mug. As she put it down and began tearing open a Splenda packet, her hand flew out a bit too far, jostling the steaming mug and spilling coffee all over the table. "Oh, shit! I'm sorry," she sobbed. "I'm just a mess. Let me get some paper towels to clean this up."

"No, no," the chaplain replied. "You just sit down. I'll do it." He went into the kitchenette to get some towels and mopped up the coffee. "Kelsey," he said without looking directly at her, "try to relax. I can see how rattled you are by all this."

"Well, I do feel like I'm going through the five stages of dying. The grief is starting to fade a little, but I'm stuck at anger."

He took his seat across from her again. "The grief hasn't faded, Kelsey. It's overwhelming you, and you're too afraid to give in to it. If it helps any, what you're feeling isn't uncommon. Many volunteers have a hard time with the first death of someone they grew close to. It happens eventually to most volunteers, but you encountered it so soon after training. It isn't the same as the patients who are with us for only a few days."

"Right. The majority. Did I maybe get too close?" Kelsey was quiet a moment. "I couldn't help it," she murmured. "It just happened."

He looked into her eyes a few moments. "Too close?"

"Marsha—you remember her from hospice class? She saw me with Stuart and said our connection made her nervous. She didn't say so, but I sensed that she thought that what he and I had was, uh, inappropriate. And near the end, some of the weekend aides thought I was his *wife*. Then Peter, he's my, my significant other, I guess…he found out about when Stuart kissed me at the police station…"

"Stuart kissed you at the police station?"

Kelsey smiled through her tears. "No, that came out wrong. See, I've been away from writing for too long, I can't even speak coherently. When we were at the police station going over everything that happened, that's when I mentioned the time that Stuart kissed me. Peter wasn't exactly thrilled. Nor was Stuart thrilled when he first met Peter and saw him touch me."

"I don't mean to take this lightly," Timothy said, "but it's beginning to sound like a soap opera."

Kelsey smiled again. "I know. Who'd ever believe any of this? But the fact remains, I can't sleep. I can't write. I can't stop crying. And I just feel so fuzzy-brained, so restless, since all this happened. I feel like something's missing, like I'm somehow not seeing something. Do you know what I mean?"

"Maybe you need help in assembling the puzzle pieces."

She nodded. "But first I need to put my finger on the anger, on the source. Am I angry at the disease? At that lunatic who killed Stuart? Or at myself?"

"At yourself? Why?"

"I should have sensed something was wrong when Stuart was so out of it that last day. I could have gotten help. Instead I just sat there reading a *Rolling Stone*, of all things, as he just slipped away." She started to cry again.

Timothy reached forward and took her hands. "Kelsey, you have nothing to feel guilty about. Who would ever imagine poison delivered in a can of Ensure?"

They were quiet for a few moments.

"Kelsey," he said, "let me ask you something. Have you ever thought about the coincidences?"

"What coincidences?"

"Let's start at the beginning. How do you think you came to be assigned to Stuart?"

"By chance, I guess. When Emily heard about Stuart, for some reason, she thought of me."

"You said you'd run into his brother and sister right after your interview. That's probably why Emily thought to call you, and not any of the other dozens of volunteers. She'd just met you."

"OK." Kelsey looked dubious.

"And she just happened to assign a woman, a new volunteer, to a very difficult case in a nursing home, where same-sex volunteers are usually assigned."

"So?"

"There's more. Weird things you've just told me."

"Weird like what?"

"Like your background in genetics, your having written that series on Huntington's disease recently. And requesting HD on your volunteer application form."

"Or ALS or Alzheimer's or Parkinson's. But right. I did put HD first."

"That's a pretty unusual request. People usually write 'dementia' or '"heart disease' or '"cancer.' And then you said that Emily told you later that that page in the file had come loose, that she didn't even know you'd had that interest when she called you."

"Yes. All that happened."

"Did you tell Emily you had any experience or knowledge of Huntington's?"

Kelsey thought back to her volunteer interview for a moment. "Well, I tried to. But she was in a hurry. She cut me off before I got to say anything."

"So don't you see how odd it all is? You actually know a great deal about this incredibly rare disease that we see in hospice only every few years. And you somehow get assigned to a patient with it right after you join up."

"Fate?" Kelsey smiled.

"It may be more than that."

"Oh, no. I don't mean any disrespect, but is this going to turn into the 'things happen for a reason' lecture? Please spare me the purpose-driven life, *Celestine Prophecy* stuff."

The chaplain couldn't help but smile. "OK, I'll be a little more specific. Did you ever think that maybe you were sent to help Stuart?"

At this Kelsey laughed out loud. "Oh, no. I'm hardly an angel."

"I didn't mean that quite so literally."

"Even if I was somehow sent here, Stuart wasn't receptive to religious thinking either, at least as far as I could tell from his records and comments from his siblings. He might have been an atheist too."

"At the risk of sounding like a Hallmark card, Kelsey, maybe sometimes things DO happen for a reason. Or at least, it may seem that way after the fact."

Kelsey was silent a few moments, an expression on her face suggesting that she was arguing with herself, and then spoke quietly. "Forget what I said. Yes, I've had those thoughts. There *were* coincidences, lots of them, almost as if I was following a script. But I can explain all of the things that happened. Except one."

"The disappearing music?"

"Yeah. That's what I meant by my frustration at not being able to explain it all."

"Sometimes we can't."

"OK, now here it comes—"

"No. Forget about God and religion, Kelsey. I can see that clouds your thinking. Let's just hold those thoughts. What else is bothering you?"

"OK. Another thing I can't explain. *How Stuart died.* I could accept death by Huntington's, or even a brain tumor from the stem cells. But murder by someone affiliated with a right-to-life group? How is it preserving life to take a life? Sabotaging stem cell research, for whatever reason, will ultimately take more lives than it saves. I need some answers. And the cops are ready to give up."

"I think you may have found it."

"Found what?"

"You may have to take off your letter 'A' after all. Did you realize that you let in a glimmer of spirituality when you questioned how Stuart's songs vanished? You even walked into a church. And listened to Connie. And now you're here."

"What's all that got to do with anything?"

"I think your growing spirituality has enabled you to more clearly see the contradiction of Stuart's life ending by the hand of someone who purports to be religious. That's a conflict. A big one."

"Maybe you're right," she said after a minute. "At least about some of it. But what can I do about it? How can I get rid of this anger?"

"I have a suggestion."

"No," she said flatly. "I'm not going to church."

The chaplain smiled. "I wouldn't do that to you. Spirituality—not religion—led you to identify the holes in the story. Okay? Now put your investigative reporter hat back on. Find out who this Damon is. Research the organization. I can't believe *Citizens Against Stem Cell Research* would use murder to stop research. It doesn't make sense. Even if you don't find him, you can find out *about* him. About them. Maybe prevent them from harming someone else or otherwise standing in the way of the research." He paused a moment and handed Kelsey the tissue box. "Kelsey, find the answers. Tell the story. And maybe then you'll find peace."

"I certainly owe that to Stuart."

"You don't owe anybody anything. Find out for yourself. It will help you heal."

"That sounds like good advice. It might solve several problems at once. Thank you, Chaplain." They stood up and hugged.

27

BIOTECH USA, FEBRUARY 24

Kelsey sat in front of her computer, iPod in, scrolling through websites and scribbling notes on a Viagra pad she'd gotten at a medical conference. Tony had been looking over the wall, watching her work for a few minutes, when she suddenly gasped. "Holy shit!"

Tony lost his balance and nearly pulled down the flimsy divider.

"What? What's the matter?" Kelsey looked up.

"Do you realize you just shouted holy shit loud enough for them to hear over in production?"

"Sorry." Kelsey took out the earbuds. "Sometimes with these things you can't tell how loud you're talking. But c'mere. Look at what I found."

Tony came around into her cubicle and peered over her shoulder, scanning the web page.

"What's all this?"

"Websites for companies offering stem-cell based therapies."

"You mean like cord blood transplants?"

"Yes, cord blood's saved and used routinely now. But some of these sites are just plain nuts. *Donate a fat sample to ensure against leukemia and lymphoma.* Here's one from a dental research institute asking parents to steal from the tooth fairy, so they can extract the kids' stem cells from the teeth. For a huge fee, of course. But look at these. Clinics offering to patch up spinal cords or hearts. Some of them even show people claiming to have found relief from paralysis or Parkinson's." She shook her head. "This is pure evil. Preying on science illiteracy while falsely raising hopes. No wonder the media coverage's regarded as all hype."

"But Kel," Tony said, "go take a look at the bigass report that just came out from *Biotech Insights*. It's over near the coffee machine. There are more than 500 absolutely legit stem cell companies. Sure, some of them are spinoffs of academic departments. But some are doing pretty cool stuff, and they're not using words like 'therapy' and 'cure.' Most of them are doing research that's only in preclinicals or phase I clinicals. Mice and safety trials. That's hardly ready for prime time."

"Sure. But how's the average Joe to know which companies are doing serious research and which are trying to sell something that doesn't exist yet? I wonder how many people have wasted their life savings pursuing false promises – then blaming science."

"I read some of the company profiles, Kel. Most deal with the so-called 'adult' stem cells and cord and bone marrow cells. Not embryonic at all."

"Ah, the unfortunately-named *adult* stem cells. It makes for good press, the distancing from the ES cells, but it's annoying to us biologists. After all, embryos have specialized cells, and adults have stem cells. Stem cells should just be called somatic when they're not embryonic. But I digress."

Tony smiled. "Yes, you do. Anyway, if these companies are pursuing somatic stem cells, and U.S. legislation eventually lightens up on the embryonic ones, won't the problem of research restriction just go away?"

"Well, no. That's the part that doesn't make it into media reports. The legislation okays fertility clinic leftovers. Fertilized ova. *That's it*. Not ES cells matched to individual patients, which is what's really needed. Somatic cell nuclear transfer, which creates cell lines that match a patient's genome, will never come out from under the shadow of 'reproductive cloning,' at least for federal funding. Not with the ever-present religious right 'vocal minority'."

"But didn't you write about that already happening?" he asked. "The Boston team using SCNT on those diabetes patients?"

"Yes. They transferred nuclei from the patients into enucleated donor eggs, and got the diabetes cell lines. With full support of the families, of course. There's a Huntington's one, too, that Peter's going to get his hands on. And others are coming from the New York Stem Cell Foundation's top secret, privately-funded lab, which they only half-jokingly call their 'underground railroad.'"

"So how soon until patients can get those cells?"

She shook her head. "Whoa, that's not the goal. At least not for the near future. We need embryonic stem cells with a Parkinson's gene or a muscular dystrophy gene knit into them so that we can recapitulate the very beginnings of a disease *in vitro*, then watch and learn what goes wrong. That sort of knowledge can then guide development of drugs or cell-based treatments. We aren't mass-producing monsters or killing babies. It's really just a tool for developmental biologists. And a very powerful one."

Tony grinned. "Hey, I haven't heard you deliver a stem cell speech in weeks. Feeling better?"

"A little. I guess."

"Well, I hesitate to sidetrack you, but is there anything new on the CSI front?"

"Not much. The cops haven't had any luck. But I'm not sure they know where to look. I've decided to find the maniac who killed Stuart by myself. His motive was apparently stem-cell related, so I thought I'd go talk to the folks at the organization he was supposedly representing."

"What's it called again?"

"CITIZENS AGAINST STEM CELL RESEARCH." She Googled it. "Here. That's them." She selected the address and some other information and printed a page. "They're off of South Street. I think I'll pay them a little visit."

"Wanna do lunch with me 'n Marsha first?"

"Sure. Just give me five minutes."

Lunch was good. Kelsey and Marsha caught up on hospice gossip while picking at their salads as Tony scarfed down soggy ketchup-drenched fries and a cheese steak.

"How can you guys eat that rabbit crap?" he asked. "That's not even food. It's chlorophyll and cell walls."

Kelsey and Marsha looked at each other and laughed. "And what you have is edible?" Marsha asked him. "Various forms of grease?"

"You don't know what you're missing." He stifled a belch. "So, Kel. How did you pull yourself out of your funk? We were gettin' worried about you."

"Believe it or not, I spoke with the chaplain from hospice." Tony actually stopped shoveling fries and Marsha's eyes bulged. "He suggested that I try to get to the bottom of Stuart's murder."

Marsha looked worried. "Is that safe? Aren't those guys anti-science nuts?"

"That's what I'd like to find out. Captain Bigelow says they've hit a dead end. But maybe I can dig up where Damon came from. What motivated him. I've been looking at the web site for *Citizens Against Stem Cell Research*, the group Damon supposedly represented."

"Supposedly?"

"Yeah. I don't know yet if he was part of their organization, or if he was acting alone. Maybe it was personal. Maybe he knew Stuart from way back when and was getting even for something. After all, I don't even know who Stuart actually was. *Before*, I mean. But if Damon's motive was to block stem cell research, for whatever reason, well, then, I'm concerned. Because it's more than just Stuart, although that's awful enough." She put her fork down and pushed the remains of her salad away. "If we're ever going to catch up with the rest of the world in this field, someone needs to track the anti-science groups and at least balance their rhetoric with facts. Up-to-date facts. And what better way than to expose them in our pages, right Tony?"

Kelsey exited the train at South and Broad and walked the three blocks to the address she'd found online. Not that she'd really needed the exact address. The storefront was hard to miss, with its plate glass window emblazoned with freshly-painted "*Citizens Against Stem Cell Research* Headquarters" above several posters taped to the glass. One read *10 Media Myths About Stem Cell Research* and listed seven or eight incorrect biological "facts." A "wanted" poster showed the face of a prominent stem cell researcher whose work had been discredited, and another poster was a blow-up of a newspaper article about the revocation of key stem cell patents. The obligatory maimed fetus photos seemed like leftovers from a Planned Parenthood protest.

Kelsey went in. A young receptionist sat at the front desk behind a nameplate that read "Claire," listening on the phone and motioning to Kelsey she'd be done in a minute. Rather than take a seat, Kelsey walked around and looked at the enlarged newspaper headlines plastered on the walls: BIOLOGISTS AGAINST LIFE. HOW MANY HAVE TO DIE? EUROPEAN GOVERNMENTS SUPPORT EMBRYOCIDE. CALIFORNIA, MARYLAND KILL EMBRYOS.

Finally Claire hung up. Kelsey walked back to the desk, holding out her hand.

"Hi," she said. "I'm Kelsey Raye, from *Biotech USA* and the *Philadelphia Reporter*. I phoned earlier?"

"Yes, please have a seat. Dr. Goldschmidt will be right with you."

"Thank you." Kelsey sat down and picked up a binder of articles on a small table. A few of her own were there, marked up with rebuttals. A door opened down a hallway, and, a short, balding, middle-aged man wearing a white lab coat approached. With him came a sharply-dressed, attractive, thirty-something blonde. Kelsey rose and they all shook hands.

"Hello. I'm Dr. Henry Goldschmidt, director of *Citizens Against Stem Cell Research*. And this is Lindsey Elkridge, who handles PR for us."

"PR? That must be interesting." Kelsey kept her voice light and friendly. "You've done a good job with the web site and all these articles. May I ask what you are a doctor of? Goldschmidt was a famous embryologist, you know."

"I didn't know that. Alas, coincidence. My Ph.D. is in 18th-century European literature."

"Mine's in genetics."

"Really. Well, why don't we go back to Lindsey's office?"

"Sure." She followed them down the hall. They turned into a lavishly appointed office. Kelsey froze in the doorway as she looked at the décor—framed accolades about the organization against a backdrop of baby-themed wallpaper.

Lindsey smiled. "Please sit down, Ms. Raye. Now what can we do for you?"

"I'm sure you know I'm the hospice volunteer who was taking care of Stuart Matheson. I'm also a reporter. Is it okay if I record our discussion?" Kelsey took out a tiny digital voice recorder and set it on the desk.

"I suppose so. Ms. Raye, we were so sorry to hear of the young man's passing."

Kelsey looked skeptical. "As I'm sure you're also aware, all of the evidence points to a man representing your organization, posing as a janitor, as the person who poisoned Stuart."

"Well," the doctor said in his smoothest voice, "as far as I know, that hasn't really been established. The victim did have a terminal illness, did he not? And that janitor did not represent our group. Lindsey, didn't two officers already come in inquiring about this?"

"Two detectives. An Asian man, and that lady who looked like Olivia Bentsen from *Law and Order*. I forget their names. I told them we don't know anything about this Damian." She turned to face Kelsey. "We don't."

"Damon," Kelsey said quietly.

"Thank you, Ms. Raye," Lindsey said frostily.

"But wasn't he carrying a sign with your organization's logo?" Kelsey persisted. "I saw him carrying it myself. So did my colleague,

Peter Holloway. If he's got your sign, that implies he's affiliated with your group. Shouldn't you have a file on him? And while you're at it, can you also check your member roster for a Myra Smithies?"

"Why? Who is she?"

"A nurse where Stuart lived. She mentioned your organization. I'm wondering if she was working with this Damon character."

"OK, I'll check." Lindsey turned around and called up the member roster on a computer, then turned her screen so Kelsey could see it. "That him?"

"Yes. I'd know those eyes anywhere. What about Smithies?" Kelsey moved back and Lindsey entered the name and sat back. A *no member listed under that name* message came back.

"That means Smithies sent for information, but never joined. And I think she showed up here once," Lindsey said. "Does that help?"

"Yes, it does. Thanks. I'm surprised. She certainly had enough money to join. Getting back to Damon, though, I'm still confused. If he was carrying your sign, and you have him on file, doesn't that make him a representative of your organization?"

Lindsey merely fidgeted, but Dr. Goldschmidt nearly erupted. "We do not, and never have, condoned violence to make our point. So if he did do this, he was acting on his own. Even if he carried our sign."

Kelsey leaned over and hit the back button and looked at Damon's photo again. "Where did this Damon Spemann, if that's really his name, come from?"

"If I'm remembering right," Lindsey replied, "he just walked in off the street. He talked to Claire about the immorality of using human embryos in research and asked about joining a protest. And I guess he bumped into that Smithies lady who never paid her dues."

"So you didn't check into his background?" Kelsey asked. "And you, or Claire, or somebody, told him about protesting at the nursing home?"

"Ms. Raye," said Goldschmidt, who was thrumming his fingers on the desk, "we don't have enough staff to check backgrounds. We tried to after the detectives visited, but we didn't get anywhere. Really, all we had planned at the nursing home was to hold up signs. That's all."

Kelsey shook her head. "But that's *not* all. Your people tried to block my way. Rather forcefully. And it wasn't just Damon."

"We didn't know that." Lindsey looked at Goldschmidt, discomfort apparent on her face.

"You didn't know that?" Kelsey asked. "There was footage on the 6 o'clock news. Want me to get it for you? This sounds a little like President Bush claiming not to know about conditions in New Orleans after Katrina hit when it had been on CNN nonstop for four days."

"Thank you, Ms. Raye." Dr. Goldschmidt stood up. "But that won't be necessary. Our people were merely trying to stop what you were doing to that poor man. Now, I really have to go return some phone calls."

"Wait a minute, *doctor*. Just what exactly is it that you think I was doing?"

"Manipulating stem cells, of course," answered Lindsey. Goldschmidt signaled her to keep quiet.

"That is NOT what I was doing. We were listening to music!"

"But weren't you taking him into a lab for experiments?"

"Not experiments, observations. Because he was getting better, and people with his disease *never do*. We were trying to find out why and how he was improving after listening to certain music. Our hypothesis is that stimulated stem or progenitor cells fueled his improvement. We were doing it to help others."

As Goldschmidt gave her a puzzled look, Lindsey blurted out, "Yes! We read all that in *World Medical Mysteries*."

Kelsey gave her a bland smile. "I'm so glad you study the scientific literature. Do you have any idea what you've done?"

"Stopped a hideous experiment?"

"Hardly. Directly or indirectly, you halted a fortuitous and promising line of research that could have provided the impetus for many studies. Not to mention condoning murder!"

"I'll have you know that a majority of our supporters belong to right-to-life groups."

"That's a comfort. What about QUALITY of life?" Kelsey stood up and gestured at the walls. "Why don't you paper a room with photographs of people with spinal cord injuries? Or multiple sclerosis? Or children with diabetes? Or spinal muscular atrophy? What we're really talking about is helping *living and breathing people*, people in pain NOW, people facing premature death. Not balls of cells that have barely even turned on their own genomes. And for your information, what was happening to Stuart was *in his own brain*, to *his own stem cells*. We didn't put them there, nor did we take them out in some gruesome experiment. And it had nothing to do with embryos. Not that you even know what a pre-implantation embryo is. You probably think it's a homunculus."

The doctor stepped forward. "What are you babbling about?"

"If your Ph.D. were in a science, DOCTOR, like mine is, maybe you'd understand. How did you come to run this outfit, anyway? What's your agenda? Who do you really represent?"

"Kelsey, can I get you something to drink?" Lindsey interjected as Goldschmidt took a deep breath.

"Thanks, Lindsey," he said. "Look, Ms. Raye. We have no idea who Damon is, murder is not part of our strategy, and we are as horrified as you are at what happened. We're on the same side! Pro-life! If we can help in any way in tracking this man down, we will, I assure you."

Deflated, Kelsey let out a sigh. "Okay. I apologize for getting so angry. I just hate the fact that some outspoken and powerful opponents of stem cell research—presidents and other politicians unfortunately included—don't seem to understand the science that they find so offensive. And I was very close to Stuart, the victim of that willful ignorance. So please," she said in a friendlier voice, "in the future, check out who you send to protests and allow to carry your signs."

"We can certainly do that. And I really am truly sorry. We never wanted this to happen. You must believe us." Goldschmidt offered his hand. Kelsey took it, then turned off the voice recorder.

"Thank you so much for your time," Kelsey said as Lindsey walked her out.

28

BIOTECH USA, MARCH 5

Kelsey sat at her desk, pounding on the keys as if they were Damon's face. She had her iPod in and was uttering sounds that only vaguely sounded like singing. It was 9 P.M., and everyone else had left, but she'd been so engrossed she didn't want to stop writing. The editor-in-chief was letting her write an editorial as well as a feature on anti-science groups. Just as she was finishing her first draft, she felt her cell phone buzzing in her pocket. She wiggled it out and snapped it open.

"Detective Coleridge! What's up? Why are you calling?"

Kelsey saved the editorial and started to shut down. "Oh, I'm sorry. I haven't checked either phone for the last several hours. I've been sort of obsessed with something I'm working on." She stood up and started to slip into her coat. "Really? I'll be there first thing in the morning. What can I bring you from Starbucks?"

꧁꧂

PHILADELPHIA POLICE HEADQUARTERS, MARCH 6

Kelsey handed Detective Coleridge a venti no whip nonfat caramel macchiato, and the two women sat down together in what passed for a lounge at the back of the station. The detective really did look an awful lot like Mariska Hargitay, the actress who played the *Law and Order* detective.

"Thanks, Kelsey. This is a treat compared to the sludge we usually drink here."

"No, thank *you*, detective. I'm sorry for missing messages yesterday, but I'd been doing some sleuthing of my own."

"Oh? It can be dangerous when citizens try to do our job, you know. And please call me Wendy."

Kelsey gave her an unapologetic look. "OK. I just thought I'd check out that anti-stem cell organization. You know, I take the pro point of view all the time, so I thought it could actually help my writing to try to see the other side. And of course I wanted to learn more about Damon and his motivations."

"And you went there alone?" The detective frowned.

"Yes."

"Maybe you should have brought your scientist friend. Are things okay with you two? I was picking up on some negative vibes at our meeting last month."

"I know you were. It was hard to miss—the Y-linked jealousy gene at full expression." Both women, quite familiar with said gene, grinned. "Well," Kelsey admitted, "things aren't *not* okay. We haven't talked very much since the big reveal in the station house about the kiss. All we've talked about, in fact, is science. Cells. Molecules. Receptors. But we have to. I'm supposed to be writing the journal report on Stuart's progress and the stem cell/music connection."

"Then I'm glad I didn't ask your friend to come down this morning. You can tell him what I'm about to tell you."

"Which is?"

"We found him."

"The actual him? Where is he? Is he here?"

"He's across the river. In Camden."

"Can I talk to him?"

"You can try, but he won't answer. He's dead."

"Dead? That's not fair. I mean, how? What happened?"

"Have you read the paper or watched CNN yet today? Hear about the big fire?"

"No. What fire?"

"There was a break-in at the Westcliff Institute."

"The cell bank across the river?"

"Yes. A man tried to break into the part of the facility that was storing skin biopsies and cheekbrush cell samples from people with neurodegenerative disorders. The guy managed to get ahold of, and destroy, the ALS collection. But even though he knew where to find the cells, he didn't realize that that part of the facility had once been a recombinant DNA lab, containment level P4."

"So he thought he'd be able to go back the way he had come in," Kelsey began.

"but he couldn't." The detective finished her sentence. "He was trapped. The fire started burning all the solvents and plastic, and he asphyxiated. The firemen found him."

"How did you figure out it was Damon? Wasn't he, well, burned?"

"The fire didn't reach him, only the fumes. The medical examiner noticed right away that his hair had recently been dyed—some of it came off on her hands. And he'd recently shaved. And get this—he was wearing only one contact lens, that made both his eyes brown. He might as well have been carrying a sign that said *I'm in disguise*."

"So he had short, neat brown hair and brown eyes? Was he a janitor there, too?"

"Yup. And there's more. He wasn't Damon Spemann. He was Jason Blattner."

"Wow. Two eye colors and holding the same job at two places that had something to do with stem cells. Coincidence? Legally, is this enough to connect him to our Damon?" Just then Kelsey's cell phone buzzed. She took it out, flipped it open and glanced at the screen, then snapped it shut.

"Oh," said Wendy, "we have more evidence."

"I'm listening."

"This is, to use one of your terms, off the record. For now. The break-in is what's on the news, but we're shielding the man's identity until we can confirm everything."

"OK, I'll keep a lid on it. Except for Peter of course." Kelsey glanced down at her phone.

"Damon put down a real address on his job application form, although the name Jason was probably false. So we went over to his place."

Kelsey leaned forward. "What did you find?"

"Well, I can't show you the evidence, or even the list of documents we found. Yet. But I can tell you that the man did his homework. He had literature from cell biology conferences, biotech company manuals, info on stem cell banks in other countries, disease organization pamphlets, Congressional testimony, and all sorts of technical papers on stem cells as well as articles in the popular press. And when I googled *Spemann*, I came up with a famous embryologist."

"Another one!"

"What?"

"Oh, nothing. The creep who runs that anti-stem cell group is also named for a famous embryologist, but didn't even know it. I can't believe hearing the name *Spemann* didn't alert me. I must've been too distraught to connect him to Hans Spemann, who invented somatic cell nuclear transfer. Decades ago. He got a Nobel prize."

"Again, what?" The detective looked lost.

"AKA cloning. Spemann invented cloning. That's just too coincidental. Our dumbass substitute janitor was no dumbass. Good work!"

"There was more. A music magazine with an article about that folksinger, you know part of the duo from LA, who has ALS, and how he donated his cells to the Westcliff Institute. Could be how Damon first heard of the place. And Kelsey, don't forget your favorite publication." Wendy grinned. "The most damning document of all."

"*World Medical Mysteries*. Of course. But I wonder why this guy was so hell-bent on sabotaging research. Was he just one of those religious types who equates a fertilized egg with a fully grown person and thinks he's saving lives?" She thought for a minute. "Or was it personal?"

"We think we may know part of that. We got his laptop, too."

"What'd you find?"

"Well, we'd still be looking if he hadn't helped us out."

"How did he do that?"

"He kept a file of correspondence with women. Two in particular. I can't go into specifics, you understand, but it involves an abortion and a miscarriage."

"So he had an agenda. Probably something about destroying human life."

"That's exactly what we're thinking. We found some anti-abortion rants, too. Seems he was one of those Planned Parenthood protestors in his spare time."

"He had motive and opportunity." Kelsey shook her head. "I think I've exhausted my *Law and Order/CSI* knowledge. What else did you find?"

"Fingerprints."

"Did they match any of the evidence, meager as it was?"

"Remember the thirty-seven crushed vanilla Ensure cans?"

"Yes."

"One of them tested positive for cyanide. And it has a partial print."

"And it matched?"

"Right on. But it didn't come up in CODIS or VICAP or any other databases. Nor was there a cold hit with a relative in prison."

Kelsey suddenly got it. "Which was what was slowing the investigation. Okay, but that just means he hasn't ever been caught and doesn't have any blood relatives who are convicted felons."

"Correct," Wendy replied, "but all that doesn't matter. The corpse at the Westcliff and the Ensure-spiker match. He's the one."

Kelsey sat back into the uncomfortable sofa, as if deflating. "You know, I'm disappointed. Not that I wanted to go through a trial, but I did want to confront him." She gave a huge sigh and blinked several times. "But maybe it's better this way. We can put that part of it to rest. I can write about it—at least when you say I can—and Peter and I can get on with the *Lancet* article and starting some preclinical work and maybe even tweaking the clinical trials."

Her cell phone buzzed again and she smiled. "And speaking of Peter, maybe it's about time I called him back." She got up to leave and gave Wendy a hug. "Let's keep in touch, okay?"

"Sure"

29

KELSEY'S DIARY

March 6

Dear Stuart,

I know it seems weird that I'm writing to you, but I feel like we have a lot of unfinished business, loose ends, and whatever other clichés you might think of. You left me too soon. Too horribly. It's almost 3 months later and it still hasn't quite sunken in. When I get off the elevator to see my new patient, for a split second I expect you to be there, sitting back in your chair and smiling at me. Yet at the same time, I feel your absence every single day. You've left a huge hole in me. Another cliché.

I'm not writing because I believe literally in an afterlife—I don't think you do, either—but I still feel your presence. Perhaps some of my confusion will lift if I say what I never got the chance to say to the real, living you. Oh how I wish I had known the you before the sickness, before that damn HD! But there's no use dwelling on that. If by some small chance there is an afterlife, you'll have your body back in working order.

I wanted you to know that I've finally gotten some answers. About what happened to you, that is. I can hardly bear to think of your last moments. Me sitting there, oblivious, reading to you, when you were struggling and unable to tell me something was so wrong. You couldn't even do the eye blink thing because I wasn't paying attention. Oh, Stuart, what can I say to you? I'm so sorry!

The man who poisoned you had two names, at least that we know of. At Ames, he was Damon Spemann. He told Elvin he'd been transferred to the second floor, Elvin believed him, and they're so mixed up down there everyone thought someone else had arranged the transfer. Then Damon just took over. He had access to the rat poison, and your food tray. He got Darwin the mouse from a local pet shop, that in turn got it from a pet broker, that ultimately got it from a specific batch from the Jackson lab, which one of Peter's students figured out by genotyping the critter.

Damon poisoned you because he wanted to make a statement about stem cell research. To try to stop it. Never mind that we weren't hacking up embryos, like he thought. He had a high school level education. He'd done a pretty good job of educating himself in biology, but not enough to realize that we weren't doing what he thought we were doing. When people get their information about science from celebrities and politicians and tabloids, not to mention stupid two-minute sound bytes from newscasters who wouldn't know a stem cell from a meatball, some of the facts get lost. I digress.

Anyway, the cops weren't having much luck in finding Damon, who vanished soon after I noticed your tattoo had stopped pulsing. I saw him leave the floor, out of the corner of my eye, but didn't remember that until later. His fingerprint, a partial, was eventually found on the Ensure can, which also had traces of cyanide. But the print didn't come up on any of the forensics databases.

Stuart, you were just a detour for Damon. That damn tabloid and maybe Nurse Smithies clued him in, distracting him from bigger plans. So he re-emerged as another janitor at a cell bank in Camden, intent on sabotaging cells donated by a folksinger with ALS, Lou Gehrig's disease. He succeeded, but got trapped in a section of hallway where smoke and toxic fumes accumulated. It was the medical examiner who identified the corpse as Damon. Or whoever he really was.

Before this happened, I visited the anti-science group Damon carried the sign for. Boy, did I let them know the extent of the damage they'd done. I doubt they understood, but I did my best. The head guy isn't even a scientist. Can you believe that??

So there it is. Peter and I have to testify before a congressional subcommittee, but since now we know you didn't die from a stem cell- induced brain tumor, but at the hands of an anti-science radical, there shouldn't be any indictment of stem cell-based treatments. Stuart, *you were improving*. We have the evidence. We hope we'll get the chance to present it. I promise you. We will find a way to go ahead with further research to find out exactly how the music and the stem cells helped you. So they can help others.

Stuart, I wanted you to know one thing before I close. I loved you, and I always will.

30

MARCH 12

Peter and Kelsey sat together on the train to Washington, D.C. When she'd called him back, Kelsey had been a little miffed to learn that he'd gone ahead and booked the trip for them. He'd tried to call her, and she hadn't answered or called back, and they really had to go, the Congressional subcommittee wasn't going to wait. When she realized that, she'd gotten too nervous to be mad. She'd been so upset that she also didn't remember whether Peter had actually offered a quasi-apology for the way their relationship had apparently stalled. Or had she dreamed it?

When they'd met at the 30th Street station, their conversation was strained, but things thawed as they talked about the science. Now, on the train, they suddenly turned to each other. Eyes locked, both blurted "I've missed you." Peter took her hands.

"I'm really glad I had us go a day early," he said. "I had a feeling if we could just go out, relax, maybe see the museums, we could get back on track. I knew you couldn't stay mad at me if I took you to the new dung beetle exhibit."

"You know me pretty well, Dr. H. I thought there was a presidential mandate or something that we be in D.C. at a specific time."

"I told you about it on the phone. Right before you hung up."

"I must have been too spaced out. In fact, I wasn't quite sure," she smiled tenderly, "but I thought you might have been trying to make amends in some way."

"Yeah, I guess I was. But I feel better now. Let's just enjoy the day, okay?"

"Sure. But I want to talk about tomorrow," she said. "Can we get that over with now? Maybe then I can actually sleep tonight. I have no idea what to expect."

"Well, I'm a veteran of hearings. I'll give my standard Stem Cells 101 talk. Again. I've given it in various forms to congressional subcommittees at least a dozen times, but the politicians seem unable to remember anything I say. I have to continually cut back on the science. It puts them to sleep." She nodded and he grinned. "Their aides are the ones who do all the background reading and summarizing, although I don't think they do much analyzing, any connecting of the dots. Most legislators don't have any science background at all. Reading summaries every few months and understanding, let alone retaining, the nuances of cell division and differentiation that are the backbone of stem cell biology is almost impossible. That's why they all seem to get stuck at the controversy. That much they can understand."

"No wonder the public knows so little. Like that doctor of English literature who runs that citizens group. He didn't have a clue about the distinction between embryonic and other stem cells."

"Yes. That's why as time goes on, it seems to me and a lot of other researchers, the knowledge level of our elected officials, and the public, grows ever more outdated. They can't keep up, ironically at a time when the U.S. lags more and more behind the rest of the world."

"You're preaching to the choir, Peter. What exactly does Stem Cells 101 cover?"

"The basics. Very watered down, of course. What a stem cell is. The concept of self-renewal, which is lost every time *The Washington Post* or *The New York Times* simplifies it into some version of 'a cell that can give rise to all the cells of the body.'"

"Well," she said, "that's not so bad. 'Gives rise' is at least quasi-accurate. If vague. It's the 'transform into any cell type' that drives me crazy. Many journalists don't realize that 'transform' in bio-speak refers to cancer."

Peter laughed. "True. I hate it when they do that, too. Anyway, after that intro, I move to important word pairs."

"Such as?"

"Totipotency and pluripotency. Embryonic stem cells versus adult stem cells."

"I prefer somatic."

"I know, but that's just more incomprehensible jargon to most people. They get 'adult,' but the toughest to explain is—"

"Let me guess. It has to be ES cells from IVF leftovers versus from SCNT."

"Right. There's enough misunderstanding about what an ES cell is. Then to try to explain that there are two very different sources of them?" He shook his head. "The problem is that the public, and especially those politicians, all use the C word instead of SCNT."

"Yes. *Cloning*. Reproductive cloning, in particular. Geez, talk about a loaded term. That one's had negative connotations for decades! I never use it in my columns for the newspaper. So, we've clearly got to avoid using it."

"Yes," he said. "Don't even *respond* to it unless you first correct them. I'll kick you under the table if you slip."

"Thanks a lot. So we'll pretend 'cloning' is like 'fart' or 'fuck' or something. A dirty word. Now let's get back to what they're going to ask me."

"Actually," he said, "you are so difficult to classify that I'm not sure. But be certain never to volunteer anything. That's just standard legal advice." He thought for a moment. "I suspect they'll ask you about Stuart. Establish how sick he was when you met him. How and when you noticed he was getting better." He paused, as if riffling through a large mental file. "Maybe they'll ask about some of the articles you've written, like that one on Batten disease. Or some of those rat spinal cord studies."

"Do you think they'll ask about cancer? If anyone truly understands what stem cells are capable of, well, it's an obvious question, isn't it?"

"It is, but if the cancer-stem cell connection isn't listed as a risk somewhere, the aides who do the research might not pick up on it. If someone does mention cancer, we just have to be honest. About how science works. How we don't know some things. That we have to find out. At least we know that Stuart didn't have a tumor. That's what I feared had happened."

"I know," she said, a catch in her voice that she hoped Peter hadn't heard. "I hope that explanation works. We're fighting the pervasive perception, the expectation that science and scientists have all the answers. That we're always 'proving' things."

"Our supporters, if they're smart, will focus on how and why ES cells would be even better than working with neural stem cells or progenitors. But don't count on it."

"Anything else I should know?"

"One thing you should remember. Predicting 'sides' can be tricky. This issue doesn't clearly follow party lines. For many people, personal tragedies trump their religious misgivings."

"Like Nancy Reagan?"

"Exactly. Old Ron was aghast at using fetal tissue to treat Parkinson's disease. But when he could no longer recognize Nancy, due to his Alzheimer's, she suddenly started chattering about the promise of stem cells. So, you never know who has a personal stake."

"Okay. Well," she said after a minute, "I think I'll survive."

"You will. Just pause before you answer a question, think it through, and remember, Dr. Raye, that you know a whole lot more than they do."

"Thanks." She gave him a squeeze.

31

Their day together at the museums did the trick, Peter and Kelsey holding hands at the Smithsonian as they looked at dioramas of giant dung beetles. Had the government known how well they were now getting along, they could have saved on the cost of one hotel room.

The first closed session before the U.S. Senate subcommittee had also gone well. Peter had expected Huntington's questions first, because most people didn't know much about the disease. He'd been prepared, with a spellbinding YouTube clip that had played on *The New York Times* website to accompany an article about a young man who knew that he'd soon start to show symptoms. Peter watched the subcommittee as they watched the man's mother thrash about her kitchen, a whirlwind of motion, flailing and jerking, at the same time a mass of smaller movements, too—she blinked, she twitched, she writhed, her face contorted, her tongue lolled in and out of her mouth. After the clip, while the senators, members of their staffs, and the invited guests were still processing the horror of the mother and the fear and dread of the son, Peter quietly recited Huntington's lore, along with appropriate Powerpoint slides.

Women burned at the stake in the Salem witch trials of 1692. The description by "horse and buggy country doctor" George Sumner Huntington in 1872 of affected members of a large family on Long Island, New York. The HD mutation tracked through 18,000 relatives living in a stilt village at Lake Maracaibo, Venezuela. The hundreds of people still living there today with HD, every one of them descended from a lone Portuguese sailor who brought the errant gene to the settlement ten generations ago. A slide showed a researcher tacking up the huge pedigree along a wall. It was that study, Peter said, that had led directly to discovery of the gene in 1993. And of course, the obligatory grainy photo of Woody Guthrie.

With images of the disease still fresh in their minds, senators, staffers, and spectators paid close attention to Peter's Stem Cell 101 lecture. He skillfully paired mocking cartoons of misconceptions with micrographs of real early human embryos—balls of identical, featureless cells. He also showed photographs of implants derived from ES cells that were clearly just sheets of cells, *not* baby body parts. The video clip of the cardiac muscle was particularly revealing as it showed a tiny collection of pulsating cells in a dish. *Not* a recognizable heart. *Not* a splayed micro-baby.

Peter showed slides to illustrate various ways to pluck cells from early embryos to start ES cell cultures while leaving the embryos viable. Other slides showed ways to salvage useful cells from doomed or even already dead early embryos. To Kelsey's astonishment, some of the naysayers still didn't get it. Even these alternatives didn't satisfy them. When one of the Republicans started yammering about the risks of preimplantation genetic diagnosis (PGD), an obvious and time-tested way to get cells while preserving the embryo, Peter shot back with statistics on the thousands of children born since 1989 after PGD indicated they were free of the diseases that ran in their families. But, given the common media depiction of the technique as a "breakthrough," the senator's response was perhaps not surprising.

Kelsey was beginning to glimpse what researchers were up against.

So that had been the morning. Things started getting a little sticky in the afternoon. Senator Brisbaine (R-Iowa) had apparently stumbled upon the fact that science is full of uncertainties. And Peter was beginning to feel as if he was reciting a mantra to the unhearing.

"So Dr. Holloway," the senator (who had started out running a grocery store) intoned, "Does the bone marrow in fact have a master stem cell, a cell type we could use instead of destroying embryos?"

"As I've said," Peter replied, "we don't necessarily have to destroy embryos. As for the master bone marrow cell, we can't know whether it exists. Not without further research. If it does exist, it is exceedingly rare, so it will take more time to identify and characterize it. So, yes, we hypothesize that such a cell exists, giving rise to the hematopoietic—I mean, blood cell—lineages. But, no, it hasn't actually been observed or isolated. We more or less infer its existence at this point from its cellular descendants."

The senator looked confused. "Cellular descendants?"

"Mature blood cells. You know, red cells, white cells, and platelets. Which of course are really cell fragments."

"Of course. However, the answer to my question is, *you don't know*. But I read that bone marrow cells are now routinely injected into the heart when a person undergoes bypass surgery because it helps the heart to heal. Bone marrow cells taken right from the patient. If that works, then why use embryo cells?"

"Well, first, embry*onic* stem cells are not *embryo* cells. ES cells are cultured cells derived from a very early embryo's cells. That means in a laboratory dish, not in an embryo. Technically, the embryo's too early to even be *considered* an embryo, because the cells haven't differentiated."

"Whatever," the senator said. "So why do we need the *embryonic* stem cells?"

Peter took a deep breath and pulled the senator back on course. "You're correct," he said. "Several centers have indeed been injecting bone marrow cells into failing hearts. But it's hardly routine. The hope is that the mesenchymal stem cells from the marrow will jump in and speed recovery of the heart, perhaps knitting new tissue. I used the word *hope* because this technique is still experimental. It's being done mostly on a case-by-case basis. Every time a patient improves, it's attributed to the stem cells. But these reports were *not* controlled clinical trials, and so other explanations were not explored. The anti-stem-cell camp has twisted these hopeful but premature conclusions to mean that embryonic stem cells weren't needed."

"They were wrong?"

"Yes, they were. In two ways. First, *The New England Journal of Medicine* recently published results of a small clinical trial attempting to validate the case reports. No effect was seen. But that just means more studies are needed."

"And secondly?"

"That's more important. The people claiming that successful adult stem cell protocols abolish the need for ES cells don't understand that ES cells will be critically important in *basic research*. Not to patch body parts like hearts. At least not yet."

"Can you explain how the embryo's cells would be used in research? I thought the focus was on healing."

"*Embryonic* stem cells." Peter felt like he was repeating himself to an extremely naïve class. "*Not embryo*. The focus is on healing if you are running a for-profit company in search of a product. But to scientists, the greatest value of ES cells will be in *in vitro* systems. In glass dishes. Cells growing in culture that can show us how diseases start, so *then* we can work on treatments."

"Can you give us an example?"

"Sure. A group from Boston just reported that ES cells from a mouse model of ALS—that's Lou Gehrig's disease—revealed that it isn't failing motor neurons that are the direct insult. It's the astrocytes that support the neurons that go haywire. Astrocytes and neurons descend from the same neural progenitors, which in turn descend from neural stem cells. In Lou Gehrig's disease, the abnormal astrocytes release a toxin that poisons the motor neurons. This lone fact sends the search for a treatment in a totally new direction."

The senator looked down at his list of questions, but found no answers there. "Mice?" he asked. "How will they help?"

"That's an example of how research is restricted. The mice had human ALS genes. It would be better, of course, to use fully human cells. Still, the public gets queasy every time a journalist latches onto the fact that we put human genes in other animals. It's done all the time."

"What about the heart work?" asked the senator, who was looking a little shocked.

"We might be able to figure out how and why the bone marrow autotransplant to the heart doesn't work if we could watch those bone marrow master stem cells form from ES cells given a cocktail to pursue the hemato—I mean blood—lineage. That is, instead of working backwards from mature blood cells to see where they come from, we could work *forwards*. From the stem cells that give rise to the ever more restricted cell lines in the bone marrow, and other tissues. That would be the dream experiment." Peter sat back and smiled.

While two or three senators had been carefully following his argument, most of them looked bored to tears. Kelsey noticed that one or two older senators were close to nodding off.

But Senator Bainbridge was still paying close attention. "What about transdifferentiation?" he asked. "I read, I believe in one of Ms. Raye's—"

"—*Dr.* Raye's—"

"I read in one of, er, her articles that certain cells from bone marrow, uh, not the elusive master stem cell which we, after all, have never seen," he looked at another page of notes, "can travel to where there's an injury, and morph into whatever's needed."

Peter nodded. "Transdifferentiation. Right. I suspect that article was from a few years ago. And, yes, it was at first hypothesized that certain bone marrow cells home to an injury, following inflammatory signals, where they then divide and their daughter cells go on to specialize as whatever cell types are required to heal the injury. This can be, for example, a blood vessel lining cell or a connective tissue cell."

"That doesn't happen?"

"Then some experiments found double the genetic load in those cells."

"Why was that important?"

"That meant that the emissaries from the bone marrow, instead of dividing to yield the cell type that was needed, fused with cells in the damaged tissue, and somehow healed them. That's why the cells had twice as much DNA as normal."

"So let me try to get this straight." The senator paused to think. "Are you telling us that there are two explanations for one observation?"

"Two *possible* explanations, yes."

The senator chuckled. "That would hardly hold up in a court of law."

"This is science," Peter replied, "not law. And that is precisely the way science works."

"I don't follow. Shouldn't there be one definitive answer for how things happen in the body? A conclusion? Proof?"

"Proofs are for math, not science. We collect *evidence*, not proof." Some of the other senators started paying closer attention. "And sometimes that evidence can point in more than one direction. Science asks questions, investigates, concludes, then refines conclusions when new information becomes available to pose further questions. It's a cycle of inquiry."

"Spare us the lecture on the scientific method," replied Senator Bainbridge. "We don't need it."

Kelsey straightened and bristled, eyes riveted on Peter, who, she could tell, was close to detonating. But he pulled himself together.

"With all due respect, Senator, I disagree. If you think we scientists provide proof, then I'm afraid you DO need to learn more about it." Two or three senators smiled. "Getting back to the point," Peter continued, "it's indeed possible that both events happen in the heart. That bone marrow stem cells replace damaged tissue *and* help the tissue to heal through cell fusion. We still do not know exactly what happens. We can't know unless we do more research."

The senator was quiet again. Then, "OK. Another question. Do all organs in the body have their own stem cells?"

"We don't know."

"Well, which ones *do* you know about?"

"Like I said, bone marrow. And cord blood, of course. Neural stem cells. Skin. Teeth have stem cells, milk duct linings, fat. Dr. Raye wrote a column about growing new parts from liposuction leftovers."

A few senators looked amused, but Bainbridge flashed them a frown.

"What about the pancreas?" he asked. "That's certainly been a focus of a lot of research and discussion. Given the prevalence of diabetes."

Peter nodded. "Yes. For a long time people thought there was a pancreatic stem cell. Or perhaps two, because it is really a dual organ, digestive and endocrine. But it's looking like there isn't one. Although the pancreas clearly has progenitor cells."

"Which are?"

"Let me go back to the slide show, Senator. See, the progenitors are the immediate descendants of stem cells. But they are less specialized than fully differentiated cells."

"Thanks for the reminder. So the pancreas situation introduces yet more uncertainty."

"But it makes sense. Lack of a true endocrine pancreatic stem cell may be why the Edmonton protocol is having problems."

"What's that?"

"Islet transplants," Peter said. "The islets are the parts of the pancreas where insulin is produced. The transplants work for awhile. But then people with diabetes need to go back on insulin. Several years had to pass before this effect could be seen. We think the transplanted islets don't provide a lasting treatment because the pancreas doesn't have its own supply of stem cells to take over."

The senator cleared his throat. "It seems that there are a lot of unanswered questions here."

"Exactly my point! That's why we need to do more research, especially in—"

"All right, Dr. Holloway." He shuffled his papers again. "Let me go in a different direction. I'd like to get a handle on some of the numbers."

"Numbers?"

"Disease prevalence. To get an idea of how compelling the need is for stem cell based therapies. That Huntington's film was most disturbing. But how many people have the disease?"

"About 30,000 in the U.S. But, Senator, you're jumping the gun. Remember how I talked about using ES cells to understand pathologies first?"

"Yes, of course. But we're *looking ahead*. Because treatments are what interest the medical consumer. And the pharmaceutical industry. And insurers. Do you know how many people, for example, have diabetes? In the U.S.?"

"Type 1?"

"The one where you need to inject insulin."

"About 2 million."

"Alzheimer's?"

"Four point five million. I have a slide of this on another PowerPoint presentation. Would you like to see it? I don't want to mix up the numbers."

"Sure."

Peter pressed keys on his laptop, and the screen filled with a list:

- *Parkinson disease*   1 million
- *Alzheimer disease*   4.5 million
- *Type 1 diabetes mellitus*   2 million
- *Spinal cord injury*   256,000
- *Huntington disease*   30,000
- *Orphan diseases*   2 million

"This is just for the U.S.," he said after everyone had read the slide. "As you can see, many millions of people could potentially be helped by anything we can learn or do using stem cells."

"Wait a minute," the Senator asked. "What happened to your apostrophe s's? Isn't it Parkinson's? Huntington's?"

"Oh, sorry," Peter shrugged. "Geneticists started the trend to remove the apostrophes with Down syndrome, oh, about 15 years ago. There are no apostrophes in genetic conditions. But it never caught on much with the media. And we tend to use the possessive in speech."

"Thank you for the editorial clarification," Senator Bainbridge said lightheartedly. "And what's an orphan disease? Why does it matter if a person has parents?" One of his aides hurried over to whisper a quick explanation.

Peter then launched into another speech he had given all too often. "The Orphan Disease Act of 1973 designated that title to any disorder that affects fewer than 200,000 individuals. Pharmaceutical companies are given financial incentives to pursue treatments for orphan diseases, which they otherwise would probably not do. All told, about 6,000 disorders have orphan status, many of them inherited and affecting our kids. In the U.S., about 25 million people have orphan diseases. The 2 million on the list who could potentially benefit from stem cell based therapies is in all likelihood a gross underestimate."

Kelsey couldn't help smiling. Peter had the facts. The Senator was looking increasingly uncomfortable.

"I'd like to see a few more numbers, if you don't mind," the senator said. "Having to do more with *reproduction*."

"That's not really my area of expertise. I deal mostly with neurodegeneration. Perhaps you should ask Dr. Raye. She's written about ARTs, I believe."

"ARTs? What is or are ARTs?"

"Sorry. Assisted reproductive technologies."

Everyone on the subcommittee turned to look at Kelsey.

"*Dr.* Raye," said Senator Bainbridge, "about how many embryos are laying frozen in *in vitro* fertilization clinics in the U.S. right now?"

"About half a million."

"And what will become of them?"

"They'll be destroyed," Kelsey said, "unless their donors can continue to pay for their upkeep. Which most people elect not to do." She paused. "Isn't it better to use them to help people?"

"*We* ask the questions. Where do you get your information?"

Kelsey frowned at the rebuke and struggled to check her rising anger. "For reproduction, usually the Alan Guttmacher Institute. But sometimes I use the National Center for Health Statistics, or the CDC. Resolve has a good web site. Resolve's an organization for infertility patients. And of course researchers in the UK are always about two decades ahead of us, so I keep up on *The Lancet* and the *British Medical Journal*. The UK is where IVF came from, and SCNT—"

"Speaking of IVF," Bainbridge interrupted her, "do you know about how many women undergo IVF each year in the U.S.? Whenever I'm in Georgetown, I see double strollers and nannies and I always think 'fertility clinic."

"Do you mean how many IVF cycles are *completed* in the U.S. each year? Many women have more than one cycle before they conceive. And, with all due respect, Senator, infertility isn't something to joke about."

The senator had the grace to nod. "OK, yes, cycles."

"It's hard to say. As you know, the infertility treatment industry is booming, at least among the well-to-do, but it is not regulated by the FDA. The statistics I've read on cycles say about 40,000. Of course, multiply that by four to eight eggs per harvest."

"Of course. Thank you. Now, returning to Dr. Holloway. I admit I'm not very good at math, but the numbers just aren't adding up. We've got 40,000 procedures that might yield a few eggs apiece, but at least 10 million people potentially lining up for eggs to house their DNA. Did I understand your distinction between needing IVF embryos, which are the immediate subject of the legislation, as well as eggs for cloning?"

Peter and Kelsey exchanged glances. "For *SCNT*," they said in unison.

"About how many eggs are needed for a clone, er, for a CNN procedure?"

Peter resisted smiling. "*SCNT*. The Koreans, who of course were discredited but still did and continue to do a lot of interesting work, were using a few hundred oocytes—that's eggs—to get a single SCNT to work. And *Advanced Cell Technologies* up in Worcester, Mass., also needed about that many."

Everyone in the room looked at Peter as if he had lapsed into a foreign language. "I think you'd better spell it out," Kelsey told him. "Literally." The audience seemed to have retained nothing from Peter's slide show.

"Oh," he said. "Sure. SCNT. Somatic cell nuclear transfer. Basically, it's using a patient's genetic instructions in a hollowed out donor egg cell, to derive replacement cells—via ES cells—that match the patient. So, theoretically, his or her immune system won't reject the cells." He gestured at the screen. "It was all in the slide show."

"Can you please enlighten us and show it again?" one of the other senators asked.

Peter quickly retrieved the slide showing how SCNT might help Michael J. Fox. "Despite the current inefficiency of nuclear transfer," he said, "improvements are likely."

"May I add something?" asked Kelsey.

"Please do."

"A parallel is the human genome project. It was completed years ahead of schedule, because along the way, technology was invented to greatly speed DNA sequencing."

Peter broke in. "And do you remember when IVF was considered nearly impossible? The headlines when Louise Joy Brown was born in 1978? The first test-tube baby? There was lots of criticism back then, too, not to mention cartoons. Comedians made jokes about her." He paused. "And today more than a *million* people are walking around who had the same beginnings as Louise. Who is, by the way, a lovely but thoroughly ordinary human being. The technique was improved, people got over the strangeness of it, and now it's routine. SCNT may go the same way. But for now, we just don't know—"

"—until you do more research." The senator gave a brief smile. "I'm beginning to get it. In the meantime, would you agree that the human egg supply isn't sufficient at present?"

"That's correct. But I'd like to throw out another number."

"And that is?

"The number of abortions each year. Kel—I mean Dr. Raye?"

"About 1.4 million."

"And why is that relevant, Dr. Holloway?" asked Senator Bainbridge.

"Because it's possible that we could harvest primordial germ cells from abortuses, and culture embryonic germ cells from them."

"Would you be so kind as to translate that into English?" a female senator broke in. "Dr. Raye, you're a journalist. Please help us."

"In a female embryo, the cells that will give rise to her eggs are set aside. These precursor cells, called primordial germ cells, can easily be collected and cultured to yield a cousin of ES cells, embryonic germ, or EG cells. They've been used in research since 1996 or so. Privately funded, of course."

"Thank you," said the senator from California.

"Seems we keep running into more and more cell types," Senator Bainbridge said. "Can these EG cells be used in place of ES cells?"

"Not yet," said Peter.

"Why not? If they've been in labs since 1996?"

Peter looked at Kelsey hesitantly, then answered. "They sometimes give rise to tumors."

Several people looked up. "That seemed to come from left field," said Senator Bainbridge, smiling again. "Now let me guess. You need to do more research?"

Peter smiled, too. "Yes. Actually, stem cells and tumor cells have some things in common, so it isn't too much of a stretch."

"OK. How else might you meet a demand for more human eggs? You can't force subordinates to donate, like the Korean doctor did."

"That's actually been a matter of much debate. Dr. Raye has written about it." He looked at her.

"It's complicated," she said. "It goes beyond the science, to matters of economics and class. But before we get into details, you should know that donating eggs isn't like donating sperm."

Several of the male senators blushed or squirmed, but Kelsey ignored them. "We all know, or can easily imagine, how sperm are donated. But to donate eggs, a woman has to give herself shots for three weeks, then have a needle pushed through her vaginal wall to retrieve the mature eggs. And she doesn't exactly feel great the whole time. Plus, the hormones she has to inject to superovulate—that means to make up to twenty eggs at a pop, compared to the normal one or two—may set her up for ovary-related health problems later. Even cancer. We just don't know yet."

Senator Bainbridge rolled his eyes and mouthed, "More research." "Where," he said aloud, "does class come in?"

"Well, if we regard egg donation as motivated by altruism, like someone donating a kidney or part of the liver to help a stranger, that would work. But if we start *paying* for eggs, like we pay for sperm, that could be a problem."

"Why?"

"The pay can be substantial," Kelsey said. "Poor women might be more tempted to go through the procedure and put themselves at risk than women of means. Plus, there's a price tag on eggs. Did you know that Harvard women are routinely offered up to $35,000 for their eggs? Hell, even I'd think about doing it for that price. That's almost a year's tuition."

A few of the senators chuckled. They were all paying attention now. "This is very interesting," one of them said.

"Continue please, Dr. Raye," said Senator Bainbridge.

"There's fear of creating a reproductive underclass of sorts. An alternative might be to consider women donating eggs as research subjects. And paying them accordingly, like paying college students to take part in psychology experiments. I remember doing that. But of course it *isn't* the same, because some women may view their eggs as potential children." She paused. "And the eggs could be donated for research, which differs from the intent in donating sperm."

"Tell them about what they're doing in the UK about egg donations," Peter interjected.

"In Britain, they match up well-to-do women who are undergoing IVF but need donor eggs with women also seeking IVF who have plenty of eggs, but can't afford the procedure. The wealthy women underwrite IVF for the money-poor, egg-rich donors, with the stipulation that they donate half of their retrieved eggs to research. Everyone wins in that scenario."

"Except, perhaps, the embryos destined for research," the senator said. "And do you really think women will volunteer to do this?"

"They're already doing so," Kelsey said. "In droves. And in Korea, hundreds of women offered to donate eggs, not coerced. In this country, plenty of young college women answer those ads and web sites looking for egg donors. There *can* be a supply, if it is handled ethically."

"And now you're going to tell me that we also need more psychosocial research. To complement the other research dollars that Dr. Holloway has pointed out are lacking."

"Well, yes!" Kelsey said, smiling.

The senator took off his glasses and sat back. "You've given us a lot to think about," he admitted. "I had no idea this would all be so fascinating. But let's take a twenty-minute break. Then we'll continue with questioning by Mr. Branch, my Republican colleague from Tennessee."

⋘∞⋙

After the break, everyone filed back in. As Kelsey and Peter took their seats, Senator Branch approached to introduce himself. Kelsey held out her hand, but the senator kept his hands behind his back, though he smiled cordially at them.

When the session resumed, Senator Branch led Kelsey through her experience with Stuart, and asked her how she connected the music to his improvement. Then Peter presented the experimental evidence of Stuart's clinical reversal, including the autopsy and cell culture results.

Kelsey couldn't get a read on how things were going. Something wasn't quite right about the senator. He seemed to be relying a lot on the rather aggressive young aide sitting next to him. When she wasn't tapping away on her laptop, she was handing over documents. The questioning went on.

"So," the senator said, "assuming that the effect you are seeing is real, if Stuart's own stem cells were stimulated enough to reverse his illness, why do we need to clone embryos?"

Peter and Kelsey cringed. "I never said anything about *cloning*," said Peter. "The correct term, as I've explained, is *SCNT*. Or just nuclear transfer. Anyway, what we really need to look at is the disease as it starts, at the molecular or cellular level. Long before we notice symptoms. Years before. By using human ES cells, generated using nuclear transfer—aka SCNT—from people with the condition in question, we should be able to recapitulate the pathogenesis in cells growing in culture. It's the same as I explained for the bone marrow cells healing the heart. And for ALS. *Not* in an embryo. *Not* in a person's body. In *glassware*."

Kelsey noticed that the senator was turning pages that the aide presented him with his left hand. He was holding his right hand beneath the table. Keeping her eyes on him, Kelsey scribbled a note and subtly moved it for Peter to see. He glanced at it and looked up at her, momentarily puzzled, then nodded.

"I'm afraid I don't understand," the senator was saying. "Why would it help to know how a disease starts?"

"Let me use another example," Peter replied. "A wonderful story. PKU. Phenylketonuria. Before the 1960s, children born with PKU were severely mentally retarded and had other problems, too. They were warehoused in institutions. Then biochemists discovered that a missing enzyme caused a certain amino acid to build up in the blood. Using blood from a newborn's heel, they invented a test for PKU and developed a special diet very low in the extra-abundant amino acid. Identifying kids at birth and having them follow this diet completely prevents the symptoms. There's even a very famous photo of three kids from one family. The older two are obviously retarded. The youngest, born after the diet was instituted but also with the disease, looks just fine. He grew up healthy. All newborns are now routinely tested for this and a few dozen other inborn errors of metabolism. Treatments, some of them dietary like for PKU, can prevent symptoms in many of these disorders."

The senator seemed distracted, still trying to shuffle papers with one hand. With a glance at Kelsey, Peter continued. "Wouldn't it be wonderful if we could treat ALS just like we do PKU? Detect it before the first inkling of muscle weakness? Then stop it in its tracks?" Peter paused. "Or maybe Parkinson's disease?"

The senator suddenly jerked backwards.

"Parkinson's disease?" he asked. "Stem cells could stop Parkinson's before it starts?"

"Possibly."

"What about in the early stages? Could stem cells ever reverse the disease?"

"Maybe not. But they might be able to halt the progression. We'll have to find out…"

"Dr. Holloway, tell me this. How bad can Parkinson's get? I'm afraid I don't know much more about it than those horrific Michael J. Fox ads from the 2006 election. And those were supposedly showing the side effects of his meds, not the disease itself."

Bingo! Kelsey said to herself.

"That's true," Peter said. "The drugs that have been used to treat Parkinson's for many years, and even some of the invasive techniques, such as deep brain stimulation, don't work forever. And we can't control where exactly they restore dopamine in the brain. So those other movements, the side effect movements, occur. But, as Mr. Fox explained, the side effects aren't as bad as the disease."

The senator was silent a few moments, clearly thinking something over. "Again, could you tell us how bad it gets?"

"Dr. Raye can tell you. She wrote an article a few years ago about a clinical trial that was discontinued, leaving several patients in the lurch. She interviewed them. She might even have the article with her." He turned to her.

"Yes, that was the GDNF trial. Let me look." She made a show of checking through the documents she'd brought along, although she'd quietly found the article soon after she noticed the senator's hand hiding.

"GDNF?" said the senator. "Another abbreviation? What's that?"

"Glial cell-line derived neurotrophic factor."

Everyone chuckled, and the senator said, "Fine, let's just stick with the letters." A few spectators gave nervous giggles. "What was that treatment?" he asked, "and what happened with the trial?"

"Did you see the movie *Awakenings*? With Robin Williams? It's a true story. Based on treating patients with a condition very similar to Parkinson's. After they got better, the treatment was taken away. And they backslid. Well, the same thing happened with GDNF. The forty-eight people in the trial had volunteered, happily, to have two holes drilled into their skulls so that a catheter could deliver GDNF from a sac sewed into their abdomens. That's how bad off they were," she said, "that they'd jumped at the chance to do that. Have holes drilled in their skulls. And most of them enjoyed near miraculous recoveries. Just like in the movie."

"So what happened? I've never heard of this."

"This happened about the same time that people started suing pharmaceutical companies over the Cox-2 inhibitors causing heart attacks."

"You mean like Vioxx?"

"Right. Well, right about then, the biotech company making GDNF found that monkeys given the drug developed some sort of brain rot, and a few of the patients had antibodies to GDNF in their blood. So the company not only discontinued the trial, they yanked the treatment from the forty-eight people, who were, by the way, quite willing to take the risk if it meant a dampening of the Parkinson's. Which they claimed it did. Besides, it's normal to make antibodies, and the unfortunate test monkeys had been given whopping doses compared to what the people got. But the execs saw what happened with Vioxx, and they pulled the plug on GDNF."

"What happened to the people?" the senator quietly asked.

"Their Parkinson's came back. A web site has their stories. That's where I got most of the information for my article. Nothing like learning about a disease straight from people who live with it every day."

"Can you read us a few?"

"Sure. I'll read the ones I used in my sidebar"

"Naomi W.: *I was diagnosed at age forty-two. Looking back, the first signs were fatigue and a vague uneasiness. My movements slowed, as if my parts were slowly locking into place. At the same time, I couldn't control some of the muscles in my hands and shoulders, hips and feet. This threw my balance off. So I learned to take a few steps fast, then stop, so I wouldn't topple over. For four years the regular drugs helped a little, but then they stopped working. I had to quit teaching, and I became homebound. I couldn't drive, couldn't do the grocery shopping. My life became a growing list of 'couldn'ts'. I became completely dependent on others by the age of fifty. I don't know what my future holds.*"

Kelsey looked up and locked eyes with the ashen Senator Branch. She then looked over at Peter, who was beaming at her. Her confidence soaring, she continued.

"Robert: Diagnosed at twenty-eight: '*At first, I experienced just a bit of clumsiness, stumbling because my feet wouldn't lift high enough to take steps. Then I noticed a fine tremor in one hand. I tried to ignore it, but it spread. Within three years, I could not control my movements. To get to the kitchen, I'd roll out of bed and onto the floor, then crawl. Everything I did was at a snail's pace.*'"

Kelsey looked up. "Family members are affected, too. It was Michael J. Fox's wife, Tracy, who first pointed out his body asymmetry, the fact that one side of him seemed frozen. Here's an excerpt from the twenty-two-year-old daughter of a man with Parkinson's."

"'*Dad was fifty-two my sophomore year, when he was diagnosed. I was living at home, and it was a good thing. He got bad fast. I'd try to stop back home whenever I could during the day to help him. Sometimes he'd be sitting in a chair, like a prisoner, unable or afraid to get up. One time I saw him crying when he didn't know I had come in. It got so he couldn't lift the utensils to eat, not even the modified ones that the occupational therapist gave him. His arms and legs would flail at the same time that his face would seem like a mask. He stopped going out, couldn't stand it when people stared. He'd drool, have to be bathed and toileted, dressed. Sleeping was nearly impossible. Because he couldn't change positions whenever he wanted to, like we all take for granted, he'd hurt. This isn't any way to live.*'"

"Is that enough?" she asked in a quiet voice.

The senator coughed and just shook his head. Then he seemed to pull himself together.

"Dr. Holloway, Dr. Raye, what do you think will happen if the government continues to restrict federal support of human embryonic stem cell research?"

Peter and Kelsey looked at each other, then he answered the question. "It will continue to be funded at the state level, especially the crucial SCNT work that even the new legislation won't cover. California, Connecticut, New York, New Jersey, they're leading the way. Massachusetts came on board when the governor changed. Organizations like the New York Stem Cell Foundation, the Broad Institute, the Stowers Institute, will continue to pick up a good chunk of the cost. More patient advocacy groups, especially representing the orphan diseases, will join the JDRF, Project ALS, the Huntington's Disease Foundation of America, and Chris Reeve and Michael J. Fox's organizations. And of course other countries have government programs, even cell banks." He counted them off on his fingers. "Israel, Canada, Australia, China, Sweden, the Czech Republic, Belgium. The list is growing. They're even centralizing, with nations pooling cell lines and other resources. While here in the good old U.S.A., depending on the political climate, we have to worry not only about funding, but about people who want to actually criminalize the research. I have a slide showing one funding structure that circumvents the lack of federal government support here."

"Can we see it?" asked the senator.

"It's just one example," Peter said as he clicked and a new image filled the screen. "Most of these disorders have unpronounceable names. They're easier to read than to say." He waited for the audience to scan the information:

> Dr. Seth Goldfinger, University of Rochester
> Current Funding:
> - National Multiple Sclerosis Society
> - Children's Ataxia Telangiectasia Foundation
> - Children's Neurobiological Solutions Foundation (Pelizaeus-Merzbacher syndrome, Krabbe disease, Tay-Sachs disease)

"Except for MS," Peter said, "these are orphan diseases. And they're all neurological. Dr. Goldfinger also gets some NIH funding, which means he has to separate all his equipment, down to the tiniest pipette. That's a lot of extra work, as I can attest."

Kelsey spoke up. "This country actually has a long history of the private sector founding and funding institutions that are taken over by the government, once their value is realized. Andrew Carnegie started the public library system. Women and children's hospitals began as private ventures. The Chicago Waterworks, even fire departments originated in the private sector. Stem cell research can go that way too."

Peter was nodding his head. "Yes, but at a cost that's not just monetary. How many stem cell researchers are losing students to the countries that wholeheartedly embrace the work? Surveys show many graduate students in the biomedical sciences in the U.S. steering clear of stem cells so they don't have to relocate. Or compromising in the systems that they work on. Mice instead of humans. Adult stem cells instead of embryonic. And we all know that grad students and postdocs do most of the science. Personally, I fear we may never catch up."

Kelsey continued. "And that means that once treatments become available—and they will—those involving SCNT will be restricted here, and costly elsewhere. We'll have Cadillac medicine. Cures for the wealthy."

After a few moments of silence, some of the senators clapped lightly. Senator Branch stood up, his hands behind his back. "Thank you," he said. "Both of you. We've learned a lot. And I, for one, am 100 percent behind human embryonic stem cell research. Given the numbers, and the horrific nature of these diseases, it isn't a crime to use these cells. It is a crime to *not* use them."

The meeting of the subcommittee ended within a few minutes.

32

"Holy shit! Kelsey, what the hell happened in there? Senator Branch was dead set against stem cell research. You heard him on NPR last month. What do you think turned him around?"

"The Parkinson's stories."

"You're right," Peter said after a minute. "I was watching him. Yeah, the patient testimonials. And he specifically asked for those stories. D'you think he's got an affected family member?"

Kelsey smiled at his slowness in catching on. "I'd say so. It's *him*."

Kelsey and Peter had actually found a quiet corner in the Capitol, behind a coffee stand. They were, at least for the moment, out of sight of lawmakers, their staffs, and the media.

"Wait a minute," Peter said. "How can you possibly know that? Is that why you scribbled that note for me to pursue Parkinson's?"

"Yup. I was afraid you were going to focus on diabetes because the numbers are larger and the patients younger. And then you veered off into ALS and PKU…" She grinned at him.

He grinned back. "I guess I do get carried away with examples. But, Kelsey, how do you know he has it? Did you get an embargoed news release and forget to tell me? Did Tony tell you when you called him during the break?"

"Nope. I'm just observant."

Peter thought a moment. "His hand."

"Right. He wouldn't shake hands with us. Or, I noticed, with anyone else. I remembered how my mother used to avoid handshakes because of her arthritis. But arthritis wouldn't have made him hide his hand. And did you notice how he had his aide do everything? He wouldn't even take notes himself? I flashed onto Michael J. Fox. His first symptom was a tremor in his pinky."

"That's right. When he was filming *Doc Hollywood*. I remember reading about that."

"So," she couldn't keep the hint of smugness out of her voice, "I figured the descriptions of advanced Parkinson's might get to him."

"Well, you figured correctly. And you were worried about testifying. Considering my tangents, you did better than I did." Peter hugged her. "Let's go get some grub," he said. "It's been a long day."

"It sure has," she agreed. "You're on."

As they went down the stairs, they came to a crowd of media vans and a huddle of microphone-poking reporters. Standing at their center was Senator Felix Branch.

"I wonder what he's telling them," Kelsey whispered.

"Wanna find out? C'mon." Peter grabbed her arm and they joined the crowd. "Hey, keep your head down," he muttered. "We don't want to distract the hordes from anything he wants to say."

Kelsey and Peter quietly stood behind the reporters.

"Senator Branch," several were shouting at the same time, "what was the outcome?"

"There isn't any outcome," he replied. "The session was just a fact-finding mission. And we got facts."

"The buzz is that you've one-eightied," said a reporter. "Yeah," said another one. "That you now support human embryo stem cell research," said a local TV news reporter. "Is that correct?" a dozen reporters asked.

"The proper word," the senator told them, "is *embryonic*. Not *embryo*. And yes, I've changed my mind. And I have an announcement to make." The microphones came closer to his face. He took a step back, then forward again. "I have Parkinson's disease," he said. "I've just been diagnosed."

After a moment of stunned silence, the crowd erupted, some reporters shouting questions, others frantically making calls on their cell phones.

"He may be a little self-serving," Peter whispered to Kelsey, "but the guy's got guts. And if it opens up the coffers for the research, who cares what the motivation is? I think things just may turn around." He took her hand. "Let's go."

33

FRANKLIN MEDICAL COLLEGE, APRIL 1

Peter was sitting at his desk, nearly hidden behind the stacks of printouts and scans, when Kelsey entered.

"Good morning, Dr. H. Is this the warehouse for spare body parts? Can I order a new hypothalamus?"

"Ha ha ha. Happy April Fool's day to you, too." He stood up and gave her a warm hug.

"If you don't have brain parts," she said, "can I give you a fibroblast and you can clone me? I'm sorry, *SCNT me*."

He lifted a stack of printouts from a chair and gestured for her to sit down. "Not quite. I've got the lab back up, but now we need more funding and someone with more gifted hands. Nuclear transfer's a bitch. Ever try it when you worked with flies way back when?"

"No, but I did imaginal disc transplants. Those little transparent Frisbee things we'd dissect out of one larva and inject into another. I'd stay off caffeine so my hands wouldn't shake, and I'd still end up blowing up my poor recipients." They laughed.

"Are you still on a high from the subcommittee meeting?"

Her grin was almost ear to ear. "We did great, don't you think? Those scans and the microarrays and the cell culture data and the music analysis. You told an incredible story."

"So did you," he said, taking her hands in his. "So did you, with your eclecticism, your breadth, your outside-but-also-inside view. Do you realize you're having a far greater impact through your writing than you probably would have if you'd stayed blowing up flies?"

Kelsey laughed and squeezed his hands. "So, boss, where do we go from here?"

"I'm not your boss. But we do have a lot of writing to do. Tons."

"I know. I've been working on the *Lancet* paper."

"And that's just a start. I got a call from an editor at *Nature Medicine*—"

"*Nature Medicine*. That's one of my favorites."

"And I thought your favorite magazine was *People*. Anyway, the *Nature Medicine* editor heard the NPR report and asked us to write a one-pager about Stuart. *Stem Cell Research* called, too. They're doing a short news item, so we won't have to turn in anything, just talk to their staffer. And, of course, there's the grant proposal for the new pilot study with the Parkinson's patients."

"That's great! Are we famous now?"

He smiled. "Well, we've come a long way from *World Medical Mysteries*."

"I should hope so." She Marsha took a document out of her bag and handed it to Peter.

"What's this?"

"A transcript. From my visit to the *Citizens Against Stem Cell Research* headquarters. It might be more along the lines of *World Medical Mysteries*, after all. Look at the highlights. Great quotes, huh?"

Peter skimmed the pages. "This is *on the record?*"

"It sure is. And you know what? Now I'm glad that idiot in the white coat who runs the organization, that linguist or whatever the heck he was, didn't take me seriously."

"How are you going to use this?"

"I'm not sure yet. Probably in the newspaper. An editorial in the magazine. Who knows? Maybe I'll write a book some day." She stood up and picked up her bag.

"Where are you off to now?" Peter asked. "I know you said this morning you were meeting Marsha, but I forgot where. And you're dressed a little nicer than usual, no offense."

"None taken. Marsha and I are part of the volunteer panel at hospice. It's training time. I'm a veteran now."

"You'll be great. Call me later."

❦

On an unseasonably warm April 1, the twelve new hospice volunteers were sitting in a semicircle in the atrium. They faced four experienced volunteers.

Emily and Lydia opened the meeting. "Thank you, Larry and Carly, for telling us about your AIDS and dementia patients," Emily said. "Now I'd like to introduce Marsha Berne, who has seen mostly a different type of patient."

Marsha gave the new volunteers a wide, welcoming smile and tossed back her black mane. "Hi. And thank you for coming to listen to us," she said, then took a deep breath. "Well, I mostly visit people who have cancer. They usually come onto the hospice program so late that they don't last very long, and that can be frustrating. I don't mean to sound heartless, because it's probably better for them when things progress swiftly. But I never get to develop much of a relationship with the people I see, not like Larry does with the AIDS patients. But I know I'm helping. They need someone to listen to them, when they can speak, and just to be there, if they can't. I think they know someone is there. Their families certainly do."

The new volunteers were transfixed by the stories they were hearing. A woman with long gray hair and wearing green corduroy overalls raised a hand. Lydia pointed to her. "Yes, Heather?"

"I have a question. Religion must come up with cancer patients. What if someone asks you to pray, and you normally don't?"

Marsha glanced over at Kelsey before replying. "That's a tough one," she said. "I'm not religious, but many patients are. I, well, I just take it one case at a time."

"But how?"

"You have to forget your own beliefs. Or lack of them. They aren't important. Not in this situation. You have to do whatever will help your patient."

Heather looked skeptical. "Isn't that a little dishonest?"

"No," Marsha and Kelsey said at the same time. "Comfort is more important," Marsha said. "Don't worry. Your instincts won't fail you."

A young man raised a hand, and Lydia nodded to him. "Yes, Juan?"

"I know I haven't even started yet," he began, "but I did tell some friends that I was going to volunteer, and they asked me how I can do something so depressing. One guy even called me a ghoul. But I don't see it that way." He looked at the other volunteers. "Am I missing something?"

"Oh," said Marsha, "we all get that. A lot. It's very common for people to think there's something wrong with us. And no, it *isn't* depressing. In fact, it's the opposite. Every patient is unique. You'll find you learn something from each one. Just wait until you hear the next story ..." Kelsey looked down, and Marsha patted her hand. "You won't believe it."

"Yes," Emily prompted her, "the next story is quite remarkable. Kelsey, why don't you tell us?"

Kelsey looked up at the class, tears starting to form. In a hushed voice, she said, "His name was Stuart...."

EPILOGUE

STUART MATHESON CENTER FOR STEM CELL MUSIC THERAPY
– TWO YEARS LATER

Kelsey and Peter, holding hands, slowly approached the front door of the new wing of the medical center. Opening day was finally here. They entered, to applause, as U2 music boomed. Standing for a moment in the center of the reception area, they looked up at the blow-ups of articles on the walls.

Case Report on the Effect of Music on Human Adult Neural Progenitor Cells in Huntington Disease. The Lancet

Music/stem cell therapy: case report inspires pilot studies. The New York Times

Adult Neural Progenitors Respond to Sound. Nature Medicine

iPods and Stem Cells: In the Name of Love. People

Clinical Trials of Music/Stem Cell Therapy Begin. The Journal of the American Medical Association

Musicians Compete for Inclusion in Stem Cell Music Therapy Trial. Guitar World

Brain Music: A Stem Cell Symphony. The New Yorker

Acoustic Activation of Adult Neural Progenitor Cells in the Basal Ganglia in Huntington Disease. Stem Cells

Music Therapy for Huntington Disease via Stem Cell Activation Validated. Science

World Medical Mysteries *Pioneers Stem Cell Cure.* World Medical Mysteries

Bono on Stem Cell Music Therapy. Newsweek

Clinical Trials of Stem Cell Music Therapy Broaden. Nature Neuroscience

Apple Underwrites iPod/Stem Cell Therapy. Business Week

Stuart Matheson Center Opens. Philadelphia Reporter

As Kelsey came to the last article, her hand at her mouth in amazement, she grabbed Peter. There was a cover of *Rolling Stone*. Superimposed on a backdrop photo of U2, scrolling forward like the beginning of a *Star Wars* film, the cover read, *"The last words that Stuart Matheson heard were from* Rolling Stone..."

"Kelsey, look." Peter gently turned her around. They were facing a huge room filled with many familiar faces. Jennifer rushed forward out of the crowd and flung herself at her sister. Kelsey could see Elvin, his dreads hard to miss, and behind him stood Senators Bainbridge and Branch. Marsha and Tony were holding hands, with Tony's other hand on a baby stroller. She saw Lydia and the stylishly-mismatched Emily, gangly Chaplain Timothy towering over everyone, and Connie, the Jesus freak nurse who'd become a good friend. Even Nurse Smithies was there, beaming. Jim Matheson and his sister, Sheila, were standing with Teri, the hospice volunteer who had come from Altoona with Jennifer. Toward the back of the crowd were Detective Coleridge, Captain Bigelow, Medical Examiner Donovan, and the rest of the criminal investigation unit. Even Dr. Goldschmidt had shown up. In a corner of the enormous room, members of Peter's current lab group were answering questions from a group of reporters.

Then Kelsey noticed several small groups of people she didn't recognize. "Peter," she said in a low voice, "who are those people? And why are they all standing?"

"Because they can," he answered. "Why don't you go over and talk with them?"

"OK, I will." But first she came to two young men wearing skiing gear. "You look familiar," she said.

"We should," one of them answered. He looked like Ashton Kutcher. "We were in *Sports Illustrated*. And on TV."

To Kelsey's puzzled look, the other man said, "Skiing accidents. We both suffered spinal cord injuries. We were paraplegics." He paused. "*Were*."

Speechless, Kelsey moved on to a group of children and teens holding a banner from the Juvenile Diabetes Research Foundation. All were clutching iPods. "Well," she said to them, "I know who you are. Bet you don't miss all those needles and pumps." The children started to chatter all at once, the closer ones trying to touch Kelsey's skirt.

"Thank you," said a little girl with huge brown eyes.

"No," Kelsey replied, "thank *you*. If it wasn't for JDRF, and the other organizations, we wouldn't be here."

Next she came to an aging hippie type holding a guitar. He was scruffy, with long, straw-like hair and light blue eyes, but quite good looking, wearing faded jeans and a Grateful Dead T-shirt that reminded Kelsey of Stuart. "And you must be the folksinger," she said. "The one who has ALS."

"The one who *had* ALS," he corrected her. "Wait till you see my fingers move on this guitar." He played the opening riff to "Alice's Restaurant."

Kelsey was approached by two elderly people she thought she recognized, but who were somehow out of context. "Who are you?" Suddenly she gasped. "No! It can't be."

"But it is." Connie and Nurse Smithies came forward, both smiling.

"Reginald?" Kelsey blurted out, "how can you even be alive?" She studied the woman's face. "And…and Mrs. Foofnagle? I don't know what Reginald had, but you were most certainly demented. You used to spend all day taking care of your dolls and stuffed hippos!"

"Reginald had a stroke," Connie said. "The music therapy undid some of the damage, but not all. He still can't speak." She turned to Mrs. Foofnagel. "But Mrs. F., why don't you tell Kelsey about yourself?"

"Yes. I did have Alzheimer's. Or so they tell me. I still live at Ames, but now I can read, and play chess. I'm teaching some of the others. Even the Parkinson's patients can play chess."

As Kelsey was trying to compose herself, Eliot Anderson, Peter's former graduate student, who had finally emerged from his curtain of hair and changed his clothes, stepped forward. His badge read *Director*. Eliot took Kelsey's hand. "How do you like our name?" he asked her with a grin. "We chose the Center for Stem Cell Music Therapy—SCMT for short—just to confuse the senators." He smiled, signaling that this was a joke, as he turned to look at the two congressional guests.

"Eliot," Kelsey couldn't help saying, "you look so different!"

"Thank you. I think. At least I can afford better clothes now." He pulled on Kelsey's hand and led her and Peter over to another knot of children.

"But we're not done. There's one more group you need to meet." He indicated the children. "These are our orphans. Orphan diseases, that is. One of them would like to say a few words."

"I think I'll need to sit down for this," Kelsey murmured. Peter found folding chairs for them both.

A little boy came forward. He was an exquisite, delicate child, about eight years old, with curly dark hair, olive skin, and intense green eyes. He held up a photograph of a boy who looked just like him, but about two years older.

"Hello, Drs. Holloway. I'm Justin. This picture is of my brother,

Graham. He died of Batten disease. A few months ago. You wrote about him, Kelsey—I mean, uh, Dr. Mrs. Holloway. Remember? You talked to me?" He took Kelsey's free hand. "Graham and me had gene therapy. And it worked. But then we couldn't have it anymore. The doctors said they ran out of money. So he got sick again. I was starting to get sick again, too, but then other doctors gave us iPods, and we had to listen to certain songs."

Justin had run out of words. He stopped and stared at the floor. When he spoke again, he could barely be heard. "It was too late for Graham," he whispered. "But it worked for me!" He gave them a smile Kelsey was sure could light up the entire complex. "Thank you for saving my life." The little boy started to cry, as did Kelsey. His parents came over. They hugged him. Then they hugged Kelsey and Peter.

After a few moments, Kelsey stood up and headed toward Detective Coleridge and the others. She was wiping at her eyes with a tissue someone had given her when she bumped into someone. She stopped and looked up, transfixed, at the handsomest man she had ever seen. He looked like the very young Richard Gere in *An Officer and a Gentleman.*

Then she gasped. Was she seeing a ghost? Sheila and Jim came up behind him.

As people gathered around them, the handsome young man took both her hands in his. Kelsey's mouth fell open as the tears started to fall again.

"You must think you're looking at my cousin Stuart," the young man said. "What Stuart would have been."

"Are you—?" She frantically tried to recall the Matheson family pedigree.

"Brian," he said. "Brian Matheson. My dad was Stuart's first cousin, Barry. He died of Huntington's. A few months after Stuart passed away. I got it, too. The mutation, that is. But I *don't* have the disease. And I won't," he said as he held up his iPod. "Thanks to you."

ISBN 142515402-6

Printed in Great Britain
by Amazon